I0573915

IGNITE MY DESIRES ROGER & LEONIE PART I

STEELE INTERNATIONAL, INC. A BILLIONAIRES ROMANCE SERIES BOOK 3

CHARMAINE LOUISE SHELTON

Ignite My Desires Roger & Leonie Part I
Copyright © 2020 by Charmaine Louise Shelton

All rights reserved. No part of this book may be reproduced or transmitted in any form or by any means, electronic or mechanical, including but not limited to photocopying, recording, or by any information storage and retrieval system without written permission from the author.

ISBN: 978-1-7352917-5-8 (Paperback)
ISBN: 978-1-7352917-4-1 (eBook)
Published by CharmaineLouise New York, Inc.
Sexy Fantasies Fulfill Your Desires Publications

Ignite My Desires Roger & Leonie Part I is a work of fiction. Names, characters, businesses, places, events, and incidents are either the product of the author's imagination or used in a fictitious manner. Any resemblance to actual persons, living or dead, or actual events is purely coincidental.

❀ Created with Vellum

CONTENTS

FREE BOOK

Get the start of the STEELE International, Inc. A Billionaires Romance Series with *Discover My Desires Sebastian & Lola Prequel* FREE!

Click Cover Below or visit **bit.ly/CLBooksNewsletter** to subscribe to my newsletter for latest news and launches, books from my author friends, and sizzling reads in book promotions. Plus, start reading the steamy billionaire romance *Series Prequel* of Sebastian Steele and Lola Lewis.

Their stories. Their discovery of unknown desires…

FREE BOOK!

EXCLUSIVE FOR SUBSCRIBERS!

ALSO BY CHARMAINE LOUISE SHELTON

STEELE INTERNATIONAL, INC.
A BILLIONAIRES ROMANCE SERIES

Discover My Desires Sebastian & Lola Prequel
(Available Exclusively to Subscribers)

Fulfill My Desires Sebastian & Lola Part I

Heighten My Desires Sebastian & Lola Part II

Ignite My Desires Roger & Leonie Part I

Stoke My Desires Roger & Leonie Part II

Justify My Desires Roger & Leonie Part III

Deepen My Desires Sebastian & Lola Part III

Capture My Desires Malcolm & Starr Part I

Embrace My Desires Malcolm & Starr Part II

Cherish My Desires Malcolm & Starr Part III

A Trilogy of Desires Sebastian & Lola Parts I-III

ABOUT STEELE INTERNATIONAL, INC. A BILLIONAIRES ROMANCE SERIES

Welcome to the titillating world of the multibillion-dollar global company and the love affairs of the family that controls it.

STEELE International, Inc. is a series of interconnecting Billionaire romance. Follow the Steele family as they fly around the world chasing the women they love and their happily ever afters. Get ready for glitz, glamour, and steamy romance books. What's better than that? The Jet-set Lifestyle has never been hotter...

The Desires Series is not for the tea set; it's for the top-shelf vodka straight up in a pretty crystal glass coterie!

Don't miss any of the sizzling romance books in the STEELE International, Inc. A Billionaires Romance Series:

Discover My Desires Sebastian & Lola Prequel
(Available Exclusively to Subscribers)

Fulfill My Desires Sebastian & Lola Part I

Heighten My Desires Sebastian & Lola Part II

Ignite My Desires Roger & Leonie Part I

Stoke My Desires Roger & Leonie Part II

Justify My Desires Roger & Leonie Part III

Deepen My Desires Sebastian & Lola Part III

Capture My Desires Malcolm & Starr Part I

Embrace My Desires Malcolm & Starr Part II

Cherish My Desires Malcolm & Starr Part III

A Trilogy of Desires Sebastian & Lola Parts I-III

A Trilogy of Desires Roger & Leonie Parts I-III

A Trilogy of Desires Malcolm & Starr Parts I-III

Series Extras

Series Playlist

ABOUT IGNITE MY DESIRES
ROGER & LEONIE PART I

Leonie The Lion Beaulieu stunning supermodel based in Paris; who's fun loving, confident, easygoing with a budding career in residential interior design. Every man wants her. But her heart's broken once.

Roger The Responsible Steele president of his family's luxury real estate empire's residential properties division; intense, focused control freak meets bubbly supermodel who upends his structured world. He let her get away once... Not this time.

Can they reignite their coup de foudre? Or won't lightning strike twice?

Roger and Leonie's second chance billionaire romance story takes you on their journey around the globe—Cabo San Lucas, Nice, Paris, New York...

Their love story is a standalone second chance romance trilogy in the series. Get a glimpse of their dynamism in other books.

Anthem: "Vogue" Madonna
https://www.youtube.com/watch?v=GuJQSAiODqI

Playlist:
https://www.youtube.com/playlist?list=
PLXwYvn0e218Bx18MlEj1svXS-8-NachjU

Visit CharmaineLouiseBooks.com

PROLOGUE

PRESENT — DUBAI, UNITED ARAB EMIRATES

ROGER

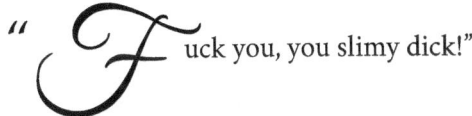uck you, you slimy dick!"

CRASH!

All I saw was red as that bastard Giovanni Mattei slid his hand up the dress of the blonde who'd been eyeing him for the past hour. We're at my future sister-in-law's opening night party for her luxury lingerie company, Lola's Coterie Dubai. The entire Steele clan is present to support her latest endeavor in her global expansion goal. Lola opened the flagship in Paris five years ago, followed by a location in London three years later.

Her initial goal to open boutiques in the United States started with New York and Las Vegas. But since meeting with STEELE Intentional, Inc. and my eldest brother Sebastian, the President of the Retail Properties Division, Lola's expansion now includes Abu Dhabi, Dubai, and Beverly Hills. Lola's Coterie Abu Dhabi opened last week, tonight is Dubai, and in a month another boutique will open in STEELE Galleria Rodeo Drive.

That fateful meeting a year ago between the two companies started a chain reaction. Sebastian and Lola dated within the week. Even moving in together. He surprised everyone since he was a notorious playboy.

Then, the spark hit me to fall for Leonie *The Lion* Beaulieu, the stunning supermodel, muse for Lola's Coterie, and Lola's best friend. Or as she calls it, *un coupe de foudre*—stroke of lightning, love at first sight. So we thought...

All I want to do right now is strike Mattei.

For the past year I've had to look at his smug face as he paraded around Monte Carlo, Las Vegas, Paris, the fucking globe with my woman on his arm.

Or at least she was for a brief two months.

The wildest two months of my life. I never knew what to expect with Leonie. One minute passionately wrapped in each other's arms, her long legs around my neck, my dick buried deep in her tight core. The next arguing about her not finishing reading assignments for her interior

2

design degree from the Paris American Academy. The next, her feline amber eyes gazing lovingly at me to only narrow in anger when I reprimanded her lack of focus. My head aches as much as my dick just from thinking about Leonie.

What a fucking rollercoaster. We held on as long as we could before an argument went further than normal. Yeah, we had smaller disagreements. Bu nothing too major. The last one, though. No cuddles and coos of apology or incredible makeup sex could bridge the chasm we created. Words said, struck a chord and there was no going back. At least not at the time.

I let her get away from me once—well, I contributed hugely to her dumping me—and I won't let it happen again. First, I have to deal with the asshole she keeps going back to, fucking Mattei. He's always waiting in the wings to capture her with his charm. Only now she's distracted with the opening, as it's a work event for her representing Lola's Coterie. Mattei takes advantage of her lack of attention to *God's Gift* and shoves his hand up another woman's dress. Asshole.

Blondie wasn't the only one who couldn't keep her eyes or hands off the Italian playboy. Add the billionaire and nobleman status and he's irresistible to certain women. And any woman is irresistible to him... Without fail he flirted right back—a wink, a sly pinch on their rump, an unnecessary brush of his groin against their ass as he passed by them. Ridiculous.

Now observing Mattei and his shenanigans pisses me off. The self-proclaimed *God Has Shown Favor* shows only disrespect for Leonie. I would hate for his stupidity to upset her on such an important night. She deserves so much more. So I can't stop myself from telling him just that.

"You could at least have enough respect for the woman you're here with, then to feel up another woman within eyesight of her."

The sleaze turns his gaze towards me. His eyes take me in from head to toe as if assessing my seriousness.

Yeah, ass, I'm serious as fuck. If she's with him, he needs to act like a man and not a randy teenager who can't control himself. It's the middle child in me that demands balance and loyalty. I want Leonie for myself, but until she's fully mine again, he will respect her.

"What I do is of no concern of yours, Steele."

I'm surprised he knows who I am since we've never spoken. He must recognize my shock as his smirk widens.

"Oh, I know who you are, Steele," he starts. "You're the loser who can't keep Leonie satisfied. So she keeps coming back to me. You see..."

He leans closer for dramatically to pseudo-whisper. But loud enough so the blonde can hear his words.

"I know how to make her cum so hard on my big dick screaming my name, she forgets all about your sorry ass."

Fuck Roger *The Responsible* who knows better than to act crazy in public. This asshole just sent me over the edge with a vision of him pounding into my woman. No... Fucking... Way.

"Fuck you, you slimy dick!"

CRASH!

In a blind rage, my fist connects with Mattei's jaw and he falls back into mannequins. As they topple to the floor, he recovers and clips me with a punch to the chest. Damn, I didn't expect the pretty boy to know how to fight. We're even at six feet, three inches. I have ten pounds of muscle on him, though. Plus, I spar regularly. I use both size and skill to my advantage.

We exchange only a few blows before my brothers Malcolm and Harris grab Mattei. Luc Montaigne, Lola's mentor, and Sebastian grab me. Security stands by, ready to step in to take over.

Still pissed, I struggle against their hold as does Mattei, who tries to shrug my brothers off. Unmatched by their combined strength, Mattei and I can only glare at each other. Itching to square off again. I give two fucks as the crowd stares on in silence. I want to finish this shit once and for all.

Until the figure of my father Morgan, the Steele Patriarch and Alpha Dom, storms over with such a wrathful look that Mattei and I stand stock-still.

Fuck. My father is pissed.

"You will cease this outrageous, infantile behavior at once and apologize to Ms. Lewis and her guests. Then leave. Do… you… understand?" Morgan issues his edict.

All eyes turn to him, including that dickhead Mattei. Morgan's Dom stare knocks us down several notches. In fact, we're below ground by the time he finishes his chastisement of us. Everyone else stands in silent awe of his power.

Morgan's words reset my out-of-control brain. I shake my head to dispel the angry red haze. Sure, Mattei was disrespectful to Leonie and said some stupid ass shit. But I never should have allowed it to get to me. It sent me on a downward spiral of jealousy, driven by an intense need to flatten him for having what is mine.

No matter the circumstances, I should have maintained command of the situation. Particularly at a highly public event held by STEELE. Before Leonie, this would never have happened. It goes against every cell in my physiology.

I gain control before Mattei and turn to seek Lola out in the crowd gathered around. I hope she's not as upset as I imagine. I spot her standing between my mother and Leonie. My younger sister Haley and Lola's assistants Blair and Billie stand near them. All have shocked expressions on their faces. Damn.

I notice Mattei tries to walk to them. But Malcolm puts his hand on his chest to stop him since he recognizes that I headed their way already. Mattei has the sense to back down.

"Lola, I apologize for my poor behavior. Please forgive me," I beseech her.

With grace, she nods her head and accepts my outstretched hand. Her eyes meet mine before she searches for Sebastian, to whom she nods, too.

I turn my attention to the other women who stare at me, surprised by my unusual outburst.

"Mother, Leonie, I ask for your forgiveness, too," I say to both of them, but my eyes lock on Leonie whose amber gaze shies away.

My shoulders rise and fall on a disappointed sigh in response to her reaction. Not wishing to prolong the situation and knowing now is not the time to address Leonie's dismissal, I turn to the guests and apologize to them. Then excuse myself from the event.

As I pass Sebastian, he squeezes my shoulder to offer me support. I nod without breaking my stride. I don't even wait to hear Mattei's apology. I have to get out of here. Try to save some face from my lack of decorum.

Minutes after I exit the boutique, I feel my mobile vibrate in my trousers' pocket. I know who it is without even checking the name on the display. I answer on the first ring.

"Sorry. That was a shitshow Lola did not deserve. Does she really forgive me? Are you going to kick my ass?"

Of course it's Sebastian. I'm sure our father told him to call me or he would. I'd rather deal with my eldest brother than the elder Steele…

I must sound like a wreck since Sebastian doesn't go in on me, as would be his right. It's his woman's event for our family's company. He's the heir apparent to CEO and Chairman of the Board. So besides being the oldest who leads his siblings, he's the future leader of our multibillion-dollar business at which each of us leads divisions. I'm thankful when Sebastian doesn't add to my ill ease.

"Yes, and no. Dad gave the guests gift cards. What the

fuck happened?" He asks.

I clue him in on the details. He tells me he understands. Baz is an Alpha male like me, although he's a Dom, too. So he understands protecting my woman's honor and my irrational possessive behavior. But he reminds me to keep my shit together in the future. Then teases me about not being responsible.

I grouse over the gibe. Then we hang up with a reminder about breakfast.

Fuck!

In my rage, I punch the wall. The plaster clatters to the floor, leaving a hole and splatters of blood. Too pissed to feel the pain, I stalk around the living room of my Rulers' Suite at STEELE Dubai I.

This shit is crazy. How can I allow myself to get so out of control that I make an ass of myself at a STEELE business function? So out of character for me—Roger *The Responsible*.

I roll my eyes in disgust at myself for letting Leonie upend my structured world. But I can't help myself. I call her mobile.

Leonie doesn't answer. What else is new…

I have no other choice than to leave a voicemail. How many will this one be? After twelve months, I've lost count. I just hope she'll listen to it and respond to me this time.

"How did we get here? Baby, I miss you. I'm so sorry. Tell me what to do. Please tell me, baby. Please…"

ROGER

"*H*ey, when did you get in?"

I lift my head to see my eldest brother, Sebastian. His gray eyes and ebony hair are just like mine, Steele family traits. Baz wears his hair slicked back, accentuating his firm jaw covered with a 5 o'clock shadow. My hair is slightly long, cut to skim my ears and neck. I keep my face clean shaven over my cleft chin. Although my olive skin tone doesn't completely hide the shadow of hair beneath the surface.

I watch him as he strolls up to my desk. He mutters to himself about me and laughs at my intense stare. Unlike my easygoing siblings, I'm the most serious of us. As the middle of five children, I'm the mediator, the one to keep the scales balanced—Roger *The Responsible* Steele. A nickname given to me by my siblings as a child.

Sebastian at thirty-five is our intrepid leader. Both as the eldest and as the heir apparent CEO and Chairman of the Board of our family's multibillion-dollar, luxury real estate development and management corporation. None of us are envious of either of his roles. We're a tight-knit family that loves and respects each other—a fiercely loyal and supportive clan.

Currently, Baz heads our Retail Properties Division of STEELE International, Inc. as the president. Our father, Morgan set to retire next year, also views Baz as the most appropriate choice to take over for our generation. Due more so to his abilities than to his age or last name.

A glance at my watch shows it's still early morning at seven. Sebastian must be on his way to his corner suite of offices. There's no missing me through the glass walls as he passes my suite next to his. I've been here for just over a half an hour, earlier than expected. Although I'm based in our Paris branch, I spend about twenty percent of my time at our headquarters in New York City.

The STEELE Tower is a modern, gray-tinted glass fifty-seven story mixed-use skyscraper on the southwest corner of Fifty-Seventh Street and Fifth Avenue within Billionaires' Row. We're on the twenty-ninth floor for the executive level where my father, second oldest brother Malcolm, Sebastian, and I have offices. Our finance and legal departments along with various conference rooms occupy the remaining space. The other divisions have designated floors below along with my younger siblings', twins Harris and Haley, STEELE Technology and Cyber Security.

As I turn to face him, my eye catches the view through the floor-to-ceiling windows. The city stretches out before me with unobstructed views. Central Park to the north, the Hudson River to the west, the East River opposite, and the rest of Manhattan to the south from Midtown to Battery Park. On a beautiful, cloudless day like this morning, the panoramas are riveting.

The interior reflects the metal our name represents. The decor—as sleek as the exterior—features platinum silk wall treatments, ebony wood floors, dove gray and white leather furniture, crystal light fixtures, Lucite tables, steel accents, and original artwork. The reception area has a spacious desk. Three attractive receptionists with headsets in their ears and custom-tailored light gray dress suits and skin-tone heels that serve as uniforms sit behind it.

The majesty of our power awes all who enter SI's offices.

I ease my stare with a smile, happy to see my brother.

"Late last night. The investors canceled our meeting because of an ill associate, so I flew out earlier than planned."

I reply as I rise from my chair and stride around the desk to give Baz a bro hug and slap on the back. My focus has been on our European projects these past few months. So I've spent less time here than usual. Baz is just as happy to see me as I am to see him.

He settles his substantial frame into the leather guest

chair opposite my desk while I lean against it. I cross my long legs clad in custom-tailored trousers at the ankles and rest my hands on the edge. At six feet, four inches, he's an inch taller than me. Both of us are fit with musculature developed from our training—Baz MMA and traditional boxing for me—with former champions.

I catch him up on the happenings with two of the new builds I'm managing in Positano, Italy and Monte Carlo, Monaco. As the president of our Residential Properties Division, I'm responsible for the global development, sales, and management of villas, estates, gated communities with clubhouses and other amenities. I have a passion for architecture, interior design, and overall aesthetic of residential structures.

As we are a multigenerational, privately owned company, each sibling works at STEELE: Malcolm, president of the Entertainment Properties Division; Harris and Haley, fraternal twins, co-founders of the subsidiary STEELE Technology and Cyber Security. Like Baz, we're not just here because of our DNA.

Our mother Michelle, or Shelley as she's known by those close to her, wasn't born into a wealthy family. She's a native New Yorker who came from a middle-class background. Fate had her employed as a shopgirl at a men's store in one of STEELE's retail properties when she met my father. They joke that it was love at first sight. Well, over thirty-six years later, they still behave like young lovers in the honeymoon stage of their relationship.

As a result of her levelheadedness because of her as she

says "normal upbringing," we interned every summer and school break at STEELE. The proper way to learn our family's business from the mailroom on the lower level to the twenty-ninth floor. Both of our parents insisted upon the best education possible. We attended private schools and received our Harvard undergraduate and MBA degrees, the family legacy school. Each of us earned the right to sit in our C-suite offices.

Sebastian fills me in on his division's meeting with Lola's Coterie that he's having with his business development team in a few hours.

"Actually, I'd appreciate you sitting in on the meeting," he says as he snaps his finger enlightened by the idea. "I could use your opinion. It's always useful to have your perspective."

He pauses and adds with a smirk, "That is if you don't mind, Roger *The Responsible*..."

"Obviously, you could use my insight after that Rockett Construction blunder..." I rib him back, referencing the sour deal he just lost to STEELE's major competitor two months ago.

Sebastian presses his lips together in a thin line. His facial expression switches to his Dom visage.

"Don't get all swole in the chest with me. That Dom shit doesn't work. I'm no sub," I chuckle.

He may be a Dom, but we're all dominant personalities —Alpha males to the core. Only Haley being female lacks that STEELE trait. She's a sweet, shy young woman protected fiercely by her older brothers. Although independent, she doesn't have the innate urge for control like us.

I fold my arms over my massive chest and cock my head to the side. We stare at each other until we crack up at our antics. We don't really need to prove ourselves. It's all in jest.

"Sure thing, bro. I accept your invitation."

Baz's mobile buzzes, interrupting our conversation. He retrieves it from his pants pocket and remarks the time is 8:20 already. Tina Nickles, one of his two assistants, texted to ask if he was running late. He types a quick response that he's in my offices and will be there in ten minutes. Between Tina and Melody Lawson, they keep a tight rein on his schedule because they know how valuable his time is and that he dislikes wasting it.

Baz returns to our conversation for a few more minutes, then says he needs to head to his offices.

"Fine, go take over the world. I have work to do anyway," I say as he strides out the door.

I use the time before the meeting to respond to communications forwarded by Françoise Faucher, my assistant in Paris. The time difference makes it early afternoon there. I have enough time to wrap up some tasks. Like Baz hates to waste time, so do I. If I can—

"Absolutely, not! I don't mind at all! In fact, while I'm in New York, I'm filming a public service announcement that encourages adolescent girls to follow their dreams!"

"Thank you—"

Her melodic laughter follows in their wake. It captivates me like a siren's song. My eyes track her through the glass wall of my office until she disappears around the corner, headed for the conference rooms.

Damn the most exquisite beauty I've ever seen walks past my office. A STEELE security staff member strides beside her. Her long legs easily keep pace with his steps, and he's well over six feet tall.

She looks so familiar. I rack my brain trying to remember where I've seen her before. It escapes me. Who is she?

The ring of my landline breaks the beauty's spell over me. I blink to clear her silken web wrapped around my mind.

"Roger Steele..."

As I head to the conference room for the meeting, I continue to scroll through my tablet.

Thanks to Google, I now know the mysterious beauty's name—Leonie *The Lion* Beaulieu. Of course she's familiar, duh. She's all over Paris, Europe, the States, the world.

The stunning supermodel stands at five feet, ten inches. With the fuck-me heels she's wearing, no wonder she kept up with the guard. Along with her nickname, her tall, voluptuous frame is her trademark.

The Parisian-born, feline beauty must be here for Sebastian's meeting with Lola's Coterie. As the brand's spokesmodel, Leonie has the perfect body to showcase the luxury lingerie. Her sensuous, statuesque figure harkens to the bombshells of yesteryear and the '90s supermodels, full bust, small waist, shapely. My dick twitches just looking at her photos—covers of *Vogue*, *Cosmopolitan*, *Sports Illustrated*.

Her golden, caramel skin reflects her biracial heritage—her mother Joséphine is Tunisian and her father Guy is French. She's the only child. Leonie means brave as a lion and Beaulieu means lovely place. I'm not a stalker, I like details and Wikipedia is just chock full of interesting tidbits.

Social media and bloggers dedicate themselves to her career and love life... Wherever she goes, men flock to her. Undoubtedly as attracted to her siren's song as I am. I swipe through the posts until I see a regular face parading her around the globe. Some schmo named Giovanni Mattei.

Thanks to Google and Wiki, I learn he's a wealthy nobleman from an aristocratic Italian family dating back to the Middle Ages and her on-again-off-again paramour. An insane urge to knock him out comes over me. The fucker.

Distracted, I walk into the conference room without lifting my eyes from my tablet's screen. The background noise of people talking and laughing suddenly stops as I open the door. I raise my gaze.

Holy... shit...

If this were a cartoon, it would be *Who Framed Roger Rabbit*. My mouth would drop open to hit the floor and my eyes would bug out of my head at the sight of Jessica Rabbit in front of me.

But it's not a cartoon, it's actual life, even if my name is

Roger. Instead of a lush cartoon woman, an equally lush lioness stands before me naked save for a scrap of silky material covering her bare mons. My mouth gapes and my eyes widen. Hell, my dick gets hard and presses uncomfortably against the zipper of my trousers. Hot damn!

"They're only breasts, *chéri!*" Leonie laughs, cupping her mouthwatering mounds in her hands as emphasis. "No need to look so stunned!"

Her brown nipples peak between her red manicured fingers, calling me to suckle the plump tips while she writhes beneath me. Unconsciously my tongue sweeps across my lips, wanting a taste of her succulent tits.

"Ahem."

Someone discreetly clears their throat and breaks the spell Leonie has cast her spell on me, again. I feel heat rise even more on my reddened face. I avert my intense stare. Then mumble an apology as I pivot to leave the room. But her siren's call draws my gaze to hers as I glance over my shoulder on my way through the door.

Her amber eyes have darkened and spark golden with interest. The predator senses her prey. Is the Alpha now in another's sight?

A slight smile plays on her full lips. My dick twitches once more when her little pink tongue darts out to moisten her full lips. Leonie must feel the pull just as much as I. Neither of us can escape it.

Damn.

I shake my head. I have to get out of here. I feel my control slipping as thoughts of carrying Leonie over my shoulder back to my office to pummel into her plays in my mind. I have the sudden urge to bury my thick cock balls deep inside of *The Lion*'s sweet pussy.

I hasten out the door as her sultry chuckle follows me.

How the hell did I walk into the wrong conference room? I lost my focus thinking about a woman... I shoot Baz a quick text to ask which one the meeting is in. His response comes immediately. I make my way to the one down the hall.

I beat Sebastian inside the room. So, I nod to members of his team, then stand to the side. It's not my meeting. I'll wait for him to lead it.

Meanwhile, I observe another gorgeous girl who must be Lola Lewis, the eponymous founder of Lola's Coterie. The petite raven-haired beauty's hazel eyes sparkle as she speaks with an older, distinguished Frenchman. Her curvy body is alluring. But doesn't attract me like my sweet Caramel Bonbon.

My gaze shifts to the door when it opens to reveal Sebastian. I notice he falters mid-stride when he enters the room. His eyes widen when he observes the brunette is now in an embrace with the Frenchman. Sebastian's reaction makes me wonder if he knows her.

Oblivious to the sudden tension in the room, Walter Smith, the director of development for the Retail Division, continues with the introductions. I was correct in my assumption; the brunette is Lola.

Lola's hazel eyes widen even more than Baz's and she flushes deeply. She too appears dumbfounded at the sight of my brother. Unconsciously, her hand moves to cover her bottom. Interesting…

Finally catching on to the lull in the room, Sebastian draws his attention from Lola to his team who watch him with curiosity in their eyes. He also notices me staring between Lola and him. His expression confirms he knows I know something is up with the two of them. Yup, my intense gaze never misses a thing. Obviously, I would catch the tension between Lola and him.

Sebastian quickly recovers and continues to stride over to Lola and Luc Montaigne the Frenchman to shake their hands. Lola starts the meeting and I join Sebastian at the table. My thoughts still distracted by Leonie and her delectable body, I barely pay any attention to the presentation. Lola and Montaigne take turns. My attention only piques when Lola announces the commencement of the fashion show.

My dick and I sit up straight at full attention.

Leonie sashays in through the door, looking like a goddess. Her hair is curled in ringlets, cascading around her face and down her back. The shiny mahogany shines beneath the lights. Her makeup is soft with a touch of nude gloss on her lips. The cups of the chemise barely contain her breasts, a hint of the dark nipples peek through. Her toned torso framed by the sheer core of the chemise, while the dainty embroidered hem grazes the tops of her thighs. A slight glimmer of gold body makeup adds sparkle to her caramel skin. As she pads around the conference room,

Leonie is the epitome of feline feminine grace and lusciousness. My dick weeps for her.

Her captivating amber eyes flick to mine as she prances on the temporary catwalk. Each time she models pieces from the collections, I can't help my intense stare. My gaze follows her every move. I'm caught in The Lion's sights.

For the first time in my life, I'm not the one in control.

LEONIE

"*Oh Chérie*, I understand. Go, go have fun with your lover, the gray-eyed wolf! Have some fun for me! Don't worry. Shoo!"

Lola hesitates in the foyer of the Presidential Suite at the St. Regis Hotel New York where we're staying for our week of business in the city.

Suite is an understatement for what's more like *une belle maisonette*. It features a large foyer that leads to the formal dining room, living room, exquisite wood-paneled library, three bedrooms, four bathrooms, powder room, and a complete kitchen. The floor-to-ceiling windows open onto large balconies with spectacular views of Central Park, Fifth Avenue, and Fifty-fifth Street. A personal butler is on call to oversee our every need. With a five-figure per night rate, it has every luxury imaginable for a home away from home. It's our preferred residence whenever either of us are in New York.

"Are you sure? We had planned to spend some nights at the latest clubs and restaurants. I feel terrible—"

"*Non*! Go! Let that Alpha Dom of yours tie you up or spank your booty or whatever you get into," I laugh, waggling my eyebrows suggestively.

For a moment, Lola's face flushes red and her hazel eyes widen at my references to her newfound sub kink. Her last lover—of over a year ago, I might add—was a Dom who spanked her before they had sex. She finally admitted it to me and how much she enjoyed his play. Not only "the release was incredible." But the punishment drove away her nerves. Good for her!

Now, I give my BFF a hug and gently push her towards the suite's front door. Lola is off for another night with the enigmatic, sexy Mr. Sebastian Steele. The billionaire playboy appears taken with her. In fact, she's just as taken with him!

"Well… If you insist!" Lola's tinkling laughter floats behind her as she heads out the door for her rendezvous.

She deserves some fun. She's so focused on growing her company these past six years we've known each other, Lola rarely takes time to enjoy herself. All day, she works in her Parisian atelier on new designs, collection themes, and plans.

Only in the last three years has she turned over the minor business affairs to her marketing and sales teams and to her assistant Blair Thomas. Lola relinquished some duties after Luc, her mentor and major investor, rationalized she focuses on the creative end of business and let others handle the rest with her final approval. Lola's Coterie has come far in the six years since she launched it.

I remember Luc insisted I meet a new lingerie designer, and I thought, *mon Dieu*, really?

At twenty-five, I was at the height of my modeling career with well-established designers pleading with my agents to book me to open and close for their shows. Global cosmetics companies clamoring for me to represent them with exclusive, multimillion-dollar, multiyear contracts. The face of *The Lion* graced hundreds of billboards and magazine covers.

So, an up-and-coming designer like Lola was far from my radar. Luckily for her, Luc knew me through mutual acquaintances and insisted that I meet with Lola. I chuckle to myself as I remember how persistent Luc was for me to give her a chance to discuss me being the spokesmodel for Lola's Coterie. The very handsome and sexy nobleman—or *Le Renard Argenté*, the Silver Fox Lola and I nicknamed Luc —can be very persuasive. How could I say, no? But really, I knew that if he said she was worth it, she must be special.

Over time, as Luc and I became more acquainted and not just people who saw each other at society functions, our friendship developed into him being my top advisor. His recommendations are purely in my best interest since he doesn't gain financially from any deals he assists me with. Luc is the personal eye whereas my agents have a commission tied to their suggestions. They strike the perfect balance.

Luc draws his knowledge from being the CEO &

Chairman of the Board of his family's multigenerational banking empire, Banque Montaigne headquartered in Paris. It has branches worldwide with New York as the United States headquarters. The banker in him added the role of financial manager to his advisor status. His wise investments turned my fifteen-year modeling career income into a multimillion-dollar fortune.

My coffers don't compare to Luc's billionaire wealth. Not only does he run his private banking empire, he's a French nobleman. A wealthy aristocrat raised in the French nobility, he's the last *duc* in his family's line.

Sadly, he became a widow when his wife Carole died in childbirth with his only son Lucas seven years prior to meeting Lola and me. He was still grieving, and Lola's Coterie became a distraction from his sorrows. It was a project different from the banking industry. So it took his mind off of his losses. Fortunately, Luc is in a better place now. Particularly since he appears to be interested in Blair and his head flight attendant Daphne Fontaine. A sweet young thing for the fifty-year-old *Renard Argenté*!

A smile plays on my face as I pad around the living room gathering the things I dropped off when I arrived back from my busy day. The meeting with STEELE International was the impetus for my trip. But I added other activities: rounds at New York's most prestigious design houses; a visit to the New York office of my modeling agency; an interview at *Vogue*; prep work for the PSA commercial I film tomorrow during which I share my dream of becoming a model and switching to residential interior design as encouragement for young girls to go for their goals. It's best to take advantage of the transatlantic trip since I'm based in Paris.

I'm thankful for the extensive travels my modeling has provided me. The fascinating cities of Singapore, Rio, St. Petersburg; the hidden gems of Koh Yao Noi, Bequia, Udaipur; the unique locations of Alta, Taranaki, Salta. I've stayed in breathtaking five-diamond hotels and resorts, spectacular multimillion-dollar villas and flats, and beautiful native accommodations immersed in the local culture. Posing for the camera has allowed me to experience various forms of residences and added to my love of design developed from childhood.

My father, Guy, is from a prominent Parisian family of merchants who date back to the Merchant Court of the eighteenth-century. From the French royal court to the grand bazaars of the Mediterranean Sea, they traveled seeking antiques, antiquities, and fabrics.

It was during one of his excursions that my father met my mother Joséphine in a souk of Tunis. She was bringing lunch to her father, who was a craftsman of ceramics intricately painted by hand. They fell in love on sight. It was a true *coupe de foudre*. Their love struck in the middle of a busy, vibrant, North African bazaar. Sounds like a romantic movie!

So my blood and DNA dictated my penchant for beautiful, extraordinary, aesthetically pleasing surroundings. As much as I've enjoyed modeling, I look forward to completing my Bachelor of Arts in interior design from the

Paris American Academy. The three-year program is taking me longer to complete due to my hectic schedule. I don't mind since I love them both. I don't let it stress me or put pressure on me. Besides, the professors and faculty understand my situation—being famous definitely has its benefits.

I have one ultimate project to present this year where I must design an entire house. *Architectural Digest* wrote a cover feature on my Parisian duplex and Monte Carlo penthouse. I did the interior design for both. They impressed AD. The editor praises my eye for detail and the combination of high-end and low-end pieces to create sumptuous, luxurious abodes reflective of the cities. The issue was their top-selling book of the year.

So despite my nerves about my project, I'm sure someone will trust me to redo their home. I'll take inspiration from my journeys and family ties.

As I walk in my bedroom of the suite, I spot my textbooks on the desk. Well, since I don't have any hot-happening plans for tonight, I might as well get some reading done. Lola teases I'm a bookworm now. Especially since I wear reading glasses.

Just as I sit on a chaise on one balcony with a glass of Réserve Jean de Lillet Blanc, my favorite aperitif, my mobile chirps with a text message.

LEVELS New York Masquerade Night Text YES to RSVP Text NO to Deline

Interesting…

Lola did gift me a seven-day guest pass to the global,

luxury, members-only BDSM/dance clubs' flagship in Manhattan's Meatpacking District. We went the first night we arrived. It was a blast! The sensual atmosphere, the writhing bodies, the pulse of the seductive music. *Incroyable!*

I chose a black enamel bracelet and Lola picked a red one. The different colored bracelets display the wearer's status to other members and guests: partnered subs wear collars given to them by their Dom; partnered Doms wear gold bracelets; available subs wear red; unattached Doms wear white; voyeurs wear black. She met her Dom Sebastian that night.

Hhhmmm.

I might as well make good use of her generosity, I laugh to myself. As I rise from my chaise, I reply YES to RSVP. With a mask on and my hair in a messy bun on top of my head, I can be incognito. Even though I didn't wear a mask the first night, I don't want people to think I make a habit of patronizing a sex club.

Plus, I garner enough attention from men regularly. I don't need them to approach me when I'm alone at this kind of club. Albeit a very safe one with applications for membership that include an initial background check with periodic random ones throughout the year, among other safety measures. However, it's usually Lola who fights off the unwanted suitors. She may be petite, but she's a feisty firecracker who uses her native New Yorker attitude to tell them to scram. Without her there, I'll stick to the shadows as a voyeur.

I'm not on the hunt for a partner at the moment. I'm taking a break from dating. Giovanni Mattei, my on-again-off-again paramour, is on the outs. He's well-built, six feet, three inches tall with lustrous curly brown hair that falls into his chocolate brown eyes adding to his rakish gorgeous look. Women flock to him in droves.

Well, I've had just about enough of his philandering playboy antics. Although he invited me to watch him race at the Grand Prix next month in Monte Carlo. I'm still undecided.

Mr. Thinks He's God Gift to Women is on my shit list. Gio is a wealthy Italian nobleman from an aristocratic family as old as the Middle Ages. Two weeks ago, he sent an oil painting from his Paris gallery that I had my eye on. I promptly returned it. Last week it was a beautiful pair of yellow diamond earrings with a note: "They remind me of your eyes right after you cum screaming on my cock." Returned to sender.

I'll give it to him, Gio—that handsome devil—definitely has the confidence of a man used to getting whatever he wants in life. He doesn't give a damn about how others view his arrogance. We've dated for two years. But I'm not tying my heart to his unfaithful one. He's not ready to settle down, and I'm not ready to settle.

For now, I'll enjoy LEVELS and select a black voyeur bracelet again to just observe. I'll live vicariously through others' hedonistic trysts tonight.

With a decisive nod, I put my textbook back on the desk. Tomorrow is another day!

I stride to the walk-in closet to select a piece of lingerie from Lola's latest collection in anticipation of her New York boutique opening. I pull out the skimpiest bit of lingerie. A delicate cream lace teddy that skims the tops of my thighs and matching barely there thong is perfect. Since a half mask will cover my face, I'll just add a touch of shiny, nude gloss to my full lips. My look completed with a sexy bed-head updo and five-inch marabou mules.

Next, a soak in the oversize bathtub to pamper my work-weary muscles with essential oils. I wash and style my hair. Then slip into the lingerie set, shoes, and a Burberry trench coat. I leave a note for Lola on her pillow to let her know where I went for the evening. Not that I expect her to return tonight since she hasn't the other nights. She'll see it in the morning before she heads to her temporary office at Banque Montaigne United States headquarters in Midtown on Park Avenue.

My heels click on the hotel lobby's marble floors as I strut from the elevators to the front doors. I pass well-dressed guests on their way to dinner or to one of the city's happening night spots. Since I don't have on my mask yet, several guests do a double take when they recognize me. Accustomed to seeing my visage graces magazine covers on the newsstands and on the billboards in Times Square, I impress even the most jaded New Yorkers. With my signature predatory smile on my face, amber eyes twinkling, I prance past the gawkers and nod at the doorman as he smiles sheepishly at me. I glide down the stairs and sweep into the chauffeured Bentley Bentayga that Leonie hired for our seven-day stay.

"Good evening, Ms. Beaulieu," the driver greets me as I settle into the plush leather seats. "Where would you like to go tonight?"

"Good evening, Stan. Please take me to LEVELS, thank you," I reply with a smile.

Stan drove Lola and me to LEVELS that first night, and I know he's driven her there to meet Sebastian. So, his face remains neutral. As the quintessential professional, he doesn't allow a judgmental expression to cross his face. I'm sure he knows LEVELS is a hedonistic establishment. Instead, he responds, "Yes, Ms. Beaulieu, right away."

ROGER

*M*y dick can't take another tug from my fist as I fantasize about driving my thick length between Leonie's luscious tits slicked with warming oil. I can't get her out of my mind. The vision of her standing naked, holding her bountiful breasts in her hands has kept me hard for days. Her ripe nipples calling for me to lave and suckle them as an act of devotion for hours. Her melodious laugh transforming into a throaty moan. Her luminous amber eyes rolling back as she bows her body, feeding her breasts deeper into my greedy mouth...

Fuck!

I need a more substantial release than my hand allows. A night at LEVELS New York offers the solution my body craves. Undoubtedly I'll find a woman who's more than willing to have a one-night tryst with one of the STEELE Quaternity, as the media has labeled my brothers and me. They've dubbed us the most sought-after of the world's eligible billionaires. Our near-limitless wealth, power, and good looks attract women like bees to honey. They clamor for a taste, even one night.

We're all guilty of not having longstanding relationships. Our work to increase STEELE International's success as the next generation takes most of our time. All of us, including our sister Haley, commit at least ten hours a day on business. In Sebastian's case, it's fourteen hours. We put pressure on ourselves, but he does it even more. I'm not far behind with twelve. We're not left with enough time a relationship requires.

Fortunately, Malcolm and our cousin Lucien Jackson opened LEVELS New York five years ago that provides just what we need. We're Global All Access Members. Other than Haley, who we forbid membership.

While completing his hospitality and culinary training at the prestigious Le Cordon Bleu in Paris, Lucien thought of a BDSM/dance club. He figured the club would fill the void for safe, uninhibited sexual activities amongst the world's wealthiest and most influential people. They convinced Sebastian a global, luxury, members-only entertainment venue focused on hedonism would add to STEELE's bottom line. Baz, the net-net guy, saw the potential and gave them the green light.

Their venture with a high profit margin proved it's bigger than "a titty bar" as Baz originally called LEVELS. Malcolm and Lucien opened additional locations in Paris and London. An idea Lucien, who's now referred to as *The Sexy Chef*, literally cooked up is worth millions.

LEVELS is one of many business partnerships that STEELE has with Jackson Corporation. World-renown for their award-winning eateries, choice cigars, and distinguished liquors and wines, their products pair well within STEELE's casinos, hotels, resorts, and residential and retail properties.

On the personal side, our mother Shelley is best friends with Lucie, the Jackson matriarch. They spent most of their adult lives together forming a closer bond than they have with their blood siblings and relatives. Not sharing DNA doesn't keep our families from being a close-knit group and Lydie, Lachlan, Lucien, and Laurent as our cousins. Connor their Patriarch has become a close friend of our father Morgan.

As my driver Eric Vogler cruises from The STEELE Tower on Fifth Avenue and Fifty-Seventh Street where I was at my penthouse to the Meatpacking District, I chuckle. Lucien and Malcolm's deliberate choice for the location adds to its allure. They selected a multi-level brick warehouse in the historic Manhattan neighborhood as a play on the area's name. Put a club where men pack their meat into willing women, and willing men allow women to pack them with their toys.

The historic reference continues with the decor. The lobby is minimal and industrial. The fixtures and furniture that appear well worn are high-end, modern replicas used to add authenticity without the grime of old pieces. The two sides have coordinating greeter stations that allow access to the separate Dine & Dance levels and the BDSM levels.

All Access members can choose from any of the seven levels. While the Dine/Dance members only have access to the party levels—Sky Lounge, Dance Club, and Level 4 Restaurant. For consistency and members' comfort, locations share the same layout with varying views:

Seven levels: 7th Sky Lounge that offers for the Meatpacking location a stunning, 360-degree view of Manhattan and across the Hudson River to New Jersey's shoreline, a bar, restaurant by day dance club by night, a coverable pool that's open during the warmer months, and a glass-retractable roof; 6th and 5th multilevel dance club with two bars and a lounge for food and drinks; 4th Level 4 Restaurant and bar open for breakfast, lunch, and dinner; 3rd has twelve private suites for members to continue their pleasure apart from the BDSM levels; 2nd Peepshow for BDSM with seating alcoves, primary stage, mini-stages, performance rooms, and a bar that serves non-alcoholic mocktails; below ground the Cellar a BDSM dungeon with mocktails bar.

Impatient to get inside, I don't wait for Eric to open my door. I hop out and stride past the queue that extends around the corner of people in expensive attire patiently await admittance to the club. Not surprising given LEVELS is for the über-wealthy and influential, too refined to behave boorishly. The hopeful patrons are not rambunctious as one would ordinarily see waiting outside a Manhattan nightclub.

I nod at the two members of the security team in custom-tailored black suits who stand outside the front doors.

"Good evening, Mr. Steele."

"Good evening," I respond as I make my way into the renovated warehouse.

I incline my head at the two stunning greeters as I step into the lobby. Their eyes gleam as brightly as their smiles when they recognize me. I don't break stride. A hard limit —no fraternizing with the staff. Instead, I press for the BDSM elevator. Once inside, I place my keycard against the panel to select the second level for Peepshow.

I stop at a greeter station in front of the doors. Another attractive staff member holds enamel bracelets. I listen as she explains the differences in the colors to two males who must be new members or guests of members: partnered subs wear collars given to them by their Dom; partnered Doms wear gold bracelets; available subs wear red; unattached Doms wear white; voyeurs wear black.

Their excitement is palpable. Interestingly, the shorter of the two selects the gold bracelet. Then attaches a silver metal chain to the black leather studded collar around the neck of his taller, more muscular partner. The Dom strides through the doors leading his sub who trails behind him.

"Good evening, Mr. Steele," smiles the greeter. "Would you like to choose a mask or do you have one of your own for Masquerade Night, Sir?"

I don't miss her emphasis on the word Sir as a sub innuendo. The rule of us not engaging with employees is not the only deterrent to dealings with her. Unlike Baz and Malcolm, Harris and I are not Doms. We're Alpha males who like control. But don't dabble as far into a D/s relationship as our older brothers. Hell, I think our father may be a Dom, which would make our mother a sub. Not the visual I need right now. I have to resolve one of my own.

"Yes, I'll take the black one, thank you," I respond in an even tone, purposefully ignoring the downward cast of her brown eyes.

I opt out of a bracelet since I will select who I want, not someone selecting me as a partner. I need not show my availability; I need to know their status. Since everyone signs a contract that includes a consensual clause, I know everyone here is open to a connection. The bracelet determines at what level.

Once my mask is in place, I walk through the doors. A cursory glance around the room already has my body relaxing in anticipation of release. With the smile of a hunter on the prowl, I enter the world of Peepshow.

Not ready to pick my willing prey for the night, I stride pass seating alcoves filled with members in various stages of sex. A main stage and several smaller platforms showcase demonstrations in bondage and edging. I continue through performance rooms with viewing windows where members watch others live their fantasies. I stop to get a drink at the bar that only serves non-alcoholic mocktails to keep everyone's minds clear.

The atmosphere is all about bacchanalia, with the melodic thrum of sensual music and the moans and groans of men and women as the backdrop to intense sexual play. The air is heavy with the scent of perfume, cologne, and sex.

As I tip my glass to my lips, my gaze lands on doors where a statuesque woman stands with a mask covering the top half of her face. Backlit by the crystal chandelier in the entry, her curvy body is on display beneath a skimpy cream-colored lingerie set. The hem of her teddy barely brushes her toned caramel thighs. The sky-high mules stress her legs for days. Her mahogany hair piled atop her head makes me want to pull the pins out to watch her glossy strands cascade down her back.

Leonie.

If she thinks wearing a mask and pulling her mane of hair in a bun can disguise her, she's mistaken. My keen eyesight detects who she is as soon as I see her. My cock comes to life in an instant, harder than it's ever been. Her siren's song calls to me once again.

As she steps onto the floor, my eyes travel to her right wrist. A black bracelet adorns it. Hhhmmm. My feline beauty is a voyeur... For now.

I observe Leonie. Determine her intentions. Is she on the hunt like me, or does she truly want to watch others in their play? I slip into the shadows, eyes trained on her every movement.

Even hidden partially by a simple black mask, *The Lion* commands attention. As she prowls around the room, several pairs of lust-filled eyes including those of a few women track my beauty as she stalks past them. Sadly for them, I have her in my sights. I will allow no one to partake of my Caramel Bonbon.

"Hello, I don't see you with anyone and your sleeve covers your wrist. Are you interested in doing a bondage and punishment scene?"

For a moment, I glance down to see a woman with waist-length blonde hair and light blue eyes staring up at me. A soft smile plays on her pouty lips. When she notices my gaze on her mouth, she darts her tongue to moisten her bottom lip suggestively. A filmy slip clings to her voluptuous figure. Taut rosy nipples press against the thin fabric.

Encouraged by my stare, she places a small hand on my broad chest. She rises to her tiptoes as she presses her lips to my ear to whisper illicit promises of pleasure.

Ordinarily I would claim her, and we'd head up to a private suite. But not tonight. Not when I have the woman whose image taunted me day and night within reach. I shake my head I'm not available at the blonde vixen. Then, stride towards Leonie who's surrounded by three men.

Not happening.

Unable to control myself, I slip my hand around her waist to rest on her flat lower belly. In a possessive hold, I angle my body directly behind hers, aligning my front to her back. A surprised gasp escapes her lips as she swings her head around to stare over her shoulder at me.

Her fuck-me heels bring her mouth on a level with

mine. I feel the warmth of her breath as the gasp slips out of her mouth. I ignore her wannabe suitors and brush my lips over hers before I bring them to the delicate shell of her ear.

"Ms. Beaulieu, what are you doing here alone?" I ask in a guttural growl.

She trembles against me. Responsive to the demanding tone of my voice, as her eyes widen in surprise. Her amber orbs search my gray ones for a sign of recognition. Subconsciously, her hand comes on top of mine, unsure of pushing me away or pulling me closer. Without a doubt, she can feel my enormous erection pressing into the crease of her firm ass.

"Wh... Wh... Who are you?" She stutters softly.

"Roger Steele," I respond, pushing my groin into her bottom on Steele, my dick as hard as the metal.

Leonie bites her plump bottom lip, and her feline eyes narrow.

Before she can respond, I move her away from the others. Leaving them to gawk after us. Leonie keeps pace with me as I stride to a corner alcove for privacy. She must want some anonymity since she wears a mask. So I will respect her wishes. As always, the woman's needs surpass my own. One of my kinks.

Seated on the semicircular red velvet banquette, our long legs touch, shooting jolts of electricity between our bodies. Leonie watches me in silence. The Queen of the Savannah analyzes her prey, waiting patiently for me to make the wrong move. I give her a moment to wonder at my behavior before I speak. In the dim light, I remove my mask.

"You haven't answered my question," I state.

Leonie's gaze sweeps across my face. She cocks her head to the side and arches her elegant eyebrow.

"What makes you think I have to answer to you, Monsieur Steele?"

Taking her challenge, I grasp her chin between my thumb and index finger to hold her face still as I bring my lips within a hair's distance of hers.

"Parce que je vous avais posé la question, et parce que je peux te donner ce que tu désires," I murmur huskily.

Once again, her eyes widen shocked by my fluency of her native tongue.

"Bof!" Leonie scoffs, shrugging her shoulders.

I can give her what she wants. Arrogant? Yes, but factual. I've never not satisfied a woman. And the way my body burns for hers, I will delight in her immensely.

"Oui mon Bonbon au Caramel, je parle couramment français," I smirk.

A seductive smile sparks across Leonie's gorgeous face, lighting her amber eyes from within. On a purr she responds, *"Est-ce un fait, Monsieur Steele?"*

"En effet, ma beauté. En effet."

When I want something, I make it mine. Methodical and determined go hand-in-hand with my intense nature.

And I want Leonie *The Lion* Beaulieu.

LEONIE

"*M*mmmmm..."

I raise my arms overhead and bow my back, pressing my hips into the mattress, thighs trembling, toes curling. My eyes close tight as a satisfied smile spreads across my face.

"Aaahhhh…"

I flop back onto the bed and open my eyes. Sunlight streams in through the windows, illuminating my bedroom at the St. Regis Hotel. With a contented sigh, I snuggle into the luxurious sheets and pull the blanket up to my chin. My mind wanders to the night Roger absconded with me at LEVELS New York a few days ago.

"Well, that sounds very interesting, monsieur. But I will have to pa—"

My words get snatched from my mouth, replaced by a startled gasp as the large hand of a man slips around my waist to rest on my lower belly. Its heat sends a zing to my core. He places his substantial body directly behind mine, aligning my back to his front.

And what a front! His chest is massive and firm. My derriere rests against his groin where his large cock stands at attention. His thick thighs press against the backs of my legs. He's so tall, we match body part to body part. His heady cologne is a sensual blend of Bulgarian rose, clary sage, and patchouli. His posture is so possessive.

I nearly swoon.

Instead, I get a grip on my raging hormones and whip my head around to stare over my shoulder at the brute. What is up with these cavemen at LEVELS? First Sebastian growls at Taylor, the head of membership, when he was giving Lola and me a tour. Now, this giant has me in his tight embrace.

Baise moi!

My five-inch mules bring our mouths so close were merely a breath apart. As though he and I are the only ones in the room, the mysterious stranger brushes his lips over mine. Then brings them to whisper in my ear.

"Ms. Beaulieu, what are you doing here alone?"

I tremble against him at his guttural growl. My body fights my mind for control as it responds to the demanding tone of his voice. Another gasp escapes as my eyes widen in surprise. Then search the gray orbs for a sign of recognition of the man behind the mask. Of its on accord, my hand comes on top of his. Do I want him to let go? Do I want to give in to his possessive behavior? My mind and body struggle to decide, unsure of pushing him away or pulling him closer. His enormous erection pressing into the crease of my ass makes the decision even harder...

"Wh... Wh... Who are you?" I whisper.

"Roger Steele," he responds, pushing his groin into my derriere on Steele.

And steel it is. Roger's dick is just like the hard metal. I allow his turgid rod to distract for a moment. I bite my lower lip trying to decide the proper action to take faced with the brother of Sebastian who's completing a deal with the company I'm the spokesmodel. Thoughts of ruining the deal for my best friend Lola with a fling with Roger swings in favor of my mind's logic and not my body's lust. A decisive mais non, Monsieur Steele!

I narrow my eyes at him to tell him just that.

Before I can open my mouth, he moves me away from the three men I was in the middle of speaking with prior to his arrival. They continue to stand in shock, watching us. Roger leads me to a corner alcove that's more private than the middle of the floor at Peepshow. He must realize I want to remain anonymous. Dieu merci pour cela!

Seated on the semicircular red velvet banquette, our long legs touch, shooting jolts of electricity between our bodies. I watch Roger in silence. The first to speak loses the advantage. I wait. In the dim light, he removes his mask.

"You haven't answered my question," he states.

My gaze sweeps across his gorgeous face. Roger Steele could be a male supermodel. His sultry gray eyes, angular cheekbones, cleft chin that begs for me to lick it. Hhhmmm... I cock my head to the side and arches my eyebrow. I can't give in to his seduction. But I can flirt.

"What makes you think I have to answer to you, Monsieur Steele?"

Roger takes my challenge. He grasps my chin between his thumb and index finger to hold my face still as he brings his lips within a hair's distance of mine.

"Parce que je vous avais posé la question, et parce que je peux te donner ce que tu désires," he murmurs huskily.

Once again, my eyes widen shocked by his fluency of my native tongue and his arrogance. He can give me what I want.

"Bof," I scoff with a Gallic shrug.

However, his confident smirk leads me to believe he is being truthful. Roger Steele knows how to satisfy a woman. My body vibrates with need. I feel my pussy moisten and clench, aching for his massive member. I shift uncomfortably on the banquette.

"Oui mon Bonbon au Caramel, je parle couramment français," he continues with his smirk.

Intrigued, a seductive smile sparks across my face as my body and mind come to an agreement. Lola's Coterie won't suffer if Roger and I have a little tryst...

"Est-ce un fait, Monsieur Steele?" I purr.

"En effet, ma beauté. En effet."

Although we moved from the Peepshow banquette to one of the private suites, our tryst turned into an evening of sharing our lives and goals. A release of our souls to the other. I've never felt so connected to a man as I do with Roger.

The connection deepened when he told me how his passion for architecture, interior design, and overall aesthetic of residential structures lead him to president of Residential Properties at STEELE. I impressed him with my decision to move into interior design after my years as a top model rather than do nothing once I retire. He told me with focus and determination, I could make a successful transition.

Not only does he have an intense stare, Roger is an intense man. Twelve hours devoted to STEELE every day drives his work ethic. Boxing sessions release the tension. He's rigid with his need for order and balance. But I'm sure there's a fun-loving man inside. There's an exceptional dominant lover present.

I squeeze my thighs together as I remember Roger's dark head nestled between them while his hooded eyes pierced mine last night. His talented tongue tuned my pussy, then played it like a fine instrument for over an hour. He had me naked, bound by silken cords, spread eagle on the bed in a suite at LEVELS. Unable to move, I could only feel my body spasm as wave after wave of orgasms rolled over me. He was relentless.

By the time Roger sat back on his haunches—like a statue chiseled by the hands of Michelangelo—I was a quivering mess lying in a puddle of my juices. His nose, mouth, and chin were wet from my climaxes. I scanned his strong shoulders, hard chest, and eight-pack abs with a happy trail that led to his massive ribbed cock. The bulbous red head leaked pre-cum. I licked my lips, wanting to taste his creamy essence.

Instead, he rose onto his knees and straddled my torso. With his thick length fisted in his hand, he tugged on it as he groaned my name. Rope after rope after rope of his seed spewed forth to cover my heaving breasts. He collapsed

45

over me, then suckled and laved my nipples as his still hard dick bobbed against my pussy entrance.

I writhed beneath Roger, aching for him to drive his staff deep inside of my core. But no.

Since I told him I only had two lovers and just ended it with the last, Roger told me we had to take it slowly. He didn't want me to rush into sex with him, then regret it. However, he promised to take care of my needs without the penetration of his glorious cock.

So, my pleas of *bais moi, bais moi maintenant* were met with his lips, tongue, and fingers.

Merde!

I roll over and scream into the downy pillow. Frustrated, I opened my big mouth about not giving in easily to suitors. Also, I fear I shared too much with my desire for genuine love like both of our parents experienced—*coup de foudre*. Roger, being the man he is, takes me at my word and refuses to go further for now.

So despite the pleasure he gave to me. I... want... more! *Je n'aurai aucun regret!*

OUR WEEK in New York City ends where we started. Gathered in the conference room at The STEELE Tower with the same cast of characters as our first meeting.

This time, Dom Pérignon Rosé Vintage 2005—somehow Baz knows Lola's favorite champagne—flows as they sign the contracts for Lola's Coterie and STEELE

International, Inc.'s multiyear, multimillion-dollar partnership.

I'm happy for my best friend. She's worked hard for her success. We're so thrilled that we do our merry dance around the table while Luc and Sebastian laugh. Roger stares, his gaze as intense as ever. Or it could be because of the sleek knit mini dress with satin stiletto boots, the tops of which rest just below my hemline. Today, I taunt him with my curves and long legs that wrapped around his head. Tonight, the wait is over.

"I'm so excited for you, *Chérie!*" I squeal and hug Lola close. "Your dreams are coming true!"

"I know!" She exclaims. "It's so awesome! We have so much to do! I can't wait to get started."

She continues and as she hugs me back.

"*Oui, petite chérie*, but no need to think of it all at this very moment," Luc interrupts as he joins us and pulls Lola in for a warm embrace. "*Jouissance du présent!* Let's have dinner tonight at Per Se, your favorite New York restaurant, to celebrate."

"Lola and I already have plans for this evening," Sebastian cuts into the conversation, staring challengingly at Luc while placing a possessive hand on Lola's lower back.

After a tense moment where they eye each other, she ends the standoff with a compromise for dinner with us at eight and desert with Baz. Perfect for what I have planned for Roger.

Lola and I are the last to arrive at the restaurant. I spy Roger immediately. Seated at the bar, I study his handsome profile as he laughs at something Luc said. I notice the women near them circle like hawks attracted to two powerful, obviously wealthy Alpha males.

Well, Roger has my name written all over him. At least I expect my scent still fills his nostrils. I giggle at the thought even as my core clenches.

As if sensing my presence, Roger turns to face us. His pupils dilate as he takes in my attire for the evening.

The white one-shoulder velvet-trimmed sequined chiffon mini dress covered in scores of iridescent sequins sparkles so brilliantly under lights. Made from chiffon, it's cut to skim my figure and has a '70s-style one-shoulder silhouette. My narrow waist defined by the velvet belt. Strappy sandals lengthen my exposed legs provocatively. A smirk curls my lips as I toss my hair, blown straight over my shoulder where it brushes the middle of my back.

As Lola and I near them, Roger stands to offer his seat to me while Blair and Luc greet us with double-cheek kisses. I turn to Roger and brush my lips against the corner of his mouth when I repeat the kiss with him.

His hands rest at the top of my derriere in an embrace. But I slip out of it to sit. A little tease never hurt. I take a sip of his drink, eyeing him with my predatory stare over the rim. His nostrils flare.

"Where's Sebastian?"

I switch my attention to Lola, who's scanning the area. Roger shifts uncomfortably next to me and looks past Lola. We follow his gaze and see Sebastian off to the side in an animated conversation with a gorgeous blonde woman who has her hand on his chest. *L'idiot!* She's the Finnish model Bridget Heimonen.

"*Le playboy occupé à une autre tâche à ce moment,*" I spit out while I glare at him.

Fortunately, Luc takes control and we head to the private room he reserved for Lola's celebratory dinner. No one pays Sebastian attention when he finally joins us. We laugh and toast, enjoying the evening. When he follows Lola to the bathroom and they don't return, I know they worked it out. I gaze across the table at Luc, who's in deep conversation with Blair. Okay, so *Le Renard Argenté* appears set, too. Now it's my turn.

Again, as though emotionally attuned to me, Roger places his hand on my upper thigh as he inclines his head to mine.

"Time for dessert," he states in a deep voice filled with desire.

Hidden by the tablecloth, his fingers slip beneath my dress and slide along my inner thighs to nudge at my silk covered seam.

I shiver, but hold firm. Placing my palm on top of his significant bulge, I murmur my response against his ear.

"Only if you give me all of you."

Roger's thick cock twitches in my hand as his breath quickens. Gruffly, he answers.

"*Comme tu le désires, mon Caramel Bonbon.*"

ROGER

"Take your dress off. I want you bare to me."

A low growl of appreciation rumbles from deep within my chest as Leonie unties the velvet belt from her narrow waist. All night my mouth watered for her puckered nipples that poked against the fabric of her little white dress. I guessed she was braless since it draped off one shoulder, revealing more of her delectable caramel skin.

When she and Lola walked up to the bar at Per Se, I wanted to drag Leonie off to my den to have my way with her. The inane idea I had of taking it slow to keep her from regretting fucking me so soon after her break up nearly killed me.

Sure, I feasted on Leonie's luscious body almost every night and tugged my junk over her naked body. But those acts do not compare to being buried balls deep inside of her delicious pussy. The little sleep that I garnered filled with fantasies of me pounding inside of her channel until I fill her with my seed.

Damn.

I'm losing my shit. Not a very responsible thought to have about sex with a relative stranger. Never have I considered unprotected intercourse with the women I've slept with in my life. There's just something about Leonie that makes my rigid stance on life bend to her whims.

Over the last few days, I let myself get caught up in her playfulness and blowing with the wind carefree attitude. She's so opposite to me. And I find my attraction to her increasing. Again, as though beyond my control.

And right now her painstakingly slow striptease has me on the edge of the precipice. Leonie's amber eyes twinkle in the ambient lighting of the bedroom in my penthouse on the fifty-second floor of THE STEELE Tower. Another against protocol move.

No woman besides my mother and sister has been to my home. My dalliances happen at LEVELS New York and Paris. Or if I'm in London at that location. Tonight, instead of going to the Meatpacking District, I instructed my driver to take us here. Leonie looked at me in surprise. But I didn't comment further. She must sense I'm not the guy to bring women to my private space. I'm not even sure why I brought her here. Except I know it feels right.

As I sit at the foot of my bed, my intense gaze slides from her hands down her torso to her long legs. As Leonie lifts the hem of her dress, a mischievous smile plays on her full lips. With a deliberate languid pace, she reveals her thighs inch by inch.

Grrrr!

In one unexpected move, I leap to my feet and lunge towards her. My hands grasp her by the waist, and I lift her from the floor. Deftly, I drop her onto the bed. She lands splayed before me. Without giving her a chance to react, I lengthen my body over hers.

One pull and the front of her dress rips open to expose her more than a handful C-cup breasts. Her brown nipples tighten in the cool air. I drop to my forearms to engulf her tit with my mouth. Forceful sucking has Leonie writhing beneath me in moments. I alternate nipping and laving her peaks, eliciting guttural mews from deep in her throat.

"Aaahhhh… Roger… Mmmmmm..."

I stroke her belly as my fingers trail to her silk-covered mound. I slip my middle finger under the elastic, and palm her bare mons with my large hand. My finger slips between her wet labia to tease her clit. The sensitive bundle of nerves swells from my artful ministrations. A quick pinch and a nip cause Leonie to bow off the bed, screaming my name as her body rocks with a powerful climax.

I continue to caress her breasts with my hungry mouth as two more fingers join the first inside of her core. Leonie is so fucking tight. Her pussy walls squeeze my digits. I need her loose enough to take the invasion of my thick, ten-inch dick.

"Are you sure you want all of me, Bonbon?" I croon in

her ear as I slide my fingers in and out of her slippery pussy.

"Mmmmmm... *Oui... Oui... Plai—*"

Her words cut short by my insistent finger fucking. Her tight walls stretch around the invasion and pulse with her impending orgasm. I plant open-mouthed kisses on her long, delicate neck, aching to mark her as mine. Claim *The Lion*.

"Rogeeerrr..."

As Leonie wails, I rise from the bed and quickly strip out of my custom-tailored suit and shirt. I toss it all to the floor, toeing my shoes and socks off my feet. Ripping my black silk boxer briefs down my muscular thighs, my hooded eyes never leave Leonie's squirming body as I roll a condom on.

Her feline eyes narrow in on her prey as they crawl over my body. Until they alight on my colossal cock. Then they widen, and her little pink tongue darts out to moisten her bottom lip. Her chest heaves on an inhalation, making her tits bounce. She widens her thighs as she lifts her arms to welcome me.

"*Mon Chéri, viens à moi,*" she purrs seductively.

My dick thumps against my stomach, pre-cum dripping from the slit.

I blaze a trail of scorching open-mouthed kisses from the arch of her foot up her inner thighs to the hollow between her breasts. Goosebumps dot her smooth skin as she shivers despite the heat of her moist body.

Pressure from my hips between her thighs urge Leonie

to open wider to accommodate my much larger frame. I settle my groin against hers, and I kiss her passionately. Her soft mewls make my member thicken and lengthen more between us. Gripping the base, I feed the broad head of my cock slowly into her core. Although she's sopping wet, I'm met by resistance.

"Open up and let me in, baby," I croon against her neck. "I need to feel your tight pussy wrapped around me."

I swipe the tip inside her folds to collect her juices for natural lube. I press forward again. Fuck... Her wet heat feels so good. Groans escape from between my lips brushing her throat.

"Ooohhh... Roger... Aaahhh, *Amoureux... Donne moi tout de toi.*"

I give her what she asks for—all of me—as I drive my dick balls deep inside until I hit her cervix. Her squeal a combination of pleasure and pain. Her hot pussy walls pulsate around my dick with each thrust that sends her sliding up the bed. She grips my biceps and holds on for the wild ride.

We've waited so long. Now, we lose each other in our rhythm. Connected as one as we ride waves of rapture.

"So, good, baby... So fucking good," I rasp against her damp neck.

The slick sounds of our bodies joining fill the room as the headboard hits the wall. Too far gone to care, I pummel into Leonie like a lust-driven fiend.

At... fucking... last.

* * *

THE ELEVATOR ARRIVES WITH A PING.

Leonie and I fall through the doors, too engrossed in a passionate kiss with our arms wrapped around each other, to notice that we're not alone. As I hike Leonie's long, shapely leg around my hip, thrusting at her pussy, I hear a cough.

"Good morning!"

I nearly drop Leonie in my haste to find the source of the unexpected greeting. She squawks, flailing her arms out to find purchase on the wall of the elevator. I lift my head to see Lola smiling, her eyes twinkling in merriment.

I swing my gaze to find Sebastian beside her with his jaw hanging open in shock. Undoubtedly since I'm *Roger The Responsible* and not prone to one-night stands nor to overt public displays of affection.

However, I'm equally surprised. It's my turn to pick my jaw up from the floor at seeing Baz with a woman coming from his penthouse two floors above mine. His cheeks flush from his attempt to suppress his laugh until Lola bursts out giggling.

Leonie joins in, her amber eyes dance in delight. She and Lola crack up and converse in French about how funny the whole situation is and how they can't believe they're so busted.

Meanwhile, Baz peers over their heads at me. I try my best to remain stoic while I study the floor indicator to avoid his inquisitive stare.

"So, what's up, man? Good night?" He ribs.

Now a flush creeps up my neck from beneath my shirt collar as I ignore his question and their gaiety.

Pressing on, he adds, "I take it the dessert was more than satisfying? A bit of sweet passion fruit filled with lots of seeds? *Succulente, n'est pas?*"

At that, Lola and Leonie's laughter increases, filling the elevator with their unrestrained guffaws and snorts. Fortunately for me, the doors open, and I grab a still laughing Leonie by the hand to drag her out of the elevator. I stalk through the lobby to the sidewalk where our cars and drivers await.

"Seriously, where are you headed?" Baz asks, looking between Leonie and me. "Lola and I plan to get her things from the hotel and bring them back here."

Leonie bugs her eyes out at Lola and starts speaking rapidly to her in French, gesturing animatedly with her hands. With a glance at Baz, Lola pulls Leonie to the side, murmuring a response. Leonie's eyes filled with concern dart to his, then back to Lola before speaking rapidly, again. I hear Luc's name mentioned with not going to be happy and too fast. Finally, I pose a question of my own to Sebastian.

"Better question, what's up with you? I've never seen you bring a woman to your home before and definitely never move them in if that's what you meant by bringing Lola's things back here."

I consider his answers. But let it go. He's a grown man and can decide for himself.

"I'm taking Leonie back to the St. Regis for her to pack while I do some work at the office before we fly back to Paris this afternoon. I'm giving her a lift since Lola and Luc are staying for the meetings."

Sebastian smirks, and like me, he lets it go. For now.

"*MERCI.*"

Leonie graces my pilot and flight crew with a dazzling, million-dollar smile as we board my Gulfstream G650 bound for Paris. Clifford stutters a response. So taken by the beauty. I drop my head to hide a smile of my own. She is breathtaking.

Even dressed casually in an Adidas tracksuit-style maxi dress and sneakers, Leonie strikes a pose. Supermodel through and through, she's flawless.

I place my hand on her lower back to guide her to the middle of the private jet for two extra-large, leather club chairs. Situated across from the burl wood console with the built-in television and entertainment center. It's my favorite spot, aside from the bedroom. We'll explore it later.

Leonie makes herself comfortable in the plush seat. Then sips Evian water from the Baccarat Crystal goblet. She notices my stare and smiles at me over the rim of the glass.

"You know the American saying, 'take a picture, it lasts longer,'" she giggles.

"I don't know if it's 'American.' But I know you've got jokes," I smirk.

Laughter bubbles up, then turns into a snort as the water tickles her nose. Her amber eyes glow with mirth.

I lean over and kiss the tip of her nose. Then on second thought slant my mouth over hers, sucking her cool tongue into my mouth. She tastes divine.

"Mmmmmm, Roger," Leonie purrs.

My dick hardens as our kiss deepens. I can't get enough of her. Our tongues parry and I slip my hand into the vee-neck of her dress to cup her bountiful breast. Just as I pinch her nipple, another slight cough intrudes. We break apart, panting.

"Pardon me, Mr. Steele," Stacey my head flight attendant says with her eyes averted. "The captain has cleared us for takeoff. So I need to collect your glasses if you don't mind, sir."

I nod, handing my tumbler to her. Leonie passes hers over, too. Once Stacey makes her way to the crew area, I press the alert button for privacy. No more unwanted interruptions for the rest of the flight. I have almost eight hours with Leonie and I don't plan on any disruptions.

I reach across her lap to secure her seatbelt. She smiles at me and kisses my cheek.

"So thoughtful of you, *Chéri. Merci.*"

During the flight we share more stories of our childhood, dreams, and challenges. Even though it's only been a week, the connection I feel for Leonie is strong, unlike with any other female.

She's a warm, loving, smart woman. I tell her again I believe her transition to interior design will be a success. She just has to stay focused and get her work done in her last year. Her lighthearted laughter fills the cabin as she slips her arms around my neck.

"Oh, *Chéri*, loosen up! You can't go through life so rigid. *Joie de vivre!*"

I smile at her and nod. A little laxity won't kill me, I suppose. Well, only a little. I join in her laughter as I pull her from her seat to lead her to the bedroom.

"Let's see how loose I can stretch your tight, little pussy, *Chérie...*"

Her laughter cuts off as a tremble runs through her body to our joined hands like a spark of lightning. Her amber eyes turn black as her pupils dilate with lust. Her breath quickens, and she nibbles on her bottom lip as she peers at me. Yeah, Leonie doesn't mind my control in the bedroom.

And I'm not about to give it up. Ever.

ROGER

"*M*r. Steele, what do you expect in a relationship? I mean in a business partnership with an interior designer."

The women in the lecture hall titter as the brunette in the front row asks her sixth question with a misspoken work, innuendo, or blatant flirtation. An American named Delia something or the other.

I sigh inwardly and glance at my Vacheron Constantin Patrimony Traditionnelle. The watch may have a lot of complications. But it easily shows another twenty minutes remain in the class.

Wonderful…

I lift my gaze to Leonie, who's barely containing her glee. Those enchanting amber eyes shine as she holds her fingers over her mouth. I cock my eyebrow at her and flex my fingers—the sign my palm itches to connect with her round bottom.

She guffaws out loud. Then pretends to cough. A male student seated beside her rubs her back and whispers in her ear. The entire class session he's used excuses to engage with her—giving her a tissue, picking up her pen, offering her a piece of candy.

Fucker.

My eyes narrow at him. This time, my fingers curl into a fist. I want to smash him.

Mine!

These past few weeks Leonie and I have been inseparable when she's in town. I've even scheduled my Positano and Monte Carlo projects' site visits for when she's off shooting in some tropical or urban locale. I'd rather spend time with her. It's worked out well. That is mostly.

We've had some disagreements about her work ethic for her studies. She uses the excuse of her modeling schedule for not completing her assignments on time. I told her just because the faculty allows her tardiness doesn't mean she should continue to miss deadlines. She accuses me of being controlling—that is, outside the bedroom.

Just the other night she went to a party instead of writing her paper due the next afternoon. She worked on it that day and submitted it last minute. But she could have finished it earlier and not rushed. Leonie doesn't see it that way. The light laughter and teasing me about my rigidness morphs into pouts and rebukes.

The upside is the incredible makeup sex. We can't go long angry with one another. So when we get back together, sparks fly. There's no holding back. Just like our first time together. Our passion ignites us.

Not everything revolves around sex in our relationship. And it is a relationship at this point. Two months is the longest I've been with the same woman. As Sebastian was so shocked to see me with Leonie since I don't do one-night stands, I'm also never with a woman longer than a couple of weeks. I'm doing a lot of firsts with Leonie.

Like now, I'm doing her a favor. I'm her show and tell—guest lecturer, she laughed—for one of her business courses at the Paris American Academy. They're discussing career paths. The pros and cons of working independently, for a firm, or at a large corporation. STEELE International is renowned. So Leonie figured she'd score cool points or "chilly points" with the professor if I did a class takeover. She pointed out the opportunity for me to meet potential new hires. Her negotiation tactics along with exuberant kisses convinced me.

The concept was good. But the women flirting with me in hopes to score a billionaire combined with the overly helpful jerk outweighs the benefits. I have to wrap this up. Before I answer the brunette's inane question, I pinpoint my gaze on Leonie and the fucker.

One glance at my expression and my balled fists, Leonie shifts away from the guy. She attempts to mollify me with a charming smile and nod of acknowledgment. The guy finally picks up she's mine when his gaze follows hers to me. I glare at him with my lip curled in a snarl and he hastens to move away from her.

Smart move, loser. I give zero fucks about what anyone may think about my possessive behavior.

I glance at my watch once more. Fifteen minutes. Then turn my attention to the eager student to answer her question. The countdown begins.

"Monsieur Steele, qu'attendez-vous dans une relation? Je veux dire dans un partenariat d'affaires avec un architecte d'intérieur," Leonie mimics the woman from earlier.

Leonie's purr zings my balls as she stands before me. She's dressed in a white round-collared, cap-sleeved blouse, navy pleated micro-mini skirt sans panties, red knee-high socks, and black patent leather, high-heel Mary Jane shoes. Her long mane pulled into a high ponytail with a red bow. Reading glasses perch on her nose.

I'm still fully clothed in my bespoke three-piece suit and A. Testoni Oxford shoes. Instead of standing at the lectern, I'm sitting at a desk in one of the Peepshow performance rooms at LEVELS Paris with the curtains drawn for privacy. No one sees Leonie in the throes of ecstasy except for me.

This LEVELS in the 7th Arrondissement Palais-Bourbon Le Faubourg inhabits the former Parisian home of a pampered courtesan to a French king. The magnificent *maison* on a tree-lined street sits behind duplicates of the original double carriage doors and features a spacious interior courtyard. They host grand soirees during the warm-weather months under the stars and strings of fairy lights.

The layout—the same as the other two locations—spreads across seven levels. As with each club, the Sky Lounge offers a view of a nearby landmark. With Paris, it's the grand Eiffel Tower resplendent in lights at night. The beauty and history of the property makes this location my favorite.

"*Oui, petite étudiante. Je fais beaucoup,*" I respond.

I plant my feet further apart to widen the space. Then pat my legs to beckon Leonie to me. She arches her elegant eyebrow and tilts her head, regarding me with her sharp, cat-like eyes.

"Come here, Caramel Bonbon, and I will answer your question," I say as I pat my thighs again.

Leonie licks her lips, then sashays towards me. The hem of her minuscule skirt sways with each movement of her hips. Her long legs close the gap between us. She pauses before me and waits for my next command.

I slip my hands around her hips to cup her firm ass. I squeeze each cheek in my palms, pulling them apart slightly. More than a handful. Perfect.

Leonie bites her plump lower lip on a moan and sways in my grip. She places her hands on my broad shoulders, leaning into me.

The curve of her full breasts peek from behind her blouse. The top buttons undone afford me a glimpse and I nuzzle my face between her mounds. I suck on her skin enough to leave a red mark. It stands in contrast to her honey-color complexion.

Mine!

My dick throbs as it presses painfully against the zipper of my trousers. I shift uncomfortably on the chair. The ache unbearable. I have to get inside of her. Now.

Wedged between my thighs, I tip my face up to hers.

"Open your blouse for me, baby."

Immediately Leonie complies. Her tits bounce free in my face. My mouth closes on her fully aroused nipple, suckling hard on the distended tip. Delectable.

"Oooh, Roger, *Amoureux*," she murmurs with her head thrown back.

I slip my index finger into her mouth and she sucks on it like a lollipop. I remove the wet digit and place it against her back entrance.

She stills, then presses her hands on my shoulders to move away.

I grip her tighter and growl against her breast. Not giving her the chance to avoid my touch. I massage the tip of my finger against her puckered hole.

"Roger…"

"Yes, baby?" I croon as I hum on her heated skin.

"I… I've never… um… I've never had anal sex," she whispers.

"Mmm mmm mmm," I purr in delight.

Yes, another first! No other man will ever have the claim of her ass.

"I'll make it so good, baby. Trust me?" I ask.

Leonie considers my words. Her hesitation is only for a moment. Yet it feels like an eternity. I would never force a woman to do anything she doesn't want to do. But I will push their limits enough for them to decide if they want to continue or stop.

"*Oui, Amoureux*," she replies confidently with a nod of her gorgeous head.

A breath I didn't realize I was holding expels from my mouth to blow warm air against her nipple. It pebbles even more. I kiss the tip softly. Then stand.

In her lower heeled shoes, I tower over Leonie. She tips her head back to search my face. I keep my expression open to ease any doubt she may have. She finds none. Able to relax fully, she smiles at me. Heat simmers in her amber eyes.

I take that as my cue to move us to the large four-poster bed with a trellis canopy. Like the rest of the clubs, Paris is just as sumptuous with high-end period furnishings, fixtures, and accents. This performance room features a school theme. Except for the armoire full of toys and the St. Andrew's Cross built into a wall, one wouldn't know they were in a BDSM club.

I play with certain elements. But tonight I'll keep it simple for Leonie's first time. My girth and ten inches are more than enough.

I sit on the bed and stand her between my thighs again. She slips her fingers into my hair, twirling the strands around them. A tug sends a jolt from my scalp to my dick as she stares at me with hooded eyes.

I draw the soft flesh on the underside of her breast into my mouth to add my second mark. She growls softly. The vibration pulses against my lips, and my cock twitches in response to her primal call.

Her clothes have to go. Now.

First, I unzip the skirt and it falls to the floor in a puddle. Holding her hand, I help her step out of the circle of fabric. Then lift her leg to drape her thigh over my shoulder. I press my nose to her pussy to inhale her sweet arousal deeply. In one long swipe of the flat of my tongue, I lave the juices collected on her lips. Delicious.

As I make a meal of her pussy, Leonie mewls and rides my face. When her inner walls quiver around my probing tongue, I pull back and swat her ass. No cumming until I give permission. The jiggle of her flesh makes my dick weep, eager to dive deep.

"Off," I growl, as I tug at her blouse.

Leonie scrambles to remove the offending garment. Her wide eyes stare at me, surprised by my aggressiveness.

Fuck.

She drives me wild. I want to claim her and fuck her like a wild beast until I wreck her pussy as she writhes beneath me. The thought urges my hand to unzip my trousers and free my turgid dick from the confines of my boxer briefs. With a groan, it springs out and thumps against my shirt-covered abs.

Leonie shivers.

I bite her inner thigh.

She squeals, folding her torso over my head, yanking my hair hard.

I take the opportunity to partake of her succulent core again. Her legs tremble from the exertion of holding back her orgasm. So, as I push my thumb into her bottom hole, I draw her engorged clit into my mouth and suck it hard.

The pleasurable pressure from the duo sensations sends her over the edge. Her body convulses as she screams my name mixed in with French curses. Satisfied, I swallow her sweet honey as my mouth floods with her release.

Soft cries come from Leonie as she pants while her body reacclimates. I slip her limp form to the mattress. Then stand to undress. Her eyes are closed as she unconsciously plays with her nipples. A smile spreads across my face, proud that I put her in a state of bliss.

As I stand there stroking my cock, Leonie's eyes flutter open. Their feline shape narrows as she assesses me. Pleased with my naked form, she draws her lower lip in her mouth with her teeth. She stretches contentedly and purrs.

"Roger, *Mon Chéri*, you're too far away. *Viens à moi maintenant.*"

With a low growl of my own, I crawl up the bed then sit back on my haunches. Her gaze drops to my bobbing cock as I stroke it once again.

"Hands and knees, Kitten," I tell her as I give my dick a last tug.

Slowly, Leonie flips over. When she's in position, I press my palm between her shoulder blades. The slight pressure is enough for her to lower to her forearms. She peeks at me over her shoulder when I wrap her ponytail around my fist and tug.

Her body bows. Beautiful.

"You look so beautiful, Pretty Kitty," I growl against the delicate shell of her ear.

Leonie mews and lifts her hips upward to brush against my groin.

I swat her ass with my free hand. She growls, wiggling her lush ass. I lower my torso over her back as I wrap my arm around her waist to pull her bottom and thighs flush to me. My thick dick slips between her cheeks.

"So good, Pretty Kitty, I promise," rumbles from my chest to her ear.

I reach into the nightstand for the lube. Then apply a generous amount to my cock and her puckered hole. As I slip my index finger in to the first knuckle, Leonie whimpers, but doesn't move away. Fuck, yes! My dick grows impossibly hard knowing she's so responsive and trusts me.

Once she's suitably prepared, I pepper her back and neck with open-mouthed kisses. She calms, and I grip my member to feed it into her body slowly. Her rear muscles push back against the invasion. So I slide my hand around her hip to caress her clit. Distracted, she allows her muscles to loosen and I slip another inch inside.

"Fuck, baby… You're so tight," I groan into her neck.

She whimpers softly, but tilts her head to give me better access to the column of her throat. I plant more kisses on her skin, humming with pleasure.

"Aaahhh… Ummm," Leonie moans as the discomfort transforms into rapture.

With one last thrust of my hips, I seat myself inside of

her fully. My balls slap her distended clit as I finger fuck her pussy. She's so wet, squelching sounds spill from her core. As I stay still to allow her rear channel to adjust to my size, I continue to plunge my fingers in her pussy. The feeling of my dick in her ass drives me crazy. I don't stop until she squirts in my hand and collapses to the bed.

I grip her hips with both hands, withdraw my dick to the tip, then thrust into her hole. Leonie cries out in wild abandon, tossing her head and bowing her back.

"That's it, Pretty Kitty. Take… every… inch," I piston with each word.

Leonie shakes as her muscles clench around my dick painfully.

With a whoop, I jackhammer my diamond hard dick into her.

"Whose is it? Who does it belong to?" I snarl, caught in her vise grip.

"Oh. Oh. Oh. Oh."

"Words, Pretty Kitty. I'll have your words!" I demand.

Leonie mewls as I feel her pussy tighten around air aroused from the pleasure she's receiving in her rear.

"*Oh, mon Dieu! Le vôtre … Le vôtre … Ooohhh,*" Leonie screams as her body quakes from the force of her climax.

Sweat glistens on her flushed skin. I lick the condensation feverishly, wanting to capture every bit of her essence. I lean over to press my front against her back possessively. Then return one hand to her pussy.

She's not done, yet. I'll wring a few more orgasms from

her before I seek my release. My balls protest as they fill with my seed. But I hold on.

"Cum for me, baby. Cum hard on my fingers. I want to feel it all the way to my dick!"

Leonie keens as another climax claims her. Two more follow on the tail of the one before. The vibrations jolt my cock, and I roar from the intensity of them.

"FUCK!!!"

"ROGER... PLEASE..."

Leonie's had enough, and I won't push her past her limit as I promised. With both hands on her hips to hold her up, I pump in and out of her tight bottom hole. My lower back tingles at the base of my spine, then shoots to my balls. My dick swells and I roar my release, digging my fingers into her soft flesh. I lose all control.

My strokes become erratic. The rhythm gone. My hips work of their own accord to guarantee every drop of my jizz empties into Leonie. Blinded and brain numbed by the sheer intensity of the euphoria, I'm rocked to my very soul.

I collapse to my side, holding Leonie close to me, still connected as one. My body doesn't want to part from her warm embrace.

She moans softly as she murmurs my name.

My fingertips stroke her flank and lower stomach to soothe her as I croon words of comfort. We settle, and my spent dick slips from her rear hole. She snuggles into me with a contented sigh.

I wrap her in my arms and nuzzle my face into her neck. Then take a deep inhale of our combined scents and the smell of our sex. Nothing is better. I fall into a peaceful sleep knowing no one will disturb us.

SOMETIME LATER, I awaken unsure of where I am until it rushes back to me. Damn. Leonie is incredible. I glance down at her now wrapped in my arms with her head and hand on my chest as I lie on my back. Idly, I trace circles on the soft skin of her back.

She murmurs something indecipherable in French and cuddles closer to me.

I think back on our time together over the last two months. The thoughts we've shared, the fun we've had, and how much she makes me happy replay in my mind. The good times transcend the disagreements.

My wish is for Leonie to be a little more serious. I've been more zany than rigid. Well, at least in my opinion. Leonie may argue not enough. I realize that I harp on her a bit—it's my nature. I just want her to succeed.

One thing's for sure, it's been the most interesting of my life. Leonie is full of surprises and I enjoy every second.

"Mmm mmm, *Chéri?*"

"*Oui, bébé?*"

"*Chéri*, stop thinking so hard! I can feel how tense you are—"

I flip us over and press her smaller body into the mattress with my larger frame. My hips spread her thighs for her to cradle me close. My burgeoning erection wedged between us. She gasps from the unexpected move and touch. I put my lips close to hers as I murmur.

"Well, then… What are you going to do about it?"

Leonie giggles and wraps her arms around my neck, gripping the hair at nape. She pulls my head down to slant her mouth to mine. Her passionate kiss sends tingles shooting through every cell of me.

Could this be our *coupe de foudre,* like our parents?

As she lifts her long legs to lock around my hips, my mind and body are in agreement.

I hope so.

LEONIE

"*Bon sang!*"

I cannot believe Roger! This is absolutely the worst thing he's ever done to make me feel less than. I want to hit him on the back of his head with my Judith Leiber minaud!

How dare he!

I glare at the mirror as though it's his reflection. As I fume in the bathroom lounge, another guest at the end-of-the-semester reception enters. One glimpse at me and she scurries back out. My face is flushed red with anger and my eyes shoot daggers. I hate that my irritation with Roger kept her from her task.

Merde!

Frustrated, I dab my face with a cool damp cloth and practice calming breaths. I lift my hair to press the soft cotton to the nape of my neck. With a sigh, I toss it into the bin, then return my gaze to the mirror. My eyes, no longer lit with anger, stare back in defeat.

I thought we were doing so well.

"HI, baby, I missed you. I'm sure you're tired. But I'd like to see you. Have dinner with me?"

I hug my mobile to my bosom, so happy to hear his baritone voice over the speaker. It's been four days since we last saw each other. Roger had to visit Positano and the Harper's Bazaar cover photoshoot took me to Mustique. Over the last six weeks, we rarely spend more than three days apart.

So although jet lag has me in bed at eight in the evening, I lift the mobile back to my lips with an affirmative answer.

"Never too tired for you, Mon Chéri," I purr seductively.

"Mmm mmm... Delighted to know," he croons in response. "I'll pick you up in half an hour."

Only moments later, we're wrapped in each other's arms standing in the foyer of my duplex. An overwhelming need to be one with the other zings through us. Roger's thickness presses against my lower belly. Moans slip from my mouth as I sway my hips to rub my mons on his burgeoning erection. His hands cup my ass to hold me in place while he grinds his pelvis into mine.

"Fuck, Bonbon. If we don't stop now, we won't leave," he growls against my lips as he steps back reluctantly.

I pout. But he only chuckles and kisses the tip of my nose.

"Later, I promise."

I clap my hands joyously when we arrive at Septime. The one Michelin star restaurant is the city's most difficult to reserve. The attraction because of its scrumptious seasonal menu and its respect for the heritage of French cuisine while moving on from traditional and more formal fine dining.

It's a favorite of mine I mentioned to Roger weeks ago. I can't believe he remembered. He's so thoughtful!

My glee dampens when as soon as we walk through the door a beautiful, raven-haired woman rushes over to pull Roger into her embrace. Her ice-blue eyes devour him as though he's the entrée du jour. And as though I cease to exist.

"Roger, Mon Amour comment vas-tu?"

He extricates himself from her clutches. But she continues to hold on to his biceps. I notice his expression glazes over like it does when he's attempting to remain civil and distant. Fortunately, he's never used that look on me.

"Hello, Anouska," he responds in French. "You appear well. Give my regards to your family."

Not deterred, she steps with him as he moves around her. With a flirtatious giggle, she responds.

"Oh, what formality, mon amour! I will not have it! Come! Tell them for yourself. We're just over here."

She slips her palm down his arm to grasp his hand, leading him into the dining room.

Que se passe-t-il!

Roger must sense my ire because his intense gray eyes turn to me, and he shakes his head.

"Anouska. Enough. I am not alone as you can see," he says, as he pulls back, dropping her hand and extending his for me to hold. "Leonie Beaulieu, this is Anouska Albert. Anouska's family does business with STEELE. Anouska, Leonie and I are dating. Say hello to your family for me. Now, if you'd excuse us."

He strides past her with me in tow. He doesn't even offer a backwards glance.

Meanwhile, I'm beyond thrilled by his declaration. I cannot wait for Roger to make good on his earlier promise of later. My body tingles in anticipation.

Later, the tingles turn to jolts of electricity as our bodies become one. While he moves deep inside of my core, he cradles my head and stares down at me intensely.

"Only you, Leonie... Mmmm mmm... baby, only you."

I WAS MISTAKEN.

Tonight, instead of supporting me, Roger lectured me in front of the faculty and some of my classmates. All because I dared to joke about handing in my final term paper three days late. I had a legitimate excuse. Work on the other side of the world in Chile with no internet access can thwart attempts at digital submissions.

Merde!

I close my eyes and inhale deeply. I will not let Roger ruin my evening. On the exhale, I lift my chin high and strut out of the bathroom. I'm *The Lion*. A successful, independent woman who doesn't take shit from anyone. Not now, never. *Non*!

"Leonie, are you all right?"

I glance to my right to find my seat mate Antonio Vasquez beside the door to the bathroom. He must have been waiting for me. How sweet of him. I smile and nod.

"Well, that was a dick move by him," he continues as he

stands to his full height of six feet two inches in front of me.

Antonio's concerned eyes search my face. Then he tucks a strand of my hair behind my ear, caressing the side of my face. He cups my chin in his large hand as his eyes drop to my mouth.

"I would never disrespect you, Leonie. You are precious," he murmurs.

Surprised, I stand transfixed by his luminous emerald stare. My lips part to respond, but he brushes his mouth against mine. I lift my hands to his chest to push him away gently. Abruptly, he's snatched away from me. I stagger from the loss of balance.

My eyes widen when I see a red-faced Roger gripping Antonio's shoulder. Then my mouth drops open when Roger punches him in the face. He reels backwards, hitting the wall. Then lunges forward. They grapple. But Roger who's a trained boxer has the advantage. His cool demeanor never waivers. His focus laser sharp. Coming out of my stupor, I call his name.

"Roger! Enough!"

He turns to pin me with his intense stare. Antonio sees an opening and hits him in the stomach. Roger doubles over from the impact.

"Fuck you, asshole! If you don't know how to treat Leonie well, then I will!"

Antonio makes to knee Roger in the head. Quickly, I push him.

"Enough I said! Both of you!"

I glare at the two Alpha Males. Antonio rubs his swollen jaw and mumbles as he heads to the men's room. Roger gives me that damnable blank stare. I close my eyes and count for ten breaths. When I open them, he's gone.

Merde!

* * *

THREE DAYS LATER, and I refuse to take Roger's calls or answer his text messages. The hurt and embarrassment too much to bear. I haven't left my duplex. Instead, assignments take priority. Whether or not it's to prove Roger wrong, I dive into my studies. In no time, I'm caught up.

Perhaps he's right. If I apply myself more, I can finish faster. I should call him—

Non!

He disrespected me in front of my instructors, peers, and the world. Thanks to camera phones, videos of my chastisement and his subsequent brawl appeared all over social and mainstream media. The Billionaire and the Bombshell splashed everywhere. The saying all publicity is good publicity may be true. But my private affairs remain just that... private. Ugh!

With a groan, I rise from the desk in my home office and stretch my arms overhead. I roll my neck in circles and my shoulders back. I rid my body of the stiffness from sitting for so long.

I need some fresh air. A walk to the café will do me a world of good. I trade my Lola's Coterie romper for a

Missoni sweater, Alaïa jeans, and Chanel ballet flats. I leave my hair in a messy bun and cover my eyes with classic Ray-Ban aviators. I toss my mobile, wallet, and keys into my 2.55 handbag and head out.

It's a beautiful afternoon. A sunny, clear blue sky and cool breeze greet me as I stroll out past my doorman. A few blocks over takes me to the hidden gem. It's only locals. No one asks me for my autograph or a photo here. Grateful for the peace, I sit at one of the outdoor tables on the quiet street. The server takes my order for a pot of green tea and a light salad.

My mobile entices me to listen and read Roger's messages. I slip it out of my handbag and turn it on. As I scroll through, my heart aches.

What the fuck, Leonie?

Mouth locked with that guy,,, Really?!?!?!

Not cool, Leonie

The tone changed with more recent text.

We need to talk

I shouldn't have spoken to you like that...

If you don't answer, I'm coming over there...

Hellooo

Similar words spoken in his voicemails. Only his tone of voice changes from angry to remorseful to demanding.

I put the mobile down with a sigh. Then stare into space as I sip my tea. I miss him. But he constantly harps on me. This time it's too much. I'm not sure it's worth his pendulous behavior.

I wish I could speak to my best friend. But Lola's busy

with the New York boutique's opening and working on the Las Vegas site. Besides, Roger is Sebastian's brother, and I don't want to cause any drama.

The vibration and chirp of a text cuts into my reverie. I flip it over and see a familiar name on the screen—Gio Mattei.

Bellissima, I haven't heard from you in forever! You didn't answer my text to come watch me race at the Grand Prix next month in Monte Carlo. You know you're my good luck charm! I'll send the jet for you. Baci, amore mio. Ciao!

Obviously I could use the distraction. Not that I'll sleep with him. *Non.* But I haven't been to my Monte Carlo penthouse in a few months... *Non!*

I have to put on my big girl panties and speak with Roger.

Another chirp, this time a text from Sebastian about surprising Lola in Las Vegas... tonight. He writes how Roger has been trying to reach me all day so we can fly over together and asks if I can make it. I respond yes right away.

A shadow looms over me just as I hit send. Odd since the rest of the area is sunny. With a frown, I glance over my shoulder to see Roger standing behind me. He looks deliciously rumpled with his thick jet black hair tousled about his head, eyes a flinty gray, and a five o'clock shadow on his normally clean-shaven jaw—gorgeous.

"Baby, I'm sorry. Please forgive me. I want to make it right."

Merde...

LEONIE

"*You* must understand how you hurt me deeply, Roger. If not, let me be clear."

I turn to face him seated on the banquette of his private jet.

"You reprimanded me as though I were a simple child and not an adult woman. You humiliated me in front of my teachers, faculty, and classmates. People I have to interact with regularly and who judge my competency. Now, they may think less of me. Why? How could you?"

We have a ten-hour flight ahead of us. I won't sit in silence or pretend nothing is wrong. It's very wrong. I stare at him expectantly.

Roger squirms. Hi eyes dart from mine to the floor.

At least he appears contrite. But he has to tell me what he was thinking to treat me in such a manner. It hurts more since he's teased me about being flighty.

I hate the stereotypical misperceptions and expectations of models: dumb; only clothes hangers; just stand there and pose prettily, not think. I serve as a mentor for girls and teens. My entire career I've fought against those beliefs and urged others to to do the same—models, designers, photographers.

Now to hear it from someone I've grown closer to than any other man...

"I apologize, Leonie. I was out of line. There's no excuse."

He takes my hands in his and stares at me intently.

"I met with the faculty and your professors. I made a public apology at each of your classes. My Human Resources team set up an annual paid internship program for two students awarded in perpetuity."

My eyes mist with tears. I turn away, ashamed to show any weakness.

Roger refuses my denial. He cups my face in his large hand. Automatically, my gaze meets his intense stare. He's so open I perceive no artifice in their gray depths. Only his sincerity and remorse shows.

"Please forgive me, baby," he murmurs.

I nod. But remember, he didn't address his other gaffe.

"Thank you for all that you've done to rectify your behavior—"

Roger leans forward to kiss me, but I put my fingers to his lips. He lifts his eyebrow in question.

"What about Antonio?" I raise my eyebrow in return and tilt my head.

His eyes darken to a steely gray, then close off. He sits

back and folds his muscular arms across his broad chest. He looks like a petulant man-child.

But I already miss the warmth of his touch. However, I will not speak first. He has to answer for his egregious conduct. Antonio's face was already swelling like a balloon!

It's a tense few minutes before Roger responds angrily.

"What about him? He was mooning all over you when I guest lectured your class. I warned him then with a glare. Next he's kissing... No correction... The two of you are kissing while you're with me—"

I cut him off, but he stops me.

"How would you have felt if Anouska flirted with me in front of you one day and later you come across us with our lips locked in a passionate kiss?"

He looks at me sharply. A dare for me to lie and say I wouldn't have behaved like he did. But I can't. Anger wouldn't describe the intensity of my reaction. I can only nod.

"You're right and wrong. I would not be happy to find you with Anouska, or anyone for that matter. But I was not kissing him—"

"You had your mouth on his and your hands on his chest. What do you call that?" Roger growls, eyes in slits.

His possessiveness makes my pussy clench. He's like a caveman claiming his mate. Crazy, but it turns me on. He must sense the electric charge in the air or my arousal because he cocks his head to the side, scanning my face. I bite the corner of my bottom lip. His nostrils flair. My pussy pulses.

Merde…

As though internally deciding, Roger takes a deep inhale. Then closes his eyes and presses his forehead to mine. He slips his hands around my waist to clasp them at my lower back.

My fingertips trace the prickly stubble along his chin to caress his powerful jaw. As I slide them into his thick hair that brushes his shirt collar, his exhale escapes as a soft sigh from his full lips. In the stillness, our breath carries like a whisper on the wind, mingling with the drone of the jet's engines.

Lulled by the rhythm, we allow our bodies and minds to reconnect. The past days dissipate with each exhale. A new start grows as we inhale. Rekindled, I slant my mouth over his. Without hesitation, Roger opens to me. Our reconnection deepens as our tongues dance.

Roger shifts on the banquette and scoops me onto his lap. My long legs bend on either side of his muscular thighs. Never breaking apart. He takes control of our kiss as he will not deny his desire. His dominance reclaims me.

"No one else gets your kisses, Leonie," he growls against my swollen lips. "They are mine and mine alone… As are you, Kitten."

I whimper and slide my heated seam along his thighs. On a groan, he slides down in the seat to notch his bulge with my pussy. Hampered by our clothing, we can only rub against fabric. The friction increases as my clit strikes his cock. The fire builds. I want more. I need more.

But no.

"I forgive you, but we can't rush into—"

Roger groans and tightens his grip on my ass to lock me in place.

Gently, I press against his chest to stand. Then straighten my clothes.

He throws his head back against the top of the banquette, his eyes squeezed shut. Long calming breaths cause his chest to rise and fall. He drags his fingers through his hair. Then leans forward and presses his forehead against my belly.

"Oh, baby," he groans as he cups my ass. "What's wrong?"

Now it's my turn to close my eyes tight. I have to be strong and not give in, as tempting as he may be. With my hands on either side of his face, I tilt it up to me. My heart bleeds when his entreating silvery eyes stare into mine.

"As much as I burn for you right now, we can't. Let's take some time off this trip. Okay, *Mon Chéri*??"

I stroke his cheek and smile encouragingly.

Roger groans as he buries his face under my sweater, nuzzling the sensitive skin. He plants a trail of open mouth kisses from my navel to between my breasts. Then blows warm air against my flesh, heating it up even more. He pulls his head out. Then stares at me intently before nodding and pulling me to sit across his lap.

I can't help but squirm as his prominent bulge rests against my ass. In response, Roger pulls me tight to his firm chest and zerbets my neck.

The tickling sensation increases my movement as

laughter bubbles from my lips. He hooks his thigh over mine. It prevents me from jumping off his lap to evade his probing fingers as they add to the tickling of his mouth.

Breathless, I squeal, "Stoppp... Rooggeerrr..."

His booming laughter joins mine as he wrestles me to the floor of the jet where he straddles me. His handsome face looms over mine. His hair falling into his sparkling eyes. He continues his onslaught with no care for my yips and yowls.

"You little temptress," he mumbles against my throat. "You rub one out on my dick, then decide we need to 'take... some... time?' Really, Kitten?"

Each poke of his fingers causes tears to spill from the corners of my eyes. They slide down my face to pool in my ears. I take a quick breath, then wheeze out a stuttered response.

"Roger, please! I can't take anymore!"

His chuckle blows more warm air onto my skin, setting me on fire even more. He sits on his heels as he smirks down at me.

"Fine. As you wish, Kitten."

Effortlessly, he rolls to the balls of his feet, then stands to hold his hand out to me. I clasp it and he lifts me up. But to emphasize his desire, he pulls my torso flush with his. I feel his still hard cock throbbing against my lower belly. Just as eager as my pussy and as denied.

"If you behave, perhaps I'll reward you," I tease, waggling my eyebrows.

On a groan, Roger buries his face in my neck for one last zerbet.

My laughter rings around the cabin.

* * *

"Is this it? Is this the space for Lola's Coterie?"

Lola asks Sebastian as she bounces on the balls of her feet, holding her beaded clutch to her chest.

Roger and I along with Luc, Blair, Tina Nickles, Walter Smith, Malcolm Steele, and Lydie Jackson gather inside of the large retail space. Tina and Walter are Sebastian's personal assistant and head of development, respectively. Lydie is a family friend of theirs who's in Vegas to meet with Malcolm.

Recently vacated by the former anchor tenant in STEELE Las Vegas' luxury mall, it's the perfect spot for Lola's Coterie. They set the mall between their two five-diamond resort and casino properties in the middle of the action of the Las Vegas Strip.

Roger and I are staying in his Bridge Penthouse, one of the twelve on the top six floors designed to attract high rollers and the über-wealthy clientele. The penthouses act as a bridge to connect the two resort properties with the mall between them from the ground level to the third floor.

Sebastian just punched in the code for the door lock. As he steps back, he gestures for Lola to enter ahead of him.

We hide in the darkened interior since the lights are off.

The paper-covered windows and doors block the inside from passersby's view. So she sidesteps to the right to let him guide the way and claps her hands in delight.

"Maybe," he teases her with a Cheshire Cat grin.

"Don't tease me."—THWACK—"My heart can't take it." She says as she hits Sebastian on the chest with her clutch.

"Okay… Okay. Wait there while I turn on the lights," he tells her and walks further into the interior towards where we stand.

It's our cue to flash the lights flash on and yell surprise. Our screams echo throughout the vast space.

Lola screeches and jumps back as we and the servers wave, clap, and stomp our feet. Sebastian joins in and swoops Lola up in the air, then carries her over to the table set for dinner. As he put her down, she fists his hair and brings his face to hers for a passionate kiss. Reluctantly, he lets her go when I grab her arm to pull her in for a hug.

"*Félicitations!*" I exclaim, beaming with my amber eyes aglow.

Luc comes over next and kisses Lola's cheeks before pulling her into an embrace. "*C'est une excellente nouvelle pour* Lola's Coterie, *petite chérie!*" He extols, hugging her, again.

Sebastian drags Lola away to introduce her to Malcolm and Lydie. I giggle at his jealousy of Luc. My skin tingles as I sense Roger's eyes on me. After spending the rest of the flight working—me with my studies and Roger with his project plans—our amorous encounter took a back seat.

When we arrived at the penthouse, we had less than

thirty minutes to change and get to the store before Sebastian brought Lola here. In our haste, we didn't have an opportunity to rekindle the flame. Although surreptitious glimpses kept the embers lit.

Now, however, Roger's eyes simmer blatantly with unquenched ardor. Sparked by our gazes meeting, he saunters over to me. His stare scorches my skin as he takes me in from head to toe.

I can't blame him since I look ravishing in my black mini dress. It's artfully ruched to create a wrap-effect skirt with long sleeves that have structured shoulder pads. The stretch-jersey gives it a close fit and is complete with an open front split that points to my core. My long legs go on forever with black point-toe pumps. The strings wrap around my ankles like a present.

Just before he reaches me, out of the corner of my eye, I see Lola hurrying in my direction. I love her outfit of a black cutout, fringed stretch-cotton and mesh, sleeveless maxi dress with matching black briefs peek out from under the sheer skirt. The plunging neckline, wispy fringe, plus delicate ties that crisscross the open back add to the sexiness. It falls demurely to a billowy, ruffled, asymmetric hem where her high strappy heels lengthen her legs.

"Malcolm's invited us to one of the resort's nightclub!" Lola gushes. "I'd love to go dancing! What a marvelous way to continue the celebration!"

She squeezes my hands between hers and we wiggle our hips, mimicking dance moves.

"I'd love to go, too!" I respond, equally excited.

"Dancing? After dinner you mean?" Roger asks with a disappointed expression on his freshly shaven face.

"Yes! We can't wait!" Lola replies, unaware of the sexual tension pinging between Roger and me.

He peers at me over her head. Then parts his lips to respond.

However, Sebastian calls everyone to the table. With a smirk, I dodge Roger's answer and loop arms with Lola. We strut to the table and take our seats. A grumpy Roger lowers himself in the chair on my other side.

Dinner is fun with Lola and I regaling everyone with stories of our exploits in growing Lola's Coterie's brand image to the fashion set. Luc chimes in with his tales. Only Roger and Sebastian appear glum.

Now in one of the resort's nightclubs, Lola and I dance in the middle of the floor. Carefree and loving life as the young, successful, and wealthy can. As always, the two of us attract the attention of every man in proximity.

Apparently the brothers had enough of Lola, me, and our admirers.

No longer sitting in our VIP area sipping glass after glass of the Jackson Special Blend Scotch, moping for the rest of the night, they stalk over to us. The other men scatter like prey, sensing the hunters.

"Okay, Dancing Queen. It's my turn," Roger growls in my ear as he slides his hands around my waist.

"Whatever do you mean, *Amoureux*?" I ask, staring up at him as I flutter my eyelashes coyly.

He spins me around so my back presses to his front as

he bends his knees to grind his pelvis into my ass. His lips trail kisses along the side of my neck as I shiver in delight. His hands slide along my flanks to grip my hips possessively. Locked in his embrace, there's no doubt I belong to him.

"Mine, Pretty Kitty. All mine!"

ROGER

"*O*h, *Mon Chéri*! This is just what I needed! A lovely break from the monotony of work, work, work, work, work as Rihanna says! Thank you!"

Leonie and I left Las Vegas for STEELE Cabo San Lucas at the spur of the moment. Might as well take advantage of being on this side of the world for a beachside rendezvous with the current year's *Sports Illustrated Swimsuit Issue* cover girl. One of many for my hot supermodel girlfriend.

She looks as tantalizing now as she does on the cover. Her long hair hangs sleek down her back from the warm ocean water. Pulled from her face, her sculpted cheekbones and swan-like neck emphasize her beauty. The itty bitty, white bikini barely contains her ample breasts and makes me want to bite her generous ass. Every man on Palmilla Beach stares mesmerized by her as Leonie frolics in the waves.

The beach features a one-mile-long stretch of gorgeous, soft white sands and blue-green swimmable waters. The five-diamond SCSL is the only resort with direct access. It's nestled near the southern tip of Palmilla Beach and commands stunning views over the turquoise water. Guests enjoy complimentary activities including snorkeling, stand-up paddleboarding, and kayaking at SCSL's very own Pelican Beach.

"Chéri! Come join me!"

I can't resist her siren's call. As I stride over to her, Leonie's feline eyes eat me alive. Memories of our love-making these last two days stir my cock. If I don't get into the water soon, everyone along the mile will see how much my Kitten excites me. As though sensing my thoughts, Leonie grins and pointedly stares at my rapidly expanding bulge.

"Happy to see me, *Amoureux*?" She teases as I dip into the water in front of her.

Beneath the waves, I cup her mons and smirk, "It's not only the ocean that has you wet, Caramel Bonbon."

She blushes at my reference to how sweet her pussy tastes. Then hisses when my thick finger slides between her folds to stroke her inner walls. I add a second to increase her fullness. Leonie rides my digits. A pinch of her clit sends her spiraling towards her climax. So caught in the throes of ecstasy, she disregards the other beachgoers.

I cover her mouth with mine to muffle the sounds of her pleasure from those around us. No one is the wiser of her release. As Leonie comes down, I nuzzle her neck, planting kisses along her feverish skin.

A hiss escapes my lips as she takes my engorged dick into her hand.

Her insistent tugs bring my release on quickly. My thighs shake as my cum spews into the water. I laugh at the thought of impregnating fish with my copious amount of seed. Leonie cocks her head questioningly. But I shake my own at the absurdity of it.

As we continue to stand in the waves, I pull her to me and she buries her face in my neck. The feel of her heart racing with mine reminds me of how close we've become over these two months. And so fast. This is the happiest I've been in a relationship with a woman in my life. Only her lack of focus mars my keenness of her.

"I don't want to leave tomorrow," Leonie whispers against my skin.

"You have your exam the next day," I murmur, rubbing her back in circles to soothe her as I think here we go. "You can't miss it."

She groans. But perks up, peeking at me.

"I could always tell my professor I had an unexpected assignment…"

What the hell? Didn't we talk about her not shirking her responsibilities? Leonie has to be more serious with her program. How can she expect to make a career out of being an interior designer if she uses flimsy excuses to not complete her assignments and coursework? I shake my head, disappointed with her behavior.

"What? Why do you have such an angry expression on your face, Roger?" She demands, pulling out of my arms.

The Lion stands fiercely akimbo in front of me. Her amber eyes no longer shine with satiety. Rather, they burn with indignation.

Too bad.

"Leonie, are you serious with me right now?" I ask, not bothering to hide my irritation.

She stares at me in defiance. Her chin tips up and her eyes narrow. With a snarl, she responds vehemently.

"I am very serious right now, Roger. Why do you stare at me in disappointment?"

Although we only got over the argument about my treatment of her at the end-of-the-semester reception, I won't back down. This is different. It's only us—no one else. Plus, she should know better than to ditch her exam. It's enough already.

"Leonie, the better question is why do you so readily, and so easily I might add, skip out on your schooling? To what end?" I query, folding my arms across my chest, as ready as she is to battle this out.

For a moment, I think her head will explode. The honey color of her face mottling with red. Followed by her eyes widening in shock. Without realizing it, I'm holding my breath. Fuck it. On an exhale, I continue.

"Right. You don't have a plausible reason. We leave as planned."

I stride back to our double chaise to gather my things. A silent Leonie appears opposite me and picks up her towel and straw bag. I can't get a read on her emotional state. For once, she's the one with the stoic expression, not me.

Without a glance in my direction, she marches back to our beachfront villa next to the resort.

I can't help but appreciate the sway of her hips. Her long, toned legs easily carry her away from me.

Fuck!

Leonie

I'm so upset with Roger. Only by sheer force of will do I keep the tears from falling. I have to get back to the villa, pack, and get the hell out of here.

His words play over and over in my mind. The sour expression on his handsome face burned a hole in my chest. Not again… Not again.

Fortunately, I make it to the front door and key in the code. I don't bother to check whether Roger is behind me. I hope not. I need to leave without further hurtful words between us. They will only make it worse. And honestly, it can't get any worse than this.

The door clicking shut behind me lets me know Roger is not with me. Was he ever?

I thank the packing gods for teaching me more is less. So, in no time, my Bottega Veneta duffle and garment bag sit on the bed waiting for me as I shower. When I walk into the bedroom wrapped in a towel, Roger is sitting beside my luggage.

We stare at one another soundlessly. I refuse to speak

first. But I wait to see what he'll say. Maybe, just maybe, he'll apologize and we can move on. When he only continues to sit and stare at me intently with those gray eyes, I rouse myself.

Not caring that he'll see me naked—nothing unusual in my profession—I drop my towel. Then don the lingerie and clothes that I left on the bed. My skin tingles with his stare. But I ignore him. As I reach for my mobile to call for one of the resort's drivers, Roger breaks the tense standoff.

"Leonie, so you're going to leave? Just like that?"

I swing to face him, skewering him with my glare.

"Are you kidding me, Roger? After all you said, you think I'll stay here with you? *Bof!*"

He frowns, his response, "No, I'm not."

I raise both of my hands palms up and shrug my shoulders while I shake my head. That's it? That's his response? Fuck it.

I turn back to my mobile and punch the numbers on the screen angrily. As I mutter to myself in French, Roger stands and takes my mobile out of my hands, disconnecting the call. Furious, I glare up at him.

"How dare you! Give it back to me... Now, Roger!" I yell.

His response shakes me to my core.

"Leonie, you were 'clear' with me on the jet. Now let me be clear with you. I want a serious-minded partner and not a wayward woman who cannot stay focused for over five minutes. You consistently flit around and avoid your studies. Coming up with excuse after lame excuse. You want people to respect you. But you cannot respect yourself."

He pauses, then continues, "It is my responsibility to return you to Paris since I brought you here. If you insist upon leaving, give me a moment and I will have the jet prepared. We can leave shortly."

With that, he hands my mobile back and pulls his out of the pocket of his swim trunks. So pompous, he doesn't even bother to look at me. He continues with his task. Roger *The Fucking Responsible* Steele to the very end.

My mouth gapes as tears spring to my eyes. This cannot be happening. Roger of all people wouldn't throw my concerns into my face so cavalierly. I clutch my chest, the pain too strong to bear.

I choke back a sob. Then take a deep breath.

"You promised me, Roger. You promised you'd never judge me or make me feel bad about myself again. You broke your promise and my heart. I can't... I won't anymore."

He turns his steely, stoic stare to regard me.

When his expression doesn't change—the one he used with Anushka and others—I know we're done. I swallow my tears and exert my Independent Woman.

"I am not some woebegone, needy woman who has to depend upon a man. I can take care of myself. Thank you very much!"

I yank my bags from the bed and storm out of the villa. Once I'm in the driveway, I call for a driver to take me to Los Cabos International Airport. While I wait for the

Mercedes-Benz G-Wagen, I pull up my private jet charter app and schedule a flight within the hour. By the time I arrive at the airport, I can board.

I use the twenty-minute drive to return emails and text messages. I'm determined not to dwell on the painful events before I can reflect on them in private. So absorbed in my tasks, I startle when the driver opens my door.

Once we're airborne, I request do not disturb. The flight attendant looks concerned for a moment before her professional demeanor falls back in place. I shake my head when she asks if I would like meal and beverage service. My stomach, too knotted to eat, gurgles in protest at the thought. She leaves me in peace.

Finally, I allow the unshed tears to fall.

My heart breaks. This is not *un coupe de foudre*.

ROGER

"*M*attei! Mattei! Mattei!"

The crowd chants. Their loud cheers erupt from the lower terrace and the deejay stops the music to announce the winning team.

Giovanni Fucking Mattei. Damn.

I watch as he grins, keeping his arm around Leonie as they pose for the cameras at the Grand Prix after party here in Monte Carlo. I barely notice Lola, who's opposite them with her arm looped through some guy on Mattei's professional racing team. Great. It's bound to piss Sebastian off.

Unbeknownst to Leonie, the party is being held at one of my new spec sites. It's a hillside villa used as the venue to showcase the property and to encourage buyers. My team expects the entire community of ten villas and a mini clubhouse to generate over a quarter billion dollars in revenue. The same project Leonie was privy to when we were together. Now she'll see it in person. But on the arm of another man.

Mattei, that slimy bastard. The one who always cheats on her is the one with whom she now parades around my fucking villa. She ran back into his arms three weeks after the Cabo fiasco.

Fine. Fuck it.

Below me, Sebastian weaves through the guests as he rushes over to the terrace wall seeking Lola. He flew in panicking after pictures of her and Leonie traipsing around Monte Carlo surfaced on the Internet.

I don't blame him. Leonie in tiny bikinis, mini dresses, fitted capris sashaying all over the place. Followed by the paparazzi. Smiling for the cameras. Never once mournful.

Another glance finds Lola laughing with Leonie, who's still glued to Mattei whose tongue is down her throat. Sebastian looks on, too. He's probably not pleased to see Lola with some other guy. I know I'm pissed with Leonie.

Again. Fine. Fuck it.

Finally, Lola's gaze sweeps around the villa and lands on the terrace where Sebastian stands glowering down at her. She does a double take when she recognizes him; her eyes widening in surprise. He merely stares at her. Even I can sense from this distance her astonishment at seeing him here. She whispers something in Leonie's ear.

She promptly lifts her shocked gaze to Sebastian. Her eyes dart around. Perhaps she's connecting the dots with

Monte Carlo, Sebastian, a villa… my project. And wonders if I'm here, too.

In my periphery, I notice Sebastian catch sight of me as I stare from a distance at Leonie and Mattei. I'm sure Sebastian can distinguish my facial expression, which may be indecipherable to a stranger. However, since I'm his brother, he can tell by the stiffness around my mouth that I'm struggling to keep a straight face and my emotions under control.

The couple I was speaking with is oblivious even as my eyes shift from them to Leonie, who's the center of attention sipping champagne amongst the jubilant racers. When the peals of her laughter rise above the music and other voices, I visibly vibrate with white heat.

"Monsieur Steele, this villa is spectacular! When do you expect the completion of construction for the other properties?"

The woman's question pulls me from my musings. I blink and return my attention to the couple. Focus, Steele! Get your head in the game! I loosen my neck to drain some pent-up tension before I respond.

"As you saw during the tour, this model villa is ready for occupancy. Of the nine other villas, three are in construction, four are in contract, and two are in the bidding process. Each property estimates three months to complete, two for an expedited surcharge."

Her husband, the founder of a Silicon Valley software company, nods as he adds, "We don't want to wait. We offer twenty million cash for this villa to close in two days. Enough time to clean up from this party—"

"And for us to enjoy before we fly back to San Jose at the end of this week." His wife interrupts as she nods emphatically.

"My team will make the arrangements tonight," I turn to my lead sales rep who then coordinates with the couple.

No sooner do I shake their hands do I feel a small palm rest on the middle of my back. I glance over my shoulder to see Verónica Casal. Another stunningly beautiful, well-known supermodel with whom I've been involved.

It's been since Leonie that I've had sex, so my dick thumps to life at the memory of Verónica's ardent fucking. Well… Hello there. No point in being a monk for someone who couldn't care less.

"*Hola guapo*," Verónica purrs seductively as she strokes my back. "It's been a while, no?"

Her chestnut eyes glint with mischief in the light. Her full red lips glisten as she licks her tongue across them. My eyes can't help but follow its trail remembering how it felt wrapped around my thick dick.

Yeah. Good plan.

"*Hola preciosa*, too long, yes," I reply with a cocky grin. "You look as delicious as ever."

Verónica preens while I take her hand to twirl her in a circle, admiring her lush curves in the form-fitting white dress she wears. Damn, her round ass is a playground. My neglected cock presses painfully against the zipper of my leather pants.

When she faces me once again, the sight of Leonie with Mattei in tow moving towards Sebastian and Lola distracts me momentarily. She appears anxious as she looks around the bustling terrace. Perhaps she is wondering if I'm here.

"Tell me, *amante*, I saw you with Leonie... But she is here with gorgeous Gio, her on-again-off-again lover. She's parading him around in front of you. So, are Leonie and you together or no?"

Irritation shoots through me like a live wire. The last shred of my desire for Leonie seared away. Roger *The Responsible* takes a back seat. Emboldened, I lean down to whisper in Verónica's ear.

"Would it stop you if we were, *preciosa*?"

"Absolutely not!" Her peal of laughter carries over the sound of the music and guests' chatter.

Out of the corner of my eye, I can tell Leonie heard Verónica and now sees us together. Leonie's cat-like gaze flashes wide with hurt. Then narrows to angry slits that send sparks in my direction. Meanwhile, I continue to whisper passionate promises in Verónica's ear. Too damn bad.

Leonie continues to glare at us until I raise my head. Then pin her with my signature intense stoic stare. Blank as fuck.

We continue to glower at each other until that jerk Mattei glides up behind Leonie. He slips his arms around her waist, burying his face in her neck. Lustily whispering in her ear.

I throw the couple a scornful look, strong enough to make even Dom Sebastian flinch. In response, Leonie lifts her chin defiantly and takes Mattei by the hand, only stopping briefly to speak to Lola. With a wistful smile, Lola shakes her head, then pins me with a scathing glare.

Sebastian says something to Leonie. She replies, attempting to keep her smile in place. I watch as she walks away with Mattei's arm wrapped around her waist tightly. It's apparent to everyone they are a couple.

I feel no remorse as I return my gaze to Verónica, who I find watching me with interest to gauge my reaction. Not to come across as a lovesick wuss, I pull her close to me letting my hard dick answer her unspoken question.

I sense Sebastian's stare. But I pretend my conversation with Verónica captivates me. I'm sure he can tell that I'm agitated by the set of my shoulders. I cannot belie my genuine emotions to my eldest brother. He knows me far too well.

"Do you have to stay any longer or can we catch up?"

I glimpse down at Verónica's upturned, heart-shaped face. Her thick inky black hair falls in waves like a frame. She is a beautiful woman. Not Leonie beautiful, but in her own right an attractive woman. I ponder whether I can escape within her voluptuous body. My cock begs me, but my mind hesitates.

"Come, *amante*, let's lose ourselves in a night of passion," her heavy-lidded eyes beckon me.

One last glance in Leonie's direction and her retreating

back with Mattei possessively holding her eases my conscious.

Decision made, I make a mental note to send a text message to my team. They must replace the mattress and bedding in the primary bedroom. I'm not so far gone that I lose sight of pleasing my clients.

LEONIE

" $\mathcal{S}$ helley is wonderful! You're lucky to have such a nice mother-in-law, *Chérie*."

I exclaim as I clink my flute to Lola's.

We parted from Shelley and Haley, her future sister-in-law, with hugs and kisses a few hours ago. Now, we're ensconced on a terrace at Lola's STEELE Tower penthouse she shares with Sebastian sipping more Dom Pérignon Rosé Vintage 2005 Champagne—her favorite. Hell, we're more than sipping, we've finished two bottles.

Lola wanted me to stay with her. But I declined, preferring to stay at her Sutton Place penthouse. I offered the excuse that being in her penthouse—I'm doing the interior design for—will allow me to get a true understanding for the space. I get she doesn't believe me. I want to avoid being in the same building as Roger.

It's been eight months since we broke up in Cabo San Lucas and almost seven since we last caught one another in Monte Carlo. It's still too raw for me. I haven't even told Lola the entire sad story. Thankfully, being the best friend that she is to me, she hasn't pressured me into discussing it.

After she told me Roger is in Paris, I agreed to spend time here after the wedding prep session. As her maid of honor, I'm a vital part of the plans, and I love it! I'm so happy for her and Sebastian. Genuine love!

So, once I realized the coast was clear, my expression went from guarded to relieved. Now, it's blissfully happy from the delectable bubbly. Yum!

"How are you and Giovanni?" Lola asks.

And like that, my stomach flips. I realize she's curious since I haven't mentioned him after she extended my plus one to him. She wants me to be happy, even on her big day when her brother-in-law will be in attendance. She deserves the truth.

I take a moment to stare beyond the glass surround at the city view for a moment. Their duplex is on the fifty-fifth and fifty-fourth floors while Roger's penthouse is on the fifty-second. Once I've gathered my thoughts, I shift in my chaise to face Lola.

"Oh, *Chérie*, I just don't know if I want to—"

Merde… Roger!

Abruptly, I sit up and swing my feet to the floor as I stare with wide eyes over Lola's shoulder at him. Surprised by my reaction, she turns to figure out the cause for my concern.

He's striding over to us with that intense gray-eyed gaze of his pinned on me. I suck in a quick inhalation of breath, startled by my body's innate reaction to him. Lola turns to face me. My normally golden-caramel complexion now ashen with my mouth opened in shock spurs her on. My petite defender as always comes to my defense.

Lola jumps to block Roger's path to me. He towers over her five-feet-five-inch frame.

"Stop!"

She puts her hands up and glares at Roger and at Sebastian, who I notice stands behind him.

"Leonie doesn't want to see you. So, please go," she tells him. Then forcefully she adds, "Now, Roger!"

He blinks away from me. His eyes cut to Lola's red-faced glare. She doesn't waiver before him. Instead, she meets his stare with her hazel eyes blazing.

"Roger, bro, you need to slow down," Baz tells him, putting his hand on Roger's shoulder to pull him back. "You're freaking them out. Not cool, man."

The air is tense. I've got to get out of here. I put my shoes back on and gather my things. I'm a bit wobbly from the champagne, but determined to leave.

"Lola, I have to go. I'll call you later," I whisper in French.

She knows I'm upset because I rarely call her Lola. Her eyes widen.

"No!"

We jump around to stare at Roger who has his hands palms forward, raised in surrender. His stare less intense, but still focused on me.

"Please, Leonie, I just want to speak with you. Just for a moment... Please," he beseeches in a voice rough with emotion.

Collectively, they hold their breath for my response. I sigh again, but nod my head in acceptance. Lola speaks, but I shake my head. She must sense I'm trying to control my emotions, so she gives me the space I request.

The glare she gives Roger would set him on fire. Sebastian turns to me and asks if I'm comfortable speaking with Roger. How kind of him to place my comfort above his brother's. I nod, again. They leave Roger and me on the terrace and head to the living room.

On the chaise Lola vacated, Roger sits forward with his elbows resting on his knees, his hands clasped together. I return to my chaise, perched on its edge with my hands folded in my lap. I don't know what to expect, so I wait for him to speak. At first we stare at each other, apparently waiting for one of us to start. Roger breaks the silence.

ROGER

"Leonie... I don't mean to upset you. I asked Sebastian if I could come over because I needed to make things right with you before their wedding. You weren't answering my calls or text messages. I had no other choice."

I catch a breath and rake my fingers through my

already mussed hair. Leonie continues to stare at me. I hope that I'm getting through to her. I need to get through to her. These past few months have been hell.

No matter what I do, I cannot stop thinking about Leonie. Missing what we had. Hating myself for fucking it up with my stupid control-freak ways. She's a grown woman who was doing fine before me.

Who am I to judge her? No one. I was wrong. I take a deep breath and press on with my plea.

"Leonie, I fucked up... Badly. I realize now I was afraid of losing control because I fell in love with you so quickly. It's never happened to me before. From the moment I looked at you outside of my office at STEELE, it was like a thunderbolt jump-started my heart for you. Only you."

Despite my dick's initial bravado to fuck Verónica, it withered and refused to stand tall at its ten inches. When I opened my eyes and saw her face instead of Leonie's, I couldn't pretend. Her scent, her voice, her touch were not those of my lover's. No one's were. My fist and visions of Leonie give me a modicum of relief.

Leonie's response to my lengthy utterance has her hands moving rapidly in agitation.

"*Non*! Not only me! You... You've been with dozens of women... from Verónica Casal to some heiress to actresses. Just stop it, Roger!"

I shake my head in denial, speaking again.

"What you observed and what happened is not what you think. True, I tried with Verónica. But only because you were with Mattei. I couldn't… We didn't have sex. As for the others, we were only together in photographs."

Leonie relaxes a bit. Her hands settle back in her lap and the unshed tears stay in place. My heart breaks. I want to pull her into my arms and never let her go. Instinctively, I perceive it's too soon. So I continue.

"If you don't want to give us a second chance, know that I am so very, very sorry. I should never have judged you and made you seem less than. You are perfect to me. Just as you are. I was the one who was wrong. Every day, I'm reminded of my loss."

I give her time to absorb my words.

"Please Leonie. For the sake of Lola and Sebastian, let's set our situation aside. Put their minds at ease about how we'll behave at their wedding. I promise I will not bother you. Okay?"

Leonie nods and stands, a sign she's ended our conversation.

I rise to stand before her, much as Lola blocked me earlier. Unable to resist, I cup Leonie's face in my hands, then tip it up towards mine. Leonie's body shudders in response when I slant my mouth over hers in a scorching kiss. The intensity of her passion makes me ache for more.

She clutches the front of my shirt in her hands as she swoons from my embrace. My mouth moves to trail kisses along her jaw and throat as I murmur words of love to her.

She trembles, then pulls away, shaking her head. Her hands no longer hold me. Rather, they push me away.

Startled by her abrupt reaction, I lose my grasp on her.

Leonie spins around, scoops up her belongings, and rushes to the door, swiping tears from her face.

"Leonie!" I call to her as I stride through the open door.

I pause when I notice Sebastian and Lola watching us. Embarrassed, I wipe a hand over my face. Then attempt to adjust my pants from the not so discreet enormous bulge at my crotch.

"Fuck," I mutter.

No one moves until Leonie tells Lola she's leaving as she hastens to the front foyer. Lola follows her. They discuss going to Lola's Sutton Place penthouse. Decision made, Lola glances back at Sebastian. He nods in under-standing. I shake my head dejectedly as I watch Leonie leave.

"What happened?" Sebastian asks as soon as the elevator door closes.

I walk back inside, straight to the liquor cabinet. I pour two tumblers of Jackson Special Blend Scotch neat. I hand one to Sebastian; we sit on the sofa. I toss back the entire glass and rise for a refill. Then on second thought carry the Waterford Crystal decanter to the coffee table.

Sebastian chuckles, "That bad, huh?"

"Yeah…"

I fill him in on every detail. Thankfully, he sits quietly as I spill my guts. Once I'm done, the relief lifts the pent-up anxiety from my chest. On a sigh, I lean back against the cushions and close my eyes. The liquor holds good in my system.

After a while, Sebastian speaks up, "Call her."

One eye pops open to stare at him. Is he serious?

"Yeah, I'm serious. You better let her know you're sorry, even if you said it already. Trust me."

His sage advice has me calling and sending text messages repeatedly since she refuses to answer. Until my last voicemail when I threaten to come over to see her in five minutes. Leonie promptly calls me back.

I apologize for upsetting her. And reinforce my agreement not to pressure her and to give her space. For the sake of peace at the wedding and out of respect for Sebastian and Lola, we hold off on any further conversations.

Sebastian was right. It made Leonie feel better. So, it made me feel better.

I played my hand. Now, we can only let it unfold.

LEONIE

J need a break after my run in with Roger. He has my head swimming. His conviction touched me more deeply than I realized.

So instead of returning to Paris as I originally planned, I continue on with Lola to Beverly Hills earlier than expected. The two of us plus Blair and Billie scheduled some much-needed girls' time before our business meetings start. They're in town for her Lola's Coterie site selection. My agents put a photo shoot and some interviews on my agenda. Haley joined us for the getaway.

The night I spoke with Roger on the terrace, Lola and I escaped to her Sutton Place penthouse. I needed time to wrap my head around what had happened. It was so out of the blue for him to be there. I know he tried to reach me multiple times in the past two months. But I wasn't at a point where I could withstand his pleas. Even now, I'm still weak for him.

Merde!

When Lola asked me if I wanted to talk about it, I finally gave in. Until then, I hadn't told her the full story, only that he was too uptight.

I spent an hour going over every detail from the meeting at STEELE to our Cabo San Lucas trip. At last, I admitted I still love him, even to myself. I can't help it, he makes my heart soar. And I guess sore, too. That's the problem… I'm afraid of being hurt… again.

Lola was concerned Roger may have acted like a brute since she saw me crying. I assured her he had said nothing untoward. It overwhelmed me.

While we drank shots of tequila, Roger called and sent text messages I refused to answer. Until his last voicemail when he threatened to come over to see me in five minutes. I promptly called him back.

He apologized for upsetting me. His agreement not to pressure me and to give me space went a long way to lessening my angst. For the sake of peace at the wedding and out of respect for Sebastian and Lola, we decided to hold off on any further conversations.

Lola told me she's fine with Giovanni being my plus one for her wedding. I wonder at Roger's reaction when I arrive with Giovanni. Two Alpha Males, one lioness…

"Leonie… Hello there… Leonie?"

Starr's gentle voice pulls my mind from rampant thoughts distracting me from my meditation session.

Focus, Leonie! Now is not the time to think about my

messed-up love life! I'm here for some rest and rejuvenation. I can figure out my relationship status with Roger and Giovanni at a later date. Anytime but now. Well, at least I hope so.

I shake my head to clear my ruminations. Then open my eyes to see not only Starr's angelic face, but Lola, Haley, Blair, and Billie peeping at me. My cheeks redden as I laugh in embarrassment.

"No judgement...!" Starr's dimples appear as she joins in.

The first stop to jumpstart our girls' time was to Starr Light Fitness & Wellness Beverly Hills for yoga and meditation classes. Lola met Starr when she hosted her first international fitness retreat on Fijian Laucala Island. Lola raved about her experience and how cool Starr is as an instructor and friend. So it's a no brainer to come to her center while we're here.

The concentration vinyasa requires prevented my mind from wandering. Instead, I tuned into my breath and the sequence of challenging asanas Starr used in the flow. The vigorous physical and mental workout was just what I needed as opposed to the slower pace of a Hatha class. Starr's dynamic teaching style made it fun.

After a few minutes in the steam room and a quick shower, we head to lunch at nearby Crustacean Beverly Hills. The modern Vietnamese fare specialties include delicious seafood that's the perfect light meal after yoga.

We settle on the gray suede seats at a banquette near the

Walk on Water. The path runs from the front door through the restaurant between tables. Interspersed with wood and weight-bearing glass, the water below appears to offer a glimpse of the ocean's depths. Aside from the cuisine, the path is the eatery's highlight.

When the server arrives, we order An Sum—Crustacean's version of dim sum—to share and salads for our meals.

"Have you spoken to Malcolm Steele, yet?" Lola asks Starr.

"No, we keep playing phone tag. Right now he's it!" She laughs. "I was unreachable in India, then traveled a few more weeks. He was away on business, followed by a holiday in Italy."

Lola explains how Starr wants to expand her business to include regular fitness retreats at five-diamond resorts around the world, preferably in unique locales. Fiji was just the start. Malcolm as head of STEELE's Entertainment Properties Division oversees their hotels and resorts. He could help Starr with a partnership.

"So at some point, I'd love to get on his calendar. Ha! Or on my mat! Give him a taste of what he's missing."

I laugh so hard that I snort.

Starr gazes at me, befuddled. And turns to Lola, who also looks confused.

Okay, not the best way to start out when first meeting someone. I clear my throat and smile.

"What you said about getting him on your mat and

showing him what he's missing sounds like a double enten-dre. Especially when the Steele men are involved!"

Lola cracks up and can't stop. Even Starr laughs, now clear on the cause of my hysteria.

"Yes," Haley starts. "My brothers can be a bit much, I must admit. Trust me, growing up with them and observing the hordes of women falling all over them was sickening!"

We laugh some more until the server swaps our appe-tizers for our main dishes. Silence descends on the table as we replenish our stores after our workout.

"*D'accord*, where do we go for our Girls' Not Out?" Leonie asks.

"The latest hot club to open is the Remy West Holly-wood," Billie who knows all the West Coast happenings responds. "Their It thing is dancers bound by ropes Shibari style suspended from the ceiling. It has a BDSM vibe if you know what I mean."

She giggles and lifts her eyebrows up and down.

Lola and I glance at each other, then snort. If only she knew we're All Access Global members of LEVELS. But then I remember Lola mentioned Patrick Rockett is AAG, too. So Billie's probably been there plenty of times with him.

Merde! We're a kinky bunch! I laugh uncontrollably.

"What did I say?" Billie asks, confused.

"Oh, Billie, nothing! It's aah… How do you say… graph-ic!" I giggle. "Let's meet at eleven in the lobby. *Oui?*"

Billie nods, accepting my save.

"What are you wearing?" Haley asks. "I have a black mini dress or a light blue sequin romper."

Fortunately, the conversation switches to a safer topic. Blair chimes in on how well the light blue would contrast with Haley's gray eyes and ebony hair. Meanwhile, Lola's eyes still twinkle with glee.

MY GIRLS and I sit in the VIP area of the Remy West Hollywood. Billie was right. This is a hot spot. The Shibari tied dancers hover inches above the crowd. The colorful silken cords artfully swathe their long, toned limbs. They blindfolded some. While others stare boldly at the revelers. The dungeon-like atmosphere adds to the BDSM theme. It's a nice attempt at a sex club. But it doesn't compare to the LEVELS locations.

Since visiting LEVELS New York, I've gone to the Paris and London locations when they have Masquerade Night. Not that I'm ashamed of my voyeurism kink, but because I prefer to remain anonymous. Besides, it adds to the thrill.

I think back to my last visit in Paris.

The feather on the mask tickles my cheek as it brushes against the side of my face with each step I take as I head deeper into Peepshow. My destination tonight is one of the performance rooms.

My erotic energy in on the floor presses against me. The sight of men and women in various throes of passion ignites my own. I'll have what they're having, I laugh as I think of the popular movie scene set in a diner in New York City. Except I won't fake my orgasm. I'll get off for real. And I cannot wait.

As I approach the selection of rooms, I slow down to inspect which has the action that I want to view tonight. The first features two men and a woman. She hangs from the ceiling by red ropes tied into a swing. Her legs spread wide and her torso angled to allow access to both her pussy and her ass. The men push her between them, impaling her on their enormous cocks. Her cries of carnal pleasure ring out over the speakers. My pussy clenches.

They're near the end, and I need a full scene to ease my ache. I move on.

I pass three other rooms also in the midst of action. A light shines above the far set of doors to a double-sided room. I quicken my pace, eager to get to the room before anyone else. Just as I arrive at the viewer's door, a man steps up to it.

He smiles at me as his bright blue eyes darken behind his mask.

"Would you like some company?" He asks in a gravelly voice.

I shake my head no and reach for the knob. He steps back to allow me entry. I return his smile as I step inside. The lock clicks and I sigh in relief.

The viewing room has a red leather sofa and a chaise to choose for seating. Along the wall an array of toys, floggers, and cords offer the viewer the opportunity to join in the activity. My fingers trial over the assortment of dildos and vibrators, each still in its sterile packaging, onetime use only. I select a clit stimulator and peel away the packaging as I stride to the chaise. I want plenty of room to stretch out and enjoy the performance.

Once settled, I press the button and the light in the playroom on the other side of the one-way window turns on. It's arranged like a bedroom in a luxury flat. A mahogany hand-carved bed with sumptuous bedding dominates the space. The sturdy four posters and lattice canopy provide various rings for attaching cords for bondage. An armoire undoubtedly contains implements for the play. A St. Andrew's Cross stands in one corner and a pommel horse in the other.

A woman walks in. She's lean and tall with long ebony hair and tawny colored eyes. The only covering on her body is a sheer white slip.

She sits on the edge of the bed and waits. A man saunters in. He's six feet and brawny with brown hair buzzed short. His coal-black eyes rake over the woman, the heat in his gaze makes her shiver visibly.

Without a word, he kneels before her and pushes her thighs apart. His mouth lowers to her pussy. She cries out and leans back on her elbows as he devours her, issuing grunts of his own. The slurping of him feasting on her juices makes mine flow.

I too lean back on one elbow. My eyes never leave the scene before me as I part my thighs and allow the cool air to hit my pussy only covered by a silk thong. My breasts grow heavy in the tight corset as my nipples press against the silk overlay.

As I continue to watch her writhe from his ministrations, my fingers pinch my puckered peaks. I refuse to give relief to my dripping pussy. It's too soon. I want the passion to build.

When she arches her back screaming through her orgasm, my eyes narrow to slits as I lift my hips and gyrate against the empty air. Sadly, I have no lover to hold me down and force me to be still in the pleasure.

The man stands open, strips his jeans off. His massive dick stands proud against his six-pack abs. He strokes it as he watches her intently. She licks her lips and beckons him to join her. He withdraws a condom from the night table beside the bed. As he returns to face her, he rolls it over his thick length.

She scoots up the bed and widens her thighs in invitation. He climbs over her and grips her hips. One back-breaking thrust and he fully seats himself deep within her pussy. Her mouth is open in a silent scream, too shocked by his brutal entry.

As he thrusts in and out of her channel, the shock morphs into a state of sheer euphoria. Wildly, she matches his movements as she bucks beneath him. His passionate dominance drives her mad.

I'm caught in a sexual thrall, riveted to the scene before me. No longer willing to hold back, I pull my thong to the side and place the stimulator on my clit. Set to the lowest level, I increase the vibrations, wanting to reach my climax as she reaches hers.

We're not too far apart as my denial only served to bring me close to the edge. A few more pumps and a few more zings, and I blast over the brink. Only then do I lose focus on them as my eyes roll back and I jackknife off of the chaise. We cry out in wild abandon as one. Then fall back as our bodies spasm from the aftershocks of mind-numbing climaxes.

My pants taper off into even breaths. I open my eyes and witness the lovers wrapped in one another's arms, snuggled close beneath the silk sheets. He strokes her face as he croons to her. She smiles at him languidly.

I blush, their connection is too intimate even for a voyeur like me. Then turn the light out to give them privacy. Their room dims to a soft ambient glow.

"Time to get our groove on one more time, Ladies!" Blair announces as she pulls Billie to her feet. "Let's go. No time to decorate the banquette!"

My reverie fades, and the Remy replaces Peepshow. I shake my head to push the vestiges away.

She's right. We've been dancing and drinking for the past three and a half hours. Girls' Night Out is fun. We enjoy each other's company and our drinks. I finish the last of my cocktail and join my friends on the dance floor. I'm going to make the most out of our GNO, too.

The DJ's music and callouts have everyone bouncing to the beat. I throw my hands up and shimmy in my black silk-satin mini dress. It's cut in a classic slip silhouette and has two shoulder straps at one side and is ruched above the thigh slit. It's one of Lola's latest designs for the evening wear collection she's creating.

"The DJ plays the best music!" Blair says as she bumps her hip against mine.

She flips her chestnut brown hair over her shoulder as she twirls on the dance floor. Catching the attention of a few guys who make their way over to us.

"Hello there, gorgeous," one of them says as he bends down to my ear. "You look familiar. Have we met?"

I peer up to get a good look at his face. He's handsome in a surfer boy type of way—sun-bleached blond hair, chocolate brown eyes, lean build. I shake my head and he cocks his head to the side, studying me for a moment.

Not interested in being dissected even by a hottie, I spin away from him and continue my dance solo. His husky laugh follows me.

He slips his hand around my waist, turning me to face him. I glance up into his smirking face.

"Not so fast, gorgeous," he smirks. "If you think you can get away from me that easily, think again."

He pulls me close and places both hands on my waist.

I just want to dance and have a good time. So I let the handsome stranger move us to the beat. After a while, he twirls me around and with bent knees; he grinds his pelvis into mine. The sensation of his hard dick against my ass breaks goosebumps across my skin.

Already keyed up from my LEVELS Paris memory, I squeeze my thighs together. The ache is strong.

We move as one for a few songs, glued back to front. His lips graze my neck and I tilt my head to allow him more access. My hands rest on top of his on my hips. His hands clutch me possessively. As the next tune begins, he whispers in my ear.

"Let's get out of here. Go make our own music, gorgeous."

Just then, I notice Sebastian grinding with Lola. I hadn't seen him arrive. They look so good together, like they belong with no one else. Lost in their own world.

That's what I want. Not some random guy. Roger's words pop into my head. Giovanni's laughter fills my ears.

I may not be sure of those two who I want. But I know for certain it's not surfer boy. Not tonight, not ever.

With a sigh, I shake my head and slip from his grip.

"Come on, gorgeous," he persists.

I step away and tell him no firmly. He nods disappointedly and walks away. I turn and make my way to Billie, Blair, and Haley. They're dancing not too far from Lola and Sebastian. The girls cheer when I reach them.

Moments later, Sebastian strides away from Lola. He leaves her standing with her mouth hanging open. She glances from him to us, apparently torn between her man and her friends. She hesitates.

"Go! Be with your boo!" Billie laughs and shoos her hands at her.

Haley, Blair, and I nod, giving Lola the thumbs up as we continue to dance.

She only hesitates a moment. Blows kisses to us. Then rushes after her man, pushing her way through the pulsating crowd.

Hell, I don't blame her. I'd do the very same thing. In fact, all of us would opt for our sexy fiancé if given the chance. Girls' Night Out is fun. Being with your friends is fun. But it doesn't compare to a night in with your more than fun lover!

"What's so funny?" Haley asks over the pulse of the music.

"Girls' Night Out or Lover Night In?" I ask, raising and lowering my hands like a scale.

Haley giggles, "That's a straightforward decision... Girl's Night Out!"

My eyes widen in surprise as I stare at her.

She giggles some more and claps her hands.

"Gotcha! Lover takes all every time!"

Billie and Blair ask what's the joke, and Haley fills them in. They laugh and high five with us in agreement. Then we dance some more, getting lost in the beat and a fun night.

ROGER

"*L*ola!"

The flashbulbs of the paparazzi's cameras light up the dark sky like fireworks. The photogs are out in full force for the opening night of Lola's Coterie Abu Dhabi. In addition to the pomp of the event, the press dubbed Sebastian and Lola *Couple of the Century* since their engagement announcement. As the first of the STEELE Quaternity to pop the question combined with Lola's fame as the top lingerie designer, their pairing makes headlines.

Add Leonie's megastardom as the brand's spokesmodel and the night couldn't get any hotter. The cool desert air can't compete with their sizzle. I watch her as stalks the red carpet towards the happy couple.

The Lion commands the crowds' attention without even glancing their way. Their shouts of her name only elicit a brief smile as she's determined to reach her best friend.

As always, Leonie's stunning beauty draws the lenses to her. She captivates in a burnt-orange sequined one-sleeve, fitted gown that reaches one knee then flares at the other like a mermaid's tail to angle down to the top of her foot. Her long legs make quick work of the red carpet in open-toe stilettos. Each sway of her hips reflects the light of the incessant flashbulbs. Her signature mane piled in a bedhead tousled style.

I notice a flicker of irritation shoot across Sebastian's face. My gaze follows his to spot fucking Mattei who must accompany Leonie. Sebastian glances around, more than likely seeking me out to give me a head's up.

No matter. I promised not to pressure her. I'm pissed he's here after all I told her about us. Briefly, I close my eyes and take a deep breath. A hand on my shoulder brings me back.

"Hey, bro, you okay?"

Malcolm just as protective of his younger siblings as Sebastian stares at me with a worried expression. He's the splitting image of Baz, except Malcolm's hair stays permanently tousled while Baz slicks his back. Both sport five o'clock shadows. Although Malcolm shaves his at times.

"Yeah, I'm good," I respond with a nod for emphasis.

"Lola! *Chérie*! How marvelous you look!"

Leonie's exclamation draws my focus back to her. She's like a magnet to my steel. I cannot resist her.

The BFFs hug and the paparazzi start their blitz again. Now that she's caught up to her friend, Leonie affords the press her full attention. She and Lola pose together and apart, ensuring their best angles.

Meanwhile, Mattei and Sebastian stand to the side. My mobile vibrates with a text message.

Listen, Mattei is here. Keep your cool, bro! It's Lola's night, don't fuck it up or else...

I type a quick response to accept his request and my promise to behave even though I'm pissed. Then I glance back up at them. I train every day with my boxing coach. So I'm at maximum strength and performance. However, Mattei is no chump, so it could get ugly real fast. And Baz would kill me. Not worth my brother's ire or upsetting my future sister-in-law.

Lola calls to Sebastian to join her and Leonie for more photos. Fortunately, Mattei keeps his distance and doesn't join them in the shots. As he stands between the two of them, the crowd goes wild. Once he notices me with Malcolm, Harris, and Haley, he calls us over to get in the pictures. The rarity of all the Steele siblings in one frame will make for excellent social media posts and traditional media coverage.

I don't hesitate when I refer to all of us as Steeles, since I won't let Leonie wander much longer. I'm sure Sebastian realizes after my drunken confession to him last month, it's only a matter to time.

As we approach, Leonie stiffens and shifts to move away. My brother won't let her. He tightens his hold on her waist. The professional in her won't cause a scene, so she relaxes at his insistence and beams for the cameras.

I take my cue. I don't hesitate to stand beside Leonie and place my arm around her possessively. I don't even acknowledge Mattei's existence. Now fully assembled, the flashes nearly blind us as the paps go crazy for the best shots.

"Luc!"

Lola calls to her mentor as she waives him over to us. He joins our group to pose for more shots.

"Lola, Leonie, Sebastian, Luc, you have news crews to speak with," Billie Chandler, one of Lola's personal assistants, says as she steps behind us.

As Leonie slips from me, I squeeze her side holding her to me longer. She glances up at me and bites her full lower lip. I ache to suck it into my mouth. Instead, I smile at her and incline my head.

"You look stunning, Pretty Kitty," I murmur in her ear.

She shivers and I hear her swallow. She's just as affected as I. Good.

I squeeze her side once more, then step back. She sways a bit, her amber eyes darkened to black. As I place my hands on her waist to steady her, she nods and pivots to follow Lola, Sebastian, and Luc. The fucker Mattei moves in. He wraps his arm around her. At first I think Leonie shifts away from him. But when I blink, they're striding away together. Again.

Fuck!

"Come on, lover boy," Malcolm teases as he grips the back of my neck.

"Damn. Am I that obvious?" I ask sheepishly, allowing him to lead me to the boutique's glass doors.

Malcolm's laugh booms around us. The corners of his eyes crinkle in delighted mischief.

"Yeah… I'd say so, little bro. But it's all good. She's a sexy one."

I jab him with my elbow in the ribs, ready to take him out. But he laughs even louder and pretends to wipe tears from his eyes.

"Stop teasing Roger, Malcolm!"

We turn to spot Haley glowering at him. Our sister, the youngest, is the most straight and narrow of the bunch after me. If I'm not the mediator, she steps in. I give her an appreciative smile and loop her arm in mine. We march through the doors leaving Malcolm and Harris laughing on the red carpet.

Half of the night I spend brooding in the corner. My gaze follows Leonie as she engages with the guests, editors, and admirers. The other half I avoid flirtatious admirers of my own.

With one Steele down, they jockey to catch one of their own. I notice Malcolm and Harris in the same predicament. Only Malcolm flirts shamelessly. Another trait he shares, or rather shared, with Sebastian is his Dom playboy tendencies.

"Lola, you impress me tremendously!"

Her tinkling laughter cuts through my musings. What is this jerk talking about?

"It's the truth! You have the figure for modeling your designs—"

"What did you just say?" Sebastian demands, moving between Lola and the jerk flirting with her.

Oh fuck! It's not me about to ruin Lola's night. I push off the wall and hustle to them. Malcolm apparently heard it, too. He's on his way over.

As we approach, the guy backs up, locking eyes with Sebastian. He's about his height and broad. Not that it matters. Baz will still knock him on his ass.

"You... Come with me," Malcolm demands.

Without waiting for the guy's response, Malcolm takes him by the arm, and I flank him. Quickly, we move him through the clusters of guests.

"Hey, what's this all about?" He struggles against Malcolm's iron grip.

"Respect. You better think long and hard before you disrespect a Steele. Now get out."

Malcolm pushes him in the direction of the two security guards who promptly remove the character from the boutique out the back.

Malcolm wipes his hands on his trousers as he watches to be sure no drama ensues. We stand shoulder to shoulder. Steele's don't take shit from anyone.

Once he's out of sight, Malcolm turns a questioning gaze towards me. He studies my face and cocks his head to the side.

"Spill."

I run my fingers through my hair and roll my neck. The tension caused by watching Leonie and Mattei all night built knots the size of golf balls. I shake my head at Malcolm.

"Okay. Then I'll tell you what I surmise. You want Leonie back. But she's schmoozing with Racer Boy, even though she's still into you. What the fuck did you do to cause her to dump you in the first place?"

As much as I want to strangle my observant older brother, I love him too much. I shake my head and shrug.

"Okay. Then let me guess… Your control-freak ways drove her away."

When I feel the heat rise on my cheeks, Malcolm chuckles.

"Bingo!"

I glance at him. His gray eyes dance with his mirth. I can't help but to join in his laughter. I feel better already. Nothing like family to make you raise your spirits when you're down.

He claps me on the shoulder and leads us out the back.

"Let's go have a drink. I can't let you knock Mattei's ass on the ground tonight. Sebastian will kill both of us. And we've had enough drama!"

TAKING MALCOLM'S ADVICE, I left Abu Dhabi the next morning. Instead of staying in the UAE for the week between that boutique opening and the one in Dubai like everyone else, I returned to Paris. Best to remove myself from the situation. Besides, I had work to do.

Now on board my jet for the return trip, I flip through page after page of images on the Internet of Leonie and Mattei. My blood boils.

Leonie at photoshoots in the desert and around the city promoting Lola's Coterie's latest collections. Attending media coverage interviews and in-boutique private parties for the city's wealthiest women. The two of them on dates for dinner at the various restaurants or at nightclubs until the early morning.

Damn. I thought I sensed a spark. Guess not.

By the time I arrive at STEELE Dubai I, I'm wound tight. There are four hours to pass before the party starts. Thankfully Sebastian flew his personal trainer and former MMA champion Borya *The War Defender* Alexeyev to the UAE. I head to the gym to spar with him.

We train occasionally when I'm in New York. My focus can't waiver with the giant Russian. So I know it's all out or get crushed when in the ring. The mood I'm in, I'll be doing the crushing.

"Oh, ho… So the little brother has come out to play, has he?"

I've barely stepped through the ropes and he's taunting me. A grunt is my only response.

"Ah… No words for me, *mal'chik*? Good."—He punches his fists together—"Let's get started, *da*."

"*Da!*"

Borya and I go at it for an hour in the ring. Then

another ninety minutes of strength training and stretching. I leave the gym reinvigorated, with my head back in the game.

Freshly showered, I meet my parents, Malcolm, Harris, and Haley for dinner. Since it's rare that we're all in one place, we take advantage of our time together. Sebastian waited for Lola, who has last-minute tasks before the party, so they can't join us.

"Hi Mom," I say as I bend over to kiss her cheek.

"Hello, honey! How was your flight?" Shelley asks, pulling me in for a hug.

I love my mother to pieces. Both of my parents are great.

"Good. How're things?" I ask as I make my way around the table greeting everyone.

"Oh lovely! Your father and I went into the desert for some dune driving. Hair-raising!" She laughs, mimicking the rollercoaster movements of the SUV.

"Glad you are back, son. How is business?" Morgan questions, always the net-net man.

"Excellent! All projects surpass projections and track on time," I respond, taking my seat beside Harris.

"Nice work, Roger as always," Morgan states. "All of you make your mother and me very proud. We have a big night ahead of us for the soon-to-be Steele. I am positive I do not have to remind you to represent our family and company well…"

His silver-gray eyes pin each of his children, ever the

Dominant. We respond in the affirmative and he nods, satisfied.

"Now, let us enjoy our meal," he signals the server.

"You will cease this outrageous, infantile behavior at once and apologize to Ms. Lewis and her guests. Then leave. Do... you... understand?" Morgan issues his edict.

All eyes turn to him, including that dickhead Mattei. Morgan's Dom stare knocks us down several notches. In fact, we're below ground by the time he finishes his chastisement of us. Everyone else stands in silent awe of his power.

Morgan's words reset my out-of-control brain. I shake my head to dispel the angry red haze. Sure, Mattei was disrespectful to Leonie and said some stupid ass shit. But I never should have allowed it to get to me. It sent me on a downward spiral of jealousy, driven by an intense need to flatten him for having what is mine.

No matter the circumstances, I should have maintained command of the situation. Particularly at a highly public event held by STEELE. Before Leonie, this would never have happened. It goes against every cell in my physiology.

I gain control before Mattei and turn to seek Lola out in the crowd gathered around. I hope she's not as upset as I imagine. I spot her standing between my mother and Leonie. My younger sister Haley and Lola's assistants Blair and Billie stand near them. All have shocked expressions on their faces. Damn.

I notice Mattei tries to walk to them. But Malcolm puts his hand on his chest to stop him since he recognizes that I headed their way already. Mattei has the sense to back down.

"Lola, I apologize for my poor behavior. Please forgive me," I beseech her.

With grace, she nods her head and accepts my outstretched hand. Her eyes meet mine before she searches for Sebastian, to whom she nods, too.

I turn my attention to the other women who stare at me, surprised by my unusual outburst.

"Mother, Leonie, I ask for your forgiveness, too," I say to both of them, but my eyes lock on Leonie whose amber gaze shies away.

My shoulders rise and fall on a disappointed sigh in response to her reaction. Not wishing to prolong the situation and knowing now is not the time to address Leonie's dismissal, I turn to the guests and apologize to them. Then excuse myself from the event.

As I pass Sebastian, he squeezes my shoulder to offer me support. I nod without breaking my stride. I don't even wait to hear Mattei's apology. I have to get out of here. Try to save some face from my lack of decorum.

Minutes after I exit the boutique, I feel my mobile vibrate in my trousers' pocket. I know who it is without even checking the name on the display. I answer on the first ring.

"Sorry. That was a shitshow Lola did not deserve. Does she really forgive me? Are you going to kick my ass?"

Of course it's Sebastian. I'm sure our father told him to call me or he would. I'd rather deal with my eldest brother than the elder Steele...

I must sound like a wreck since Sebastian doesn't go in on me, as would be his right. It's his woman's event for our family's company. He's the heir apparent to CEO and Chairman of the Board. So besides being the oldest who leads his siblings, he's the future leader of our multibillion-dollar business at which each of us leads divisions. I'm thankful when Sebastian doesn't add to my ill ease.

"Yes, and no. Dad gave the guests gift cards. What the fuck happened?" He asks.

I clue him in on the details. He tells me he understands. Baz is an Alpha male like me, although he's a Dom, too. So he understands protecting my woman's honor and my irrational possessive behavior. But he reminds me to keep my shit together in the future. Then teases me about not being responsible.

I grouse over the gibe. Then we hang up with a reminder about breakfast.

FUCK!

In my rage, I punch the wall. The plaster clatters to the floor, leaving a hole and splatters of blood. Too pissed to feel the pain, I stalk around the living room of my Rulers' Suite at STEELE Dubai I.

This shit is crazy. How can I allow myself to get so out of control that I make an ass of myself at a STEELE business function? So out of character for me—Roger *The Responsible.*

I roll my eyes in disgust at myself for letting Leonie upend my structured world. But I can't help myself. I call her mobile.

Leonie doesn't answer. What else is new…

I have no other choice than to leave a voicemail. How many will this one be? After twelve months, I've lost count. I just hope she'll listen to it and respond to me this time.

"How did we get here? Baby, I miss you. I'm so sorry. Tell me what to do. Please tell me, baby. Please…"

LEONIE

"*How* *ow did we get here? Baby, I miss you. I'm so sorry. Tell me what to do. Please tell me, baby. Please...*"

My heart breaks again. This time not from the pain, but for the ache Roger puts in me. I want him. I want him more than anything in my life. If not for the hurt he caused, I would run to his suite in a heartbeat.

It's the fiftieth time I've listened to his message in the few hours since he left the party. I still cannot believe he fought Gio. And in the middle of the guests. It's so unlike Roger. His rage was palpable. No one has said what happened.

After Roger apologized, Mattei stepped forward. Ever the Italian nobleman, he exuded charm as he bowed to Shelley, Lola, and me, then to the crowd. He increased his accent as he issued his apology. He reminded me of a statesman at the Colosseum.

When he took my hand in his and kissed it with a flourish, I couldn't meet his eyes no more than I could Roger's. Gio's words of love crooned in my ear made my stomach churn with bile. *Non*! I shook my head. Denied, he pivoted and strutted out of the boutique without a backwards glance.

Typical. He always gets flippant when I don't go along with his wants. Too bad. Not this time.

Not when Roger told me he fell in love with me from the start. I felt the same… I still do.

"How did we get here? Baby, I miss you. I'm so sorry. Tell me what to do. Please tell me, baby. Please..."

I sigh and hug the mobile to my bosom as I roll over onto my back in the empty bed of my Rulers' Suite. How I wish Roger were here with me. Held in his powerful arms, close to his firm chest where his heartbeats the same pulse as mine.

Merde…

I close my eyes and let the mobile slip to the mattress. My fingertips skim across the tops of my full breasts to cup their weight. The turgid, toffee nipples poke against the cool silk sheets. A gasp escapes from between my lips as I pinch and tug them. A zing of electricity shoots to my pussy. I bow off of the bed. My long wavy hair tumbles down my back. Aaahhh…

One hand slides between my mounds to skitter across the soft skin of my flat belly. The destination weeps drops of my essence in anticipation of the pleasurable release. My breath catches as my palm covers my bare mons while one finger slips inside of my throbbing pussy. Ssssss...

One does not compare to Roger's massive girth and length. I... need... more.

A second and a third digit join the first. I jackknife as they stroke my G-spot. Fuuuck...

Relentlessly, I probe my dripping pussy. Shivers rack my heated body when the juices slide down my butt cheeks to collect beneath me.

"Roger, oh Roger," I moan piteously, my lone cries ring out in the silent room.

My heels dig into the mattress as I lift my hips to meet the thrusts of my fingers. Deeper into my core they drive.

It's not enough!

Frustrated, I flip onto my knees and reach for BOB, the travel version. Not quite Roger, but closer than my slim fingers. My dripping pussy swallows the battery-operated boyfriend. Mmm mmm...

I toss my mane over my shoulder and lower my chest to the mattress, keeping my ass high in the air. The angle pushes the buzzing vibrator deep within my pussy, nearly to my cervix. Rhythmic thrusts match the movement of my hips as I charge towards my climax. My pussy muscles clench as my thighs shake.

"Oh... Oh... Oh... Oooooh..."

I wail as my orgasm pulsates through my core. Subsequent spasms rock me. Once sated, I collapse to the bed. BOB drops from my hand. I lie in a heap. Moments later, I pull the sheets back over my cooling body and curl into a ball.

As my musky scent fills the air, thoughts of Roger fill my dreams.

"Lola, darling, you had Sebastian and the boys ready to run to the suite! Sebastian was beside himself! He told me, 'damn tradition!'"

Shelley laughs as we sit in the STEELE Dubai I Spa waiting for our manicures and pedicures to dry. After a full day of beauty treatments, they have pampered us into silky smooth, ultra-relaxed, glammed-up dolls. All to prepare for Lola and Sebastian's wedding. Although all of us knew it was tonight, he surprised Lola.

"Yes! Luc called me hyperventilating!" Chortles Blair Thomas, Lola's other personal assistant. "I thought we'd have to ring for the medic to resuscitate them!"

Shelley, Haley, Billie, and I join in on their laughter. We're loud as our voices echo around the nails room. But it doesn't matter since Sebastian reserved the entire spa just for Lola.

"Pardon me, Ms. Lewis."

One of the spa aestheticians stands at the door. A rose wrapped in white silk held in her outstretched hand.

"How romantic," sighs Billie with a wistful look in her big green eyes. "I'm so happy for you!"

"Shelley, you raised a good man," Blair chimes in.

"Thank you, Blair," Shelley responds and lifts her glass of citrus-infused water in toast. "May you all marry your romantic, good man!"

She smiles and glances at each of us. But she winks at me. I blush and avert my eyes. Does she know about Roger and me?

"Ladies, we hope you enjoyed your spa sessions! You seem sufficiently rejuvenated! The restaurant awaits you!" The manager announces.

"Excellent, right on schedule," Shelley responds. "We'll have your bridesmaids' luncheon. Then Lola, you can rest for two hours before the glam squad arrives."

The five-star treatment continues when we arrive at the restaurant and sit at the best table overlooking the dazzling water. We turn to Lola when she speaks.

"I want to thank all of you for all that you've done to help me with my wedding and for being such a supportive mother-in-law and friends," she tells everyone "I have special gifts for you. But I didn't know this was happening now. So they're in New York. I promise to give them to you as soon as I return."

"Oh, darling! We knew your wedding would be here all along. So we planned for everything to be in Dubai. Plus, your bridesmaids' gifts!"

"Thank you! Thank you!"

Lola hands out each of our gifts. I tear up when I hold my pair of diamond drop earrings up to sparkle in the light. They're bigger than the others. Instead of one drop, mine has three.

"*Merci, Chérie,*" I whisper as I hug Lola close.

The last gift is for Shelley.

"Lola… This is so thoughtful… Thank you, darling," she says, holding back her tears as she looks at the beautifully framed photograph of Lola and Sebastian. "This will sit in the center of the living room table amongst our photos."

We continue to enjoy ourselves through the rest of the luncheon. Our laughter peals across the room as we trade stories of our love lives. We decline dessert and end with tea.

"Lola, time to rest before getting you ready," Shelley announces with a raised eyebrow, tapping the bezel of her Chopard L.U.C. XP Esprit by Fleurier Peony watch.

"You look so beautiful, Lola!" I gush as I touch a handkerchief under my teary eyes. "T*u es magnifique, Chérie!*"

"Oh, how absolutely stunning and sexy!" Haley exclaims.

"Simply divine," sighs Blair.

"Sebastian will snatch you away before the ceremony even starts!" Laughs Billie.

We leave Lola to have a moment to herself before she becomes Mrs. Sebastian Steele. Lucky girl…

As I stand outside of the room, my mind drifts to thoughts of my wedding. Would it be just as grand? Will I glow with such pure love and happiness? Will Roger be my groom…

When Lola emerges from the room, I rouse myself and hand her bouquet to her. Then give her air kisses. I adjust her train to flow perfectly behind her sensational gown and fluff the heirloom veil into place.

I love Lola dearly. My sister and best friend has found her genuine love at last. I am beyond excited for them.

As we line up behind the rest of the bridal party, my skin tingles. I lift my gaze to find Roger, who's one of Sebastian's groomsmen, gray eyes focused on me intently. So engrossed, he almost misses his cue to walk down the aisle. Blair has to nudge him to shift his focus from me. When she turns to see what he's captured his attention, I blush and avert my eyes.

I glance over my shoulder at Lola with a smile before I too glide down today's catwalk. Once again, my eyes meet Roger's as the doors shut for Lola's grand entrance.

ROGER

"—*O*ur turn… Roger? Roger, we have to go."

An elbow poked into my side brings my attention from Leonie to my bridal party partner, Blair. Her cerulean blue eyes gaze up at me questioningly. Then she peers over her shoulder to see Leonie blush as she turns to Lola hastily.

A small smile plays on Blairs rosebud lips when she faces front again. Her eyes brighten as though she knows something is going on between Leonie and me. I arch my brow at Blair. But she loops her arm through mine again and proceeds through the doors. We're only slightly off in our timing.

The sight of Sebastian waiting anxiously for his bride makes me think of Leonie. Does she love me? She didn't respond with words of her love for me when I told her I fell in love with her from the first moment. Hell, she was just gallivanting around Abu Dhabi and Dubai with Mattei. So who knows?

Fortunately, Sebastian squashed any chance of that slimy dick being at their wedding. Sebastian was adamant. No one fucks with his family. He didn't give a damn if Leonie wanted him here. However, Lola assured him Mattei wasn't coming. Thank fuck!

Blair and I take our places at the altar just in time for me to admire Leonie as she glides down the aisle. Her strapless column gown flows around her in a swirl of silk organza layers in various orange and fuchsia hues. Her glossy mahogany hair swept up stresses her long neck. Her amber eyes sparkle more than the ornate diamond earrings. Gorgeous.

I wonder what type of bride she'd make: regal like her namesake; elegant; demure; mine...

Low chuckles from Malcolm and Harris who stand near me makes me realize I spoke mine aloud. Leonie's lips turn up in a smile, but she avoids my gaze. Progress.

Sebastian's sharp intake of air is all the announcement we need to know Lola stands at the top of the aisle. She is breathtaking. My heart swells with joy for my brother. He takes care of all of us. Now he has someone who can take care of him.

I want the same. He may only have eyes for Lola. But only Leonie captures me. Once again our eyes meet. I gaze at her unwaveringly to display my love for her without words. This time, she doesn't shy away. She returns my stare until Lola hands her bouquet to Leonie.

Throughout the ceremony, Leonie and I exchange furtive glances. My jealousy spikes when Malcolm dramatically offers his arm to Leonie before they walk back up the aisle. Although they're best man and maid of honor, it reminds me of someone else being her groom. I don't like it at all.

Mine!

We make it through the wedding party and family photos without a brawl—if not, Morgan and Sebastian would banish me forever. Now at the reception, Leonie stands before Lola and Sebastian like the Queen of the Savannah. She exudes feline grace. Her toast is touching with a story of how she and Lola first met and now are sisters for life. Lola dabs her eyes and blows kisses to her best friend.

Also overwhelmed, Leonie's voice waivers as her eyes brim with tears. I rise from my chair to comfort her. But Malcolm—who's giving his toast next—steps beside Leonie. He pulls her into an embrace as he whispers in her ear.

I freeze. My face must resemble stone. Only my intense stare riveted on Malcolm proves I'm not a statue. Now he's rubbing Leonie's back.

What... the... fuck...

Fortunately, Leonie collects herself and disentangles from Malcolm's arms. She returns to the table. My steely gaze tracks her every move. When she's close, my limbs function for me to stand and help her into her chair. She touches my chest and briefly leans against me with a sigh.

Thank you.

Relief along with the heat from Leonie's body courses through my veins as the stone turns to mush. My baby is back.

Not caring we're in a ballroom full of three hundred guests, I press my forehead against Leonie's.

"I love you, Kitten. I love you so much."

She bites her lower lip to keep the tears from falling. But they spill from the corners. I kiss each one. Her body trembles in my arms.

"I... I love you too, *Amoureux*," she whispers.

My heart leaps. I have to restrain myself from swinging Leonie around and whooping my victory.

She must sense my thoughts because she places her palms on my chest and shakes her head. Her amber eyes twinkle. Then she pulls me down to sit in our chairs.

Malcolm's voice cuts through. He regales us with a fairy tale story of Sebastian's miscreant behavior until the Lovely Lola saved him from imminent doom. Everyone roars with laughter while Sebastian rolls his eyes at the charmer. Malcolm laughs, and the meal continues.

Throughput the night, Leonie helps Lola change clothes and does her maid of honor duties with gusto. We don't have a moment to discuss our exchange. She does glance sideways at me and I stare at her.

When Sebastian whisks Lola off the dance floor hours later, I stride over to Leonie. She's still dancing with Starr Knight, another of Lola's friends. She owns the Beverly Hills-based fitness studio and wellness center Starr Light

Fitness & Wellness. Interestingly, Malcolm hasn't been able to keep his hungry eyes off of her. Oh, brother.

I place my hand on Leonie's lower back. She turns around and smiles.

"Lola and Sebastian left. Do you have to stay?" I ask, not wanting to pressure her.

She raises her finger to gesture for a moment. Turning back to Starr, she whispers in her ear. Starr nods and smiles at me. She is a beauty with her flawless chestnut-colored skin and long, curly, dark brown hair with matching brown eyes. Not to mention her killer body. Damn, no wonder Malcolm has her in his sights.

As stunning as Starr may be, I only want Leonie. Thankfully, she places her hand in mine. I smile at Starr. Then lead Leonie out of the ballroom.

She's quiet as we walk through the lobby. When guests approach to offer congratulations for Sebastian and Lola, Leonie charms them with her witty words. Otherwise, she maintains a subdued demeanor. It makes me nervous, and I'm not one who ruffles easily.

Not wanting to spook her, I remain just as silent. But smile encouragingly when I notice her peeking at me surreptitiously. A return smile twitches at the corners of her mouth before she looks away.

Finally alone on the elevator reserved for accessing the Rulers Suites, I slip my arms around Leonie's waist and press my forehead against hers. Thankfully, she allows me to hold her close and even wraps her arms around my neck. We remain locked in place until the elevator doors ping to open on my floor.

Once again I take her hand in mine, clasping our fingers together. She squeezes and smiles up at me. That slight gesture adds a buoyancy to my step and eases the last of my tension.

I pause at my door.

"Are you sure?"

The beatific smile that spreads across Leonie's face zings my heart. But I must hear her verbalize her agreement.

"Words, Pretty Kitty," I request.

"*Oui, Amoureux. Absolument,*" she purrs.

I cup Leonie's face and capture her full lips in a passionate, breathtaking kiss.

She melts against me and tangles my hair in her fingers. Her soft mewls make my cock lengthen and thicken with need. When she feels it press against her belly, she moans and tightens her grip on my hair. Her tugs on my scalp add a touch of pain to the pleasure, and I growl low in my throat. She mewls in deference to my dominance.

Unable to withstand another second, I wind one arm around her waist, locking her to my side as I punch in the passkey code for the door. She's not getting away again. We're all in.

I carry her like she's my bride over the threshold straight to the bedroom. She peppers my face and neck with kisses as she growls impatiently. I chuckle and she growls some more.

"Don't tease me, *Amoureux*! I've missed you so much!" Leonie chides as she giggles.

"I missed you, too, baby. More than you can imagine," I murmur with my lips pressed in her hair.

She tightens her arms around my neck and buries her face as she sighs contentedly. Yeah, she was just as worried as I. No more worries anymore; I vow.

I stride through the bedroom door to the massive bed. As soon as I set Leonie on her feet, she slips her hands inside my classic, bespoke tuxedo to remove it. Eagerly, we strip one another of our garments, laughing as they fall to the floor in a heap around us.

At last, Leonie stands before me, no longer a vision. Her glorious, naked body so real, so mine. As my intense hooded gaze travels over her, my dick hardens painfully. Her exquisite face flush with excitement. Her bountiful breasts heavy, the puckered tips rise and fall with her breaths. The curve of her hips call for my hands to grip them. Long, toned legs tremble. The scent of her arousal carries through the air to ignite my desire.

I tilt my head back, close my eyes, and take a deep inhale. I need a moment to collect myself before I pounce. Slowly, I re-focus on her.

Leonie's feline eyes devour me. My dick twitches from her predatory gaze. She turns and struts to the bed, casting a sidelong stare at me. I watch transfixed as she crawls to the middle. Her round ass high and her head low, *The Lion* on the prowl. She languorously rolls to her back, leans on her elbows, and parts her thighs for me.

Her pussy glistens in the soft light from the bedside lamps.

"Roger, *Chéri, Amoureux,*" she coos as she beckons me with a crook of her long finger.

Like one of Pavlov's dogs, I salivate and lope over to her.

She laughs, a low, seductive rumble in the back of her throat. Her amber eyes glow.

"Here, Kitty, Kitty, Kitty," I call as I crawl over her lush body.

My lips land on her succulent mouth as my groin notches with her warm, welcoming embrace. We groan in unison as our heated flesh meets. Erotic energy zaps all around us. The air crackles with our frisson of fervency.

"Roger... Please," Leonie implores, eager for more.

I kiss the tip of her nose. Then rise to get a condom.

Leonie places her small hand on my broad chest to stop me. A shake of her head brings me alarm.

"What's wrong?" I ask, concerned by the uncertainty on her face.

She shakes her head, and her hair tumbles from the pins holding it up. I reach over and remove them. Then run my fingers through her glossy tresses, enjoying their silky touch. She peeks at me sheepishly. I lift my eyebrows.

"I... I want to feel you inside of me with nothing between us," she rushes on when my eyes widen. "I took a test a few years ago. And I don't have any STIs. But if you don't want to or can't—"

A test a few years ago isn't enough since she's been with

that fucker Mattei. I shake my head and sit back on my haunches.

"I had a test after we broke up and I don't have any either."—I shake my head again when her eyes brighten—"But you haven't had one recently, and Mattei... I don't trust that fucker."

I finish on an angry growl. The nightmare of him inside of Leonie like he boasted before I knocked him on his ass burns my brain cells. I shake my head vehemently to dispel it.

"—had sex with him... Roger?"

Leonie's questioning tone of voice cuts through. I didn't hear a word she said.

"Did you hear me?" She asks as she sits up.

"No," I reply.

She kneels in front of me and cradles my face in both of her hands. A soft smile plays on her lips.

"Roger, *Amoureux*, you are my second lover. I had sex once before you, when I was twenty-one. It's time to do it, I'm a woman, I thought... Disastrous. I have never had sex with Giovanni Mattei."

Stunned, my mouth gapes open. How the hell is that possible? Really? Thinking back, I recall how tight she was around my dick. A shudder runs through me at the memory.

"It's possible," Leonie giggles.

Fuck, I spoke out loud...

"In fact, you nearly split me in two. But you felt so good. So, so good... Mmm mmm," she purrs. "Giovanni and I fooled around, *oui*. But never had intercourse. That's why he was with so many other women. He thought I would get jealous and give in. *Bof*! I used him for some relief and he kept others from pursuing me. I wasn't interested in an actual relationship. My career came first. That is until you, *Chéri*. You changed everything."

Fuck... me! Talk about a boost to a guy's ego! Only once before? That fucker lied! Hell yeah!

I whoop and lift Leonie into my arms, crushing her to my chest as my mouth descends on hers.

Her delighted giggles prevent us from kissing truly. So, I zerbet her face and neck. Her giggles turn into uncontrollable snorts as she squirms on my lap. But I refuse to let her go.

This woman is mine, all mine!

ROGER

"*L*eonie is a special gift of her mother and mine. Madame Beaulieu and I tried for many years to conceive. Many painful miscarriages and the resulting agony finally gave fruit to our *magnifique petite fille*. After she was born, we could not have any more children. She means everything to us."

Monsieur Beaulieu pauses conversing in his native tongue and pins me with a stare so intense it makes mine look like goo-goo eyes. He continues after what feels like hours, but was merely a moment.

"Leonie's mother and I never approved of that Giovanni Mattei character. *Non!* Leonie assured us it was not serious. She never brought him to meet us—no man, in fact. Although unbeknownst to Leonie, I met Mattei one night to tell him what I tell you now."

He leans forward. His obsidian eyes bore into mine.

"Do not fuck my daughter over or you will pay the price."

He rivets me in place for a full minute. Then sits back as Leonie and her mother return from the restaurant's ladies' room.

Instantly, his demeanor softens as he rises to help his wife into her chair and kisses her cheek lovingly. From behind her, he dings me with another look as I help Leonie into her seat beside me.

Guy Beaulieu is one tough-as-fuck man. Outwardly, he's the impeccable, wealthy businessman from a long line of prominent Parisian merchants who trace their lineage to the eighteenth-century. His brawny frame stands at six feet, four inches, still physically fit for a man in his sixties. Leonie tells me he's studied jujutsu for decades. He's just as comfortable in the French salons as in the back alleys. I hardly want him after me. Damn.

"Roger *chéri*, you appear ill at ease. Did my husband scare you to death with his threats?" Madame Beaulieu laughs, her amber eyes twinkling so like her daughter's.

She's the opposite of her husband. Petite, soft, warm. Her ebony hair cut in a stylish curly bob frames her fawn-colored, oval-shaped face. Pouty lips turn up in a joyful smile. Her daughter is as radiant as she. In her early fifties, she could model as much as *The Lion*.

Leonie gapes at her father, "*Papa, non! Tu as promis!*"

Guy smiles indulgently at his gift, a smile that graces Leonie's face all the time. He shakes his head and holds out his hand for hers. She places her hand in his much larger one and he squeezes it.

"Don't you worry, *Mon Trésor*, if Monsieur Steele cannot handle me... *Bof*... He is not deserving of you!"

"*Oh, Papa!*" Leonie sighs.

I watch their interaction. It reminds me of my family's loyalty and love. I don't blame her father. He is correct. I would do the same for my daughter. A smile blooms on my face at the thought of having a baby with Leonie. But then I remember what Monsieur Beaulieu said about their difficulties. I pray Leonie and I don't suffer the same heartache. It would kill me.

I ignore those negative thoughts. Then cup Leonie's face and ease her disquiet.

"My love, your father is correct. You deserve a man and not a boy. Trust me when I say I am a man and your happiness is my top priority."

Monsieur Beaulieu sits back in his chair with a grunt. But nods his head in appreciation of my declaration. Madame Beaulieu smiles warmly.

"*Ça c'est bon*," Leonie murmurs as she leans into my side.

Dinner continues on a lighter note. I guess Monsieur Beaulieu accepts me. I enjoy his company. He's so like my father. I respect his stern countenance. And Leonie adores him. Daddy's Little Girl. I smile again, thinking of our children. She may not realize it yet. But I'm not letting her get away this time. She's mine forever. I'll just give her some time.

"Madame Beaulieu—"

"Don't be silly, Roger, *chéri*! Call me Josy!" She insists.

"*Merci*, Josy," I return her smile. "Leonie tells me you enjoy baking and make the best double-chocolate soufflés."

Josy claps her hands in delight.

"Absolutely! My favorite pastime! You must come to our home for Sunday brunch and I will make them especially for you, Roger. *Oui, Mon Amour?*"

She turns to Guy, and he smiles at her with such unbridled love I have to glance away, afraid of intruding on their private moment. Leonie grasps my hand and grins at me. I kiss her cheek softly. One day, I think to myself.

When the check arrives, guy insists on paying. A dominant move. But I give in to him as he is Leonie's father. I admire him already. Even if he didn't command it.

We depart with hugs and kisses. Promises of Sunday brunch next weekend at their ancestral mansion on the outskirts of Paris confirms his acceptance of me. We shake firmly and he nods. I won't fuck this up.

Eric, my driver, opens the door to my steel-gray Rolls-Royce Corniche. Leonie smiles at him graciously and slips inside. I nod and ask him to take us to my flat. It's a duplex penthouse on the thirty-first and thirty-second floors of The STEELE Tower Paris in the Front de Seine district of Beaugrenelle in the *quinzième*.

The property, like New York City, is mixed-use with commercial and residential space plus the largest mall in Paris. The views of the Seine and of the Eiffel Tower are incredible, especially at night when the spectacular light display flits across the monumental iron structure.

The past month we've alternated nights at her penthouse and mine. Little by little she's left personal items in my bathroom and I made space for her clothes in the dressing room. I've done the same at her place. I'll give her some time. But eventually, she's moving in with me.

"*Amoureux*, dinner was *fantastique!*" Leonie says as she cuddles against my side.

I wrap my arm around her shoulder and she lays her head on my chest, her palm rests on my abs. I kiss her hair and inhale her classic sultry perfume, Dior's Pure Poison. She tells me it makes her feel powerful, like a woman who commands attention. The blend of florals with amber and musk is the perfect balance of femininity and masculinity. It's imprinted on my brain.

"Yes, my love. And your parents remind me of mine."

I put my fingertip to her lips when she sits up with a frown.

"Your father behaved exactly as I would with our daughter's boyfriend," I continue.

Leonie's eyes widen. I cock my head questioningly. Then realize I said, "our daughter." I hold my breath and await her response.

She scans my face. I keep a neutral expression and display no guile. Satisfied, Leonie leans back against me. The remainder of the ride we spend in comfortable silence, each lost in thought. I stare out the window as I rub Leonie's arm, getting as much relaxation from it as she receives.

Eric pulls into the garage and opens the door. Leonie

and I head to the private elevator that takes us to my family's floors only. My parents maintain a penthouse on the floor below mine, and a second one below theirs, my siblings use when in Paris. I key in my code, and the lift speeds to our destination.

"Would you like a glass of Réserve Jean de Lillet Blanc?" I ask Leonie.

I added cases of her favorite aperitif to my liquor collection. I prefer the Jackson Special Blend Scotch neat. It's become our habit to relax on the terrace with our drinks in the evenings.

"*Oui, Mon Chéri.* I'm going to change. I'll meet you out there," she says as she walks up the stairs.

I remove my tie and toss it with my suit jacket onto the sofa as I pass. After I pour our selections, I sit on the double chaise and kick off my shoes. The Eiffel Tower is aglow with glittering clear lights. The brilliance reminds me of diamonds sparkling in the inky night sky.

Lost in thought, I don't notice Leonie's return until she sits beside me and pulls a cashmere blanket over us. She takes a sip of her Lille*t* as she smiles at me over the rim. Her amber eyes outdazzle the Eiffel Tower.

She places our glasses on the table and crawls onto my lap. Straddling my thighs, she captures my mouth with hers. The taste of passion fruit dances on my tastebuds. As bold in flavor as Leonie's desire for me. I wrap my arms tightly around her waist and loose myself in our rekindled love.

* * *

Le Beaulieu Manoir is the family's ancestral home on the westernmost part of the outskirts of Paris in Neuilly-Auteuil-Passy. The majestic property features manicured park-like grounds, stables, tennis court, swimming pool and cabana, and a palatial French Rococo mansion. A part of the 16th arrondissement, it's in the wealthiest neighborhood.

They built the hamlet between the thirteenth and seventeenth centuries. Later, during the reign of Louis XV, it became a fashionable country retreat for French elites. The Beaulieu's twenty acres of land border Bois de Boulogne with parts of the acreage awarded to their ancestors by the monarch.

Even as I glance around and marvel at its beauty, I can't get rid of my concerns.

"Relax, *Mon Chéri*," Leonie says as she squeezes my hand. "My *Maman* adores you and my *Papa*... Well, he doesn't dislike you!"

She giggles and kisses my cheek.

Her joke eases some of my tension. I want her father to at least respect the fact I'm serious about Leonie and not some schmo like Mattei. Guy cannot put me in the same category as that dick.

Leonie and I made good on our acceptance to Sunday brunch Josy extended to us at dinner last week. I'm taking it as an opportunity for her parents to get better acquainted with me and to prove I'm worthy of their *Trésor*.

The large, ornate hand carved door opens. I expected a butler, but Josy rushes out to greet us.

"Bienvenue! Bienvenue!" She exclaims as she pulls Leonie in for a hug and kisses her cheeks.

Josy turns to me and cups my face as she greets me with double kisses, too. She's a gorgeous woman who Leonie will more than likely continue to resemble as she grows older.

"Come, Guy had to take a call. He'll join us shortly," she says as she leads us through the door.

The interior decor is just as impressive as the outside. The furniture, paintings, and sculpture mimic the light elements with curves and natural patterns to form the delicacy and playfulness influenced by Rococo designs.

The Beaulieus as wealthy merchants who traveled the world for the most luxurious items are clear. The mixture of Asian, North African, and Russian influences appears in the tapestries, wall panels, and fabrics. The modern era shows through in accessories, other artwork, and air-conditioning and heating systems. It's extraordinary.

We walk past beautifully appointed salons to an all-glass solarium that overlooks the rear rose garden. They set a table for our brunch and a sideboard arranged for a buffet-style service. The delicious aroma of savory and sweet dishes fills the air. Spices, meats, and baked goods blend to make my mouth water.

"Oh *Maman*! You've outdone yourself today! *Merci*," Leonie says as she hugs her mother.

"You cooked all of this yourself, Josy?" I ask, astonished at the amount and variety of foods.

She smiles and nods, "*Oui*! On Sundays and Mondays, we give the staff the days off. I prefer to cook and bake, anyway. I grew up learning our family's recipes from my *Maman* and *Grand-mère*."

Josy turns to Leonie and laughs.

"Now this one, she preferred to follow her *Papa* and *Grand-père* around the shops and bazaars!"

I join in her laughter.

"That explains Leonie's not so grand attempts at cooking for us!"

Leonie pouts and mutters under her breath. I kiss her forehead to settle the frown on her face, and she giggles.

"Bienvenue au manoir Beaulieu!"

Guy's voice booms in the solarium.

We turn to find him striding into the room, ever the man of the estate. He's impeccably dressed in bespoke blazer, shirt, and trousers with Gucci loafers. He hugs Leonie and gives her kisses. Then faces me.

His obsidian eyes pierce my gray orbs as he takes me in. With a nod, he extends his hand, and I meet him to give a firm shake. He nods again in appreciation and claps me on the back.

"Come, let us eat," he commands.

Guy is so like my father Morgan. I wonder how the two men will get along as I line up at the sideboard.

As expected, the food is delicious. Traditional Tunisian dishes and Continental fare offer more than enough options. I spot deserts, but not Josy's famous double-chocolate soufflés. I hope they're in the oven.

"This is delicious, Josy. Thank you so much," I tell her, meaning every word.

She beams, and Guy rubs her neck.

The intimate touch reminds me of Leonie and me. She must sense my thoughts as she slips her hand in mine under the table. I smile at her, and she winks at me.

Our meal continues with lively discussions on current events, the arts, and business. Guy asks how Beaulieu Enterprises, SAS can partner with STEELE International, Inc. I tell him Sebastian is on his honeymoon. But I will speak with him when he returns. I assure Guy with his company's goods and STEELE's properties we should be able to come to an agreement. He's satisfied and looks forward to meeting Sebastian.

Later, Leonie and I stroll through the grounds. She points out where she fell from her horse and how she helped her mother plant flowers. She explains although she was an only child, her parents more than made up for her lack of siblings by letting her friends spend time at their estate.

I envision Leonie playing with our children on these ancestral lands, and my heart soars. I pull her close and kiss the top of her head as I stare into our future.

LEONIE

"*A*ntonio?"

I walk into the Human Resources Department at STEELE Paris for my third interview as a part-time junior designer to find my former seat mate in the waiting area. Next to him is the female student who was flirting shamelessly with Roger when he guest lectured my class. I don't remember her name since we never interacted. No matter, I smile pleasantly.

Post the fiasco with Roger, Antonio changed seats. Now, he only offers brief nods to me whenever I greet him. Not that I blame Antonio. His face was a mess. Roger paid for his medical costs and gave him a sum of money in recompense. I guess it goes further with the internships Roger set up. Antonio and the other student must interview for the first slots.

"Bonjour, it's nice to see you. Are you interviewing for

the internships?" I ask as I sit across from them in the gray leather Louis XV style chair.

I place my Hermès attaché and portfolio on the floor, then smooth the skirt of my green Versace suit. The color highlights my coloring and the gold silk shirt makes my amber eyes pop. STEELE is a modern company that fits well with my style and work ethic.

Since Roger and I broke up, I redoubled my efforts to complete my bachelor's degree. I accomplished my coursework and my final project of Lola's Sutton Place penthouse two months ago. My grade average shot up to 3.9. I'll graduate with honors. I missed this years' ceremony. But will take part six months from now in the one at the end of this term.

I haven't given up my modeling career, yet. I plan to transition between now and graduation, starting with a part-time junior designer position. Roger urged me to interview at STEELE after he saw my designs and Lola's place. Suitably impressed, he insisted I was ready for STEELE and would do well. He even teased me about being more responsible than him. I had to laugh since now we're together and he shared his genuine feelings with me; I understand better. And he was right. Once I focused truly, I finished quickly.

C'est la vie!

"Oh, bonjour, Leonie."

Antonio sounds far less enthusiastic about our unexpected meeting than I. He turns back to the other student, but her eyes survey me. I figure since I didn't address her, too. So, I smile and extend my hand.

"Hello, we never formally met. I'm Leonie Beau—"

"Oh, I know who you are… Who doesn't?" She sneers, then turns to Antonio. "If she's interviewing for the internship, we might as well leave. She's dating the president. So of course she'll get it."

So taken aback by her vehement display, my mouth drops open. My gaze shifts from her to Antonio, who has the decency to redden from embarrassment. He grips her arm and pulls her back to the sofa. Then brings his gaze to mine.

"Leonie, please disregard Delia. She's just nervous. We are here for the internship interviews," he states as he flashes a warning look at her. "Leonie Beaulieu this is Delia Shaw. Delia, Leonie."

I fix my face and re-extend my hand. I try not to let anyone get the better of me. My reputation is my livelihood.

"Hello, Delia. Not that what you assume would happen is correct, I am not interviewing for the internships. I wish you both luck."

I nod at Antonio and sit back in my chair. Just as I reach for my mobile to avoid further conversation, a woman appears at my side.

"Bonjour, Ms. Beaulieu. Please come with me."

I smile at her and gather my bags. As I stand, I glance at Antonio and Delia. He smiles and wishes me good luck. Delia has a pinched expression, but nods when Antonio nudges her. I beam brightly—never let them see you sweat —and follow the assistant.

Suddenly nervous, I touch my hair to be sure every strand remains slicked in the bun at the nape of my neck. The suit is sexy. But it's the combination of my reading glasses and hairstyle that keeps it professional.

Hhhmmm... Perhaps a scene at LEVELS Paris with me as librarian and Roger as naughty schoolboy—

Distracted, I bump into the assistant and apologize profusely. She takes it in stride and opens an office door to usher me inside.

A man in his late fifties rises from behind an Empire era burled-elm desk. As elegant as the piece, the man exudes a confident, dignified persona. Monsieur Bernard Bonnay, the vice president of Human Resources, greets me with a firm handshake.

"Bonjour, Mademoiselle Beaulieu," he starts. "It's a pleasure to meet you. Please have a seat."

"*Enchanté*, Monsieur Bonnay," I respond, gripping his hand with sufficient firmness.

We settle in our seats, him behind his desk and me in a visitor's chair that matches the wood. I cross my legs. The flesh-tone Manolo Blahnik stiletto bounces with my nerves. I shift to cross at my ankles to hide the movement.

Monsieur Bonnay smiles warmly, "No need for nerves, mademoiselle. You've impressed everyone with your designs and ideas. This meeting is merely a formality."

My thoughts drift to Delia's nasty remarks. Did I only make it this far because of Roger? Do they really find my work up to the standards of STEELE? How will others perceive me? The turmoil adds to my nerves.

Merde…

"—about your inspiration. The pairings intrigue me."

I tune in just in time to answer appropriately. Once the conversation moves to my work and love of design, I relax. The interview goes quickly. The end of the hour catches us unaware until Monsieur Bonnay's assistant knocks at his door. His next appointment awaits.

"Well, Mademoiselle Beaulieu, welcome to STEELE! My assistant will help you with the paperwork. You may complete it in one of the conference rooms. We scheduled a lunch to introduce you to the rest of the team on Monday. Please let us know if that date conflicts with your schedule. *Bonne chance!*"

My cheeks hurt from the wide grin. Excitedly, I shake Monsieur Bonnay's hand when we stop at the door of his office. He and his assistant smile just as broadly.

"Right this way, Mademoiselle Beaulieu," she says, gesturing down the hall with a manilla folder full of papers.

So ecstatic, I practically skip behind her. We enter a glass-walled conference room with a long walnut and brass table styled after the Louis XIV period and brown leather chairs with brass fittings. The decor throughout the offices fits well with Paris and pays homage to its history.

We confirm my workdays as Monday through Wednesday, job description, salary, and benefits. It's so odd for me since I've never had to deal with this onboarding process. I love it!

Once I complete the paperwork, she takes me to the security office for my photo ID. Now, in front of a camera... This is the norm, I giggle to myself. The two burly men become mush when they see me. One asks for a selfie. I oblige happily. My father taught me it's always good to make friends in all areas of a company.

Just as we walk to the elevator—thankfully I don't see Antonio and Delia—my mobile vibrates in my attaché. The assistant leaves me with more words of welcome and good luck. The name on the display increases my grin. Roger, *Mon Amour.*

"Hi," I answer breathlessly.

"Hi, Bonbon. How did it go?" He asks in the deep baritone that makes me shiver.

"Excellent! I got the position and start on Monday!" I exclaim, bouncing on the balls of my feet.

His deep chuckle zips through me.

"Congratulations! We must celebrate with dinner tonight at L'Ambroisie!"

"Oui, oui! Mon préféré, merci, Mon Amour!"

The three Michelin star restaurant is my favorite in Paris. The food of the gods bursts with flavor, perfectly executed by Chef Pacaud. It's in a regal townhouse on Place des Vosges in the Marais district.

Roger pauses, triggered. His sexual tension travels through my mobile.

"Take my private elevator on your left up to twenty. I'll send it down. You deserve a full congratulations now, Pretty Kitty," he rumbles.

As I ride up to the executive offices, my heart races and my pussy drips in anticipation of our taboo office tryst. I laugh out loud when I picture Dalia's face. Hater!

The next bubble of laughter gets trapped in my throat when the elevator doors ping open. Roger's dominating figure stands before me. His intense gray eyes peer into me from his gorgeous chiseled face. A smirk plays on his full lips. His collar-length hair begs for me to tug it as I pull his mouth to mine.

The bespoke, navy pinstripe, three-piece suit fits his muscular physique to perfection. Broad chest covered by the custom shirt, vest, and jacket. Long legs encased in the finest Italian wool. Black leather Oxfords adorn his great feet. Big hands, great feet, massive dick…

I rub my thighs together to ease the ache as I step out of the elevator. Roger notices my unmet desire and growls deep in his chest. His eyes darken to slate in an instant. *Mon loup* is on the prowl. My lion bows before him.

Roger takes my hand and leads me past the three receptionists and offices to his in the far corner. We step inside. Immediately, he strides to his desk to press the buttons to turn the transparent glass walls opaque and to lock the double wooden doors.

He lifts me with ease to sit on his desk. Then rucks up my skirt to stand between my thighs. They tremble.

"Congratulations, Leonie, my love," he croons against my open lips as he slides his long fingers along my inner thighs. "You deserve the position."

He nips my lower lip and I yelp. Thankfully, his office is

soundproof. The tips of her fingers graze the silk gusset of my already moist panties. He growls in appreciation as he slips two fingers beneath the thin fabric. Hardly a barrier from Roger's determined digits.

"Aaahhh, *Amoureux*, *merci*," I pant as his fingers plunder my wet pussy, the sound and scent of my arousal clear in the room.

His lips plot a path of open-moutheded kisses along my jaw to my neck where he draws the sensitive skin into his mouth and sucks. He marks me as his. The sharp pain makes me cry out.

I dig my fingers in the back of his neck, unsure if I want to push him away or pull him closer. The pistoning strokes of his thick invasion make me buck against his hand.

When his other hand reaches for the back zipper of my skirt, I open it for him. Roger slips his thumb in my mouth. My cue to suck on it. Then he slips it inside the back of my panties to press against my bottom hole.

I rise from the table. Only to have gravity push his thumb past the rings of muscle into my ass when I land back down.

"Ssssss… Ooohhh," I hiss and cry out, even as my body squirms to take him further.

"Will you do your very best, Pretty Kitty?" Roger rasps in my ear. "Or will I have to punish your misbehavior?"

His threat of pleasure mixed with pain sends me over the edge. I keen in response as his fingers continue to pump in and out of my holes. The alternating thrusts coordinated for maximum gratification. He covers my last one with his mouth. He absorbs my screams of ecstasy.

As my body quakes with the aftershocks, Roger doesn't let up. Instead, he adds two more fingers to each hole. I writhe uncontrollably from the onslaught of sensation. Wantonly, I crave more. I meet each of his thrusts with my own. I match his movements and taking him deeper within each part of me.

"So good... So good..." I cry out in French, no longer able to think coherently enough to translate my native tongue.

"You deserve every orgasm, Kitten. Every... single... one..." Roger punctuates each word with a pistoning stroke, purposefully hitting my G-spot.

"*Medre...*"

I wail as the fourth orgasm rocks through my body. My hips undulate of their own accord. Mindlessly, I let my body take over as my damp forehead falls against Roger's broad chest.

"There, there, Pretty Kitten. I have you..." he croons against my hair, no longer neatly slicked back.

I lose count of the number of orgasms he's wrung from my body. My inner thighs press against the sides of his muscular legs, trying to close and prevent any more of his ministrations. I'm done.

"Have I sufficiently shown you how very proud I am of you, Leonie love?" Roger murmurs.

I can only nod. Too spent to make my mouth form

words. Fortunately, Roger only chuckles and doesn't demand my "words."

Gently, he extricates his fingers from my body. He places the ones were in my pussy against my lips. Without hesitation, I open for him. Then moan as I taste my sweet essence coating his skin. I lick his fingers clean with relish as our eyes meet above his hand.

His hooded gaze draws another climax from me. I close my eyes and shiver in delight. He chuckles.

Once he's satisfied with my efforts, he pinches my chin between the same fingers and kisses me deeply. Groaning as he savors my flavor, still fresh on my tongue.

"Good girl," he murmurs as he steps back.

Roger's intense gaze takes me in from head to toe. A smirk from witnessing me come undone for him plays on his handsome face, flush from his arousal.

I slide off the desk and drop to my knees to offer him my thanks. But he shakes his head and pulls me to my feet.

Cradling my face in his hands, Roger murmurs, "That was for you, my love. Pleasure for your success. Your satisfaction is all that I desire."

I close my eyes and nuzzle against one of his palm.

I love this man more than words can ever express.

ROGER

"*H*ello Mr. Steele."

I glance up from the monitor for my laptop to the unknown voice at the door of my office. My eyes must be computer weary. I blink to clear my vision. The daymare doesn't change.

It's the American brunette from Leonie's class. The same one who tweaked my last nerve with her inane questions. Her attempt at flirting with me then, and now her presence in my office makes my hackles raise.

Where in the hell is my assistant Françoise?

Sure, I have an open-door policy. But it's for employees, not an intern. At least I suspect she's one of the two interns Bonnay recently hired.

Please don't let my conciliatory offer turn sour. Too late to retract it. And if she went through the proper process, I have no reason to terminate her internship.

I have to tread lightly. But firmly shut down any notion she has of continuing her flirtatious actions.

A glance at the clock lets me know hours have passed since I started reviewing these documents, and it's Françoise's lunchtime. No wonder she's not at her desk.

Fuck.

The intern saunters into my office like she belongs in my inner sanctum. She stops to stand before my desk. Unfortunately, my hesitancy gave her an opening. Sliding her fingers along the very low cut of her tightly fitted wrap dress, she lets her eyes sweep across my face and upper body.

My skin crawls.

My suit jacket hangs on the valet in the corner, my tie with top button loosened hangs at my throat, and I rolled my sleeves up over my forearms. Sometimes the French cuffs and links prove hindrances when I have a lot to type. I tousled my hair from running my hands through it while deep in thought over these contracts.

Obviously this woman appreciates my unkempt appearance. She pokes the tip of her tongue out to moisten her overly glossy red lips as she fixates on mine.

Inwardly, I groan in annoyance. No way does she appeal to me. I force my eyes to not roll in disgust. I inhale, then exhale to avoid snapping her head off for intruding and flirting, again.

Time to put a stop to her shenanigans. Once and for all. It's enough already. I have work to do. No time for a misguided, delusional intern.

"You seem to need some assistance… I can help ease your load," she says, rounding the corner of my desk.

"That is precisely why Monsieur Steele has a more than capable personal assistant and not a recently hired intern who is out of her depth, Ms. Shaw."

The disapproving voice of Françoise cracks through my office like a whip. The intern stops cold in her tracks. The lash of Françoise's reprimand prevents any forward motion.

A flicker of irritation runs over the intern's face before she fixes her expression into a neutral one. She pivots to face my assistant who has a bag of food in her hand and a scowl on her face.

Françoise has worked for me since I started as president here five years ago. She's in her mid-fifties and takes no shit from anyone—including me. Her work ethic, above reproach, keeps her at the top of my list of the company's best employees. She's an asset. And right now, an invaluable one.

"Let me be crystal clear, Ms. Shaw. You are not to enter Monsieur Steele's offices at any time. In fact, you do not have clearance for the executive floor. We will go to security to correct your ID access immediately. Then proceed to Human Resources for them to brief you on protocol."

Without taking her stern gaze from the intern, Françoise puts the bag on my conference table.

"Monsieur Steele, I brought lunch for you," she says, still pinning the intern with her cold eyes.

"*Merci*, Madame Faucher," I reply and move to the table as far away as possible from the intern.

"Now, right this way, Ms. Shaw," Françoise commands as she blocks her from me and points to the door with her outstretched hand.

From the corner of my eye, I see the intern lift her chin and stride out of my office without glancing at Françoise or me.

My assistant, or rather savior, arches her eyebrow at me before she marches out the door.

Crisis averted.

The sound of my mobile brings my attention back to my desk. A smile dispels the vexation. It's the ringtone I use for Leone.

"Ciao, Kitten," I answer.

"Ciao *Amore Mio*," she purrs.

Another of her attributes I love. She's fluent in French, English, Italian, German, and Spanish. Often we'll converse in French and Italian since I speak those languages fluently, too. We're inspired by one of our favorite movies, *A Fish Called Wanda*. When Leonie purrs any of them seductively in her husky voice, my dick hardens.

Now she sounds breathless and not from our exertions. What is she doing, I wonder?

"If you don't stop seducing me, I'm going to scream in the throes of passion right on this treadmill!" She teases.

Ah yes, the gym. Leonie stays fit through Pilates, yoga, cardio, and strength training. She doesn't take her natural beauty for granted. She enhances it with regular exercise and clean eating. When she swallows my jizz, she laughs and calls it protein.

"What's so funny?" She asks.

"Thinking of your favorite protein," I chuckle.

Leonie roars heartily. I'm sure every man in the vicinity stares at her. Especially with sweat glistening on her skin. Fuckers.

"Are we still on for dinner tonight with your friends?" She asks.

I forgot we're having dinner with Joel Bailey and his long-time girlfriend, Hettie Fuchs. Joel and I met at a business function years ago and hit it off. They've been dating for a few years now. He's an investor in real estate and she's an attorney who specializes in commercial property law. They live in The STEELE Tower a few floors below me.

"Yes. Why?" I ask.

I hear the speed slow down and Leonie swipe a towel over her face.

"I want to be sure I have something to wear," she responds, her voice muffled by the towel.

Now, I chuckle. The clotheshorse wants to be sure she has something to wear? Hysterical! Leonie has taken over three-quarters of my closet in two months. I've had to move some of my out-of-season pieces to one of the guest rooms. I told her she already has her first STEELE design assignment: redo our closets. She laughed and kissed me on the cheek as she put another suit in my hand for removal. Gotta love her.

"Not funny! They're your closest friends outside of your family. I want them to like me!" She says.

I clear my throat. I won't tease her. She's serious. I've had over a year to become acquainted with her closest friends, Luc and of course Lola. We decided to spend time with everyone, so we're comfortable on both sides.

"We're going to Brasserie Lipp. I'm changing into a sport coat, shirt, and trousers with loafers. Does that help?" I ask.

Leonie is quiet and I can tell she's contemplating her outfit, so I give her a moment. The background sound changes to soft music. She must be in the locker room.

"Okay, I'll pick up a dress I had my eye on. I love you! *Caio!*"

And just like that, she's gone. A quick breath of fresh air that my soul needs.

* * *

"LEONIE, I love your dress! The pink pattern is gorgeous!"

I agree.

She's achieved her goal. Joel and Hettie adore her. All throughout drinks and dinner, they exchanged stories and found commonalities in the schools they attended and holiday spots they enjoy. She and Hettie already have plans for lunch and shopping this weekend. Plus skiing in Verbier come winter.

And yes, the airy silk floral-print crepe de chine mini dress is elegant and more than suitable to meet her boyfriend's closest friends. The pussy-bow tied at the high neck and flowy blouson sleeves balance the above the knee hemline. Leonie appears both demure and sexy. I can't wait to unwrap her later.

I glance from the two women to Joel. He wears a smug expression. I raise my eyebrows and cock my head in question. He smirks and leans towards me.

"I'll clear my calendar," he says only loud enough for me to hear.

"Okaaay…" I respond.

Joel hums the Wedding March and wiggles his left ring finger.

"Like I said, I'll clear my calendar. I give you at max five months," he laughs as he clinks his beer goblet to mine.

"I'll toast to that, my friend," I respond with a laugh.

"What are we toasting?" Hettie asks, flitting her gaze from Joel to me and back.

"To the best is yet to come, my dear. The best is yet to come," he responds, winking at me over his glass.

"*Prost! Zum Wohl!*" Leonie chimes in as she clinks her glass of Lillet with Hettie's snifter of brandy and our goblets.

Her laughter rings above the hum of conversations, music, and utensils on dishes. She glows with jubilance, more intoxicating than the most potent liquor.

I gaze adoringly at the love of my life. Joel is right. It won't be much longer.

And I cannot wait.

LEONIE

"*W*hat the hell, Leonie?!"
Merde…

Roger storms into my new dressing room—I made good on the redesign of our closets—waving my mobile around. His nostrils flare and his eyes narrow to slits. I fear he'll have a coronary as bright red as he appears from the skin exposed by his unbuttoned shirt to his hairline. He yells like a crazy caveman.

When he shoves my mobile towards me, it explains his rage. A text message from Giovanni flashes boldly across the locked screen:

Bellissima amore mia, I can't wait to see you…

Nervously, I swallow. I didn't want Roger to find out in this manner. My plan was to tell him during breakfast, make light of it. Now, it weighs heavily in the tense air between us.

Giovanni has been blowing up my mobile for the past

three weeks. Ever since the bloggers and media picked up on my relationship with Roger. They were especially voracious for the story since Roger and Giovanni fought at Lola's Coterie Dubai opening, where I appeared as spokesmodel. The love triangle angle proves irresistible.

Now, I'm once again irresistible to Giovanni...

Too bad. He pissed me off for the last time. It wasn't only the fight. His touching that guest at the party right in front of me was the last straw. We may not have had a monogamous relationship—on his end—but he never dared to throw his sidepieces in my face. To hell with our "understanding."

At first, I ignored his calls and messages. Yesterday, when he showed up at my agents' offices and made a scene, I finally gave in to meet him for lunch. It's over. I plan to disillusion him of any notions of our reuniting. Then inform him to back the fuck off.

I had avoided telling Roger right away since I didn't want to upset him. But I did anyway.

Merde...

"Hellooo... Earth to Leonie!"

Roger continues, irked further by my delayed response.

I close my eyes, take a deep inhale, and slowly let the air out as my gaze meets stormy gray eyes. The tinge of hurt in their depths makes me lose my breath. I will not allow Giovanni to damage my genuine relationship with Roger. *Non!*

"Roger, *Mon Cœur*," I start as I take the mobile with the

offensive text message from his hand and place it on the island. "Please forgive me—"

His breath hitches sharply. I swivel my gaze back to him. His gray eyes widened in shock.

Fuck, he must think I'm breaking up with him... again. I shake my head forcefully while I hold his between my hands. His eyes flicker everywhere, but at me. I pull his face closer to mine, making it impossible for him to avoid my gaze. Once his intense glare focuses on me, I continue.

"You misunderstand and it's my fault. I should have told you yesterday. I am sorry."

Roger relaxes a smidgen. But his gaze remains hostile.

I brush my lips over his mouth and sigh as I press my forehead to his. I breathe deeply of his warm breath, letting it soak into me. Strengthen me. Our souls need this connection.

I stand upright and lock eyes with him.

"I agreed to meet with Giovanni because he's been pestering me for over three weeks. I declined his calls and ignored his text messages. Until yesterday. He made a scene at my agents' offices. They were going to press charges. But I told them I would speak with him and tell him to back off since I am with you."

Roger bristles as the words tumble from my mouth. His face deepens in color. He's about to explode.

"What do you mean? That asshole has been harassing you for weeks... Then threatens your agents... And... you... do... not... tell... me?!"

He sputters and wrenches from my hold. He paces the

dressing room as he mutters curses and pulls at his hair. Every few steps, Roger faces me and scowls. Then resumes his tirade.

I stand quietly. He needs to bow off the steam. And I really can't blame him. I'd react the same way.

After a good five minutes, Roger pulls his mobile from his trousers pocket and jabs in his code before he jabs the surface again.

"Do it. Do it now!"

I blink in shock. Who is he speaking to? What are they going to do?

Roger takes a deep breath. Puts his mobile back in his pocket. Runs his fingers through his hair. Then turns to me. The storm moved on from his eyes. Instead, they're slate gray and hooded with raw desire. He regards me for a moment. His gaze traveling from my head to my toes, then back to my eyes. Sexual tension replaces the angry vibes.

I shudder under his perusal.

He prowls towards me.

Uh, oh...

Without a word, he yanks the sash on my silk dressing gown and rips it from my naked body. The soft material caresses my skin as it slips down my body to pool at my feet.

My nipples pebble and my pussy floods.

In one swoop of his forearm, Roger clears the island of the accessories and my mobile on top. He grabs my waist and plops me down on the cool marble surface. My heated pussy trembles. From the abrupt change in temperature or in anticipation, I'm unsure. All I know is that I desire this man. A lot.

Roger plants his palms on my inner thighs and pushes them apart. His eyes never leave mine as he lowers his mouth to my dripping seam. One long lick sends a jolt of electricity straight to my core. I lock my ankles behind his head and grip his hair. He thwarts my attempt to pull him closer to my core with three successive spanks to my pussy lips.

"Ooowww!" I yowl.

Holy shit! He's never done that before. A spanking on my ass, *oui*. But my sensitive bits, *mais non*!

A lapping sound replaces the squelching caused by his fingers meeting my wet pussy. Roger devours me. His tongue sweeps in and around my inner channel. I jump when the tip probes the rough texture of my G-spot. Then cry out in wild abandon as I quake with my climax.

Roger's fingers join his tongue. He drives them in and out. Then scissors the digits to stretch me.

My inner walls clench, aware that the strike of his massive cock comes next. I rock my pussy against his palm like a cat in heat. Then throw my head back and scream as another orgasm throws me over the edge.

The sound of the zipper teeth separating and the pressure of his heavy dick against my thigh jerks me back to attention. My gaze falls to the space between us. Roger's enormous dick strains. Every ridge and vein stands out in relief against the velvety soft skin. A drop of pre-cum glistens on the slit of the bulbous head.

My mouth waters.

Still silent, Roger grips the base in his fist and rubs it against my swollen flesh. My juices coat his length in natural lube. He angles the tip at my entrance, braces his other hand at my ass, and plunges his dick inside. The hand at my rear locks me in place as he fills me root to tip.

Roger swallows my scream with a savage kiss. His tongue plunges into my mouth. It sweeps in to conquer. It matches the brutal thrusts of his hips.

I keen from the invasions. But I keep pace with both ends.

Roger's grunts and the slapping of his semen-filled balls against my ass fill the air. I writhe against him, aching for more. I need to feel his possessive punishment. I need to atone for my sin.

My forehead drops to his broad shoulder as my hands gain purchase in his thick hair. His grunts deepen to growls when I pull on his scalp. I know he relishes the pain.

Roger's feral dominance masters my desire. I cum one explosion after the other until I beg for him to stop.

Instead, he lifts me in his arms, widens his stance, and jackhammers up into my core. His muscular arms and thighs hold me aloft easily. I bounce on his thick dick as he chases his release.

With a mighty roar, Roger slams me down on his massive girth one last time. He holds me securely in place. Our bodies locked together. Inseparable.

I feel his cock swell and jerk inside of my depths as his

seed fills my womb. Triggered, my pussy clamps repeatedly. It milks every drop of his essence into me. This orgasm wrings the last of my strength from me. Sated, I collapse in his arms.

"You are mine, Leonie. Only mine. I will allow no man to lay claim to you ever again." Roger rasps in my ear.

It's the last thing I hear before darkness pulls me under.

My last thought as my pussy tightens around its mate: *oui, Mon Cœur. Oui.*

LEONIE

*I*t's been a month.

Whomever Roger spoke with on the mobile. Whatever he had done. I haven't heard a peep from Giovanni Mattei. Not a voicemail, text message, smoke signal, nothing. He's disappeared from my life completely. Thank goodness!

Roger still refuses to tell me what happened. Just to trust him and not to worry. I trust him explicitly. So, no worries plague me whatsoever.

We've been back together for three months and it couldn't get better. He's even asked me to move in since we spend most of our time at his penthouse. I go by my duplex to pick up more things to bring back to his!

Mais non.

Billie's adage plays loudly in my mind: why pay for the cow if you can get the milk for free? Her hard-to-get tactic works wonders on her boy toy, Patrick Rockett. Her words of wisdom added to Lola's initial fiasco after moving in with Sebastian keep me from taking that step. Not yet.

I know Roger loves me. But I need more of a commitment. For now, it's all good.

Another bright note is my work at STEELE. The Interior Design Team treats me as being a worthy part of them. They know Roger is my boyfriend. But no one judges me or treats me in a certain kind of way. Every day that they appreciate my contributions proves Delia's snide comments erroneous.

Over the three months, I see her in the office on Wednesdays, one of her two days with Thursday being the other. She's asked me out to lunch a few times. But I don't trust her motives. Roger told me about her incident in his office. Bless Françoise!

Antonio has extended lunch invitations to me, too. I decline them without hesitation. His internship is with the Technical Design Team since he's a computer wiz and specializes in AutoCAD software. Even when our paths cross during the research and sketching process, I maintain my distance. No need to poke the bear named Roger Steele.

As far as my modeling goes, I re-negotiated my exclusive beauty contract with the top cosmetics company in the industry. Since I represented them, their revenue increased by thirty percent over three years.

The extended contract for five more years increases my multimillion-dollar fee over one hundred percent and includes corporate stock valued in the millions. Thanks to Luc and his business acumen, it's a historic deal.

My contract with Lola's Coterie also extended for five more years. She wanted longer. But I told her a fresh face would be good for the brand since I'll be thirty-six by the end of it. Not that ageism plays a role. I'll still be just as fabulous, if not more so! Luc had us compromise with a clause added for a review at the end of the five years.

My agents booked me for the best runway shows for this year's and next year's seasons. My signature feline prowl still rules the catwalk. Younger models try to emulate it or ask for my guidance that I happily provide. I am the acknowledged Queen. RAWR!

Roger and I have a busy social life, too. We've spent a few weekends with my parents, during which my mother fills him with different deserts and pastries. He loves it. Even my father accepts him. They've met at my father's club and he's introduced him to some members. Roger is under consideration for membership.

Other times, we hang out with Joel and Hettie. Either movie or game night at Roger's penthouse or at their half-floor flat. Hettie and I go to the gym and shopping together. She's attended one of my mentorship sessions to discuss her career with the girls.

Our schedules keep us busy.

Now, Lola and Sebastian returned from their two-month-long honeymoon. They're in Paris for a few days. Lola to catch up on work with Luc and her team at her flagship. Sebastian to check in on STEELE Paris as part of his newly appointed CEO and Chairman of the Board positions. Hot Power Couple!

Roger and I plan to have dinner with them, then go to LEVELS Paris for Masquerade Night. Neither man wants others to recognize their women. So, now Roger and I only go when members wear masks, or else we sneak in through the employee entrance and straight to his private suite. Possessive much?

All in all, my world is delightful and I'm thankful for it.

Lola's ringtone blasts through my musings. She's here! Excited, I answer her call.

"Hey, *Chérie*! Are you downstairs?" I ask.

"Hey, Girl! Yes! Sebastian went to Roger's office for some last-minute meeting. I'm on my way up to you," she responds.

I rush to the entry foyer to meet my BFF. As soon as the family's private elevator doors opens, we fall into each other's arms. It's been too long. The most time we've ever been apart and not spoken since becoming friends seven years ago.

"I missed you so much," Lola sniffles as she dabs at her eyes

She lost her parents in a tragic car accident when she was seventeen. With no other relatives, Luc and I were all she had until Sebastian and the Steele clan fifteen months ago. My parents adore Lola and adopted her as a second daughter. But understandably it's not the same as having one's own parents.

"I missed you, too," I sigh, then tease her. "Too busy being spanked and banged by Captain Caveman to think of your BFF, I suppose…"

We look at each other and burst out in loud guffaws that lead into uncontrollable snorts. I grab her arm and pull her through the penthouse's front doors and out to the main terrace. A bottle of Dom P. chills in a champagne bucket.

"*Voilà!*" I wave my hand to present Lola's favorite champagne to her.

She claps and bounds over to pop the cork. As she pours the tasty bubbly, she arches her eyebrow at me and smirks.

"So… Nice place you have here. You seem rather comfy, eh?"

I bite my lower lip to hold back a giggle. She continues to stare after she hands a flute to me. I try to hold out, but fail. A laugh bursts forth and my eyes fill will with joyful tears as I clink glasses with her.

"Ah, yes, here's to the end of the STEELE Quaternity and to the new Steele Duo!" Lola toasts as she joins in my laughter.

The champagne tickles my nose when I take a sip.

"Here, here!" I agree wholeheartedly.

I claim Roger as much as he claims me.

Lola and I fall onto chaises and sip the first glass in silence. Years of camaraderie allow us to enjoy the solitude with no need to rush and fill it with unnecessary words. Lola adds more of the champagne to our flutes. Then shifts on her chaise to face me. I angle myself towards her too.

"So, tell me—"

"How was your—"

We laugh some more for speaking at the same time. Lola inclines her head for me to go on.

"Tell me! How was your honeymoon? Shelley said you went island hopping. How romantic!"

Lola's face beams as she swoons against the back of the chaise. Her hazel eyes glow with an inner flame so heightened by love that she radiates from within. I know how she feels; I smile to myself.

"It was unbelievable! Sebastian arranged the most spectacular trip! One I will never forget."

She recounts the various tropical locales they traveled to over the two months. Her detailed tales of the sunrises, sunsets, private beaches, fresh food with local flavors, take me on a voyeuristic journey. I don't blame her when she says was reluctant to return.

"Now, it's your turn to spill..." Lola says pointedly as she tops off our flutes once again.

I take a slow sip and peer over the rim to tease her. She throws a pillow at me, and I laugh. I recount every iota from the night of her wedding to this morning. Well, I left out the incredible shower sex—TMI!

Sebastian's booming voice interrupts our giggles.

"Oh, so different from the last time you two were on a terrace sipping Dom Pérignon..."

Lola and I glance over at him and Roger, who laughs jovially as he punches his older brother in the arm playfully. They tussle and end with Roger in a headlock, getting a nudgie in the head. He pushes Sebastian off and strides over to give Lola a kiss on the cheek. Then drops onto the chaise next to me, planting a big, wet kiss on my lips.

Sebastian and Lola laugh. He comes over and kisses my cheek before pulling Lola onto his lap on her chaise. His gray eyes hold the same burning light as Lola's as he gazes at her.

I'm so happy for my best friend and Sebastian.

"Well, Sis, how's it going?" Sebastian says as he pierces me with his penetrating stare.

I'm surprised by his choice of descriptive label for me. Does he mean because Lola and I are like sisters? Or is he referring to my relationship with Roger and thus with him? I open my mouth. Then close it, not sure how to answer.

Roger throws the pillow back at Sebastian. But he ducks. He chuckles as he speaks again.

"Well, you and Lola are sisters, *non?*" He asks, his face barely holding onto the neutral expression.

"Ass," Roger mumbles as he takes my flute and drains the glass.

Lola titters and refills it. Roger promptly drinks it down, and Sebastian laughs.

Well, I'm glad they all think it's hilarious. I feel as though I'm missing something from their private joke. I take the fresh glass from Roger and tilt it back. The delicious bubbly fills me. Then glare at each of them in turn. They laugh uproariously.

Roger pulls me onto his lap and kisses the top of my

head. I wrap my arms around his waist as I burrow into his chest and sigh. Content with the bliss of my life.

* * *

"TELL me what makes your pussy weep, Pretty Kitty."

Roger rumbles in my ear as I squirm on the seat between his muscular thighs as we sit on the dark red leather banquette. His rock-hard cock presses against the crack of my ass. I squirm some more.

We're at Peepshow in LEVELS Paris. We finished dinner at Arpège and came here with Lola and Sebastian almost an hour ago. Time is hard to track when feeding my voyeur kink.

My eyes framed by an ornate gold half-mask that has peacock's feathers across the top like a headdress widen as I glance around the room. I changed into an ass-skimming, silk georgette negligee. The cream sheer material hides nothing, including my puckered nipples and swollen pussy lips. Gold, six-inch mules adorn my feet.

Roger gifted me a stunning pair of yellow diamond chandelier earrings. They glitter in the low light as my head swivels, taking in the hedonistic sights surrounding us.

The other seating alcoves filled with members in various stages of sex draw my attention first. The lusty sounds of women and men as they climax fills the air. A main stage and several smaller platforms showcase demonstrations in bondage and edging.

The atmosphere is all about bacchanalia with the melodic thrum of sensual music. Somewhere amongst it all or in one of the performance rooms, Lola and Sebastian disappeared.

I yelp when Roger nips the delicate shell of my ear.

"Tell me," he demands on a growl.

My body vibrates with the sensation. I mewl and press further into his firm chest. My nails dig into his thick thighs. His growl deepens. My pussy throbs.

"Th... The man on his knees servicing his Dom... just over there," I pant, pointing my chin towards the left.

A naked man whose eyes blindfolded by a white silk cloth kneels before a giant, muscular man with a crew cut and tight leather pants. His motorcycle boots stand far apart to brace him as he drills his enormous dick down his sub's throat. One hand holds the man's head in place while the other swings a flogger against the man's back. Both men groan in pleasure.

Roger chuckles against my neck. Then sucks some skin into his mouth. Another mark to claim me.

Since being a member at LEVELS, my sexual appetite has expanded to include unthought of desires and things that never intrigued me before. The men case in point.

I look to my right and see a woman dangling from the ceiling caught like a butterfly bound in the web of Shibari rope. Her partner taunts her engorged nipples and pussy lips with hot red wax. The woman shrills as a drop lands on her clit.

Merde...

My pussy winces. Not for me... Yet.

Roger hooks his feet around my ankles and pulls my legs apart.

I squeak in surprise.

Two of his thick fingers crawl across my inner thigh. Then breach my pussy entrance.

I arch my back and raise my hips to give him better access to my achy core.

Roger's other hand presses down on my hip and the top of my thigh to keep me still. He fucks me with his fingers until I break with a toe-curling orgasm.

I toss my head back. My body bucks against his hand as he draws another orgasm from my core. My entire body quivers from the intensity of the ecstasy. My screams join the others to rebound off the walls and ceiling as we reach our climaxes in unison.

"Good, Little Kitty," Roger croons as he pats my plundered pussy lovingly. "Good, Little Kitty."

I purr my pleasure as I lap his fingers clean.

ROGER

*"D*amn, it must be in the water!"

"Hell, as long as it's not in my Jackson Reserve, I'm good. Let those three keep the water!"

"I'll drink to that, bro!"

Everyone laughs at Malcolm's and our cousin Lucien Jackson's banter. They along with Sebastian, Joel, and myself enjoy a Guys' Night Out at Jackson Smoke&Scotch a new lounge Lucien opened last month on Rue Saint-Honoré.

The legendary Place Vendôme/St. Honoré area is the place to see and be seen. Where money is no object for the people it attracts. Old society, fashionistas, and celebrities frequent the nearby high-chic spots to shop, drink, and dine.

It's the latest addition to Jackson Corporation's luxury establishments created by *The Sexy Chef* as legions of his female followers dubbed Lucien. They slated locations in

London, New York, and Los Angeles for over the next six months. Another hot property for the Jacksons to add to their list.

"Funny, you were chasing after Starr Knight at my wedding," Sebastian says as he blows out smoke from his Jackson Cuban Cigar.

All heads swing to Malcolm, curious to know who sparked the interest of the Dom playboy enough for him to give chase. It's the reverse—he can't keep women from their pursuit of him. His face flushes and he takes a swig of his Scotch. He mumbles an answer with the snifter at his lips.

"Pardon… Say again? We didn't hear you, Lover Boy, er, playboy…" Sebastian teases him relentlessly as only an older brother can.

Malcolm, now recovered, cradles the Baccarat crystal snifter in his palms as he smirks at Sebastian. His gray eyes flash with devilment.

"I don't know what you're talking about," Malcolm scoffs. "You must have been floating in the clouds, struck by Cupid's arrow."

He makes goo-goo eyes and bats his eyelashes coyly at Sebastian.

We crack up, Baz included. His cheeks even redden with embarrassment. Poor guy. Malcolm's got him down pat.

"Say what you want, Hettie and I have a good thing going… As it is. No signs of marriage on our horizon," Joel states with a decisive nod between puffs of his cigar. "I'm way too young to commit for the rest of my life."

Lucien and Malcolm clink glasses with Joel adding robust cheers and here, here.

I shake my head and chuckle as I sip my Scotch. The burn feels good going down, then settles in my stomach with warmth. But not as warm as I felt buried deep inside of Leonie's lush paradise this morning.

One of the best parts about her spending the night is waking up to bury myself within her body: mouth, pussy, ass. She's a supercharged magnet that pulls me in every time. I shift in my leather club chair as my cock stiffens at the thought of Leonie. Damn.

So far she's denied me the pleasure of moving in with me. Skipping past my many hints and outright requests. As much time as she spends at my penthouse, she might as well just give in. I know she wants to.

Some mornings I pretend I'm still asleep, but I sense Leonie's amber gaze on my face. She traces her fingertips across my cheek or along the cleft in my chin. Her soft murmurs of love in French fills me with such incredible joy. One time I opened my eyes, and she startled, then slipped out of bed without a word. She didn't mention the moment at all. She's not quite there, but she's almost ready.

And I'm a patient man.

"Laugh all you want. I was just like you. Probably worse," Sebastian starts, eyeing each of his hecklers. "It'll happen to you, too. And I'm going to be the one yucking it up."

Malcolm, Lucien, and Joel's eyes widen at Sebastian's proclamation. Then they burst out in hysterical laughter. Lucien wipes his eyes while Joel doubles over. Sebastian and I can't help but to join them.

The conversation progresses to business and sports, typical guy talk. Malcolm and Lucien update us on their latest project Jackson Hole at STEELE. They're high-end, international beach bars with restaurants in jet-set hot spots. The first location at our resort in Monte Carlo opened a few months ago, and the next scheduled for Cannes. It's already popular with reservations and private parties booked months in advance.

I tell them Leonie and I will go to Monte Carlo since we planned a trip there the following weekend. It's been a while since either of us has visited. We'll stay at her penthouse as it's closer to the action than my hillside villa. We expect a refreshing, fun-filled break.

"No, sir! Paris Saint-Germain will win," exclaims Lucien.

Joel throws his head back and roars with laughter.

"How about a friendly wager? Liverpool FC by one," he responds.

Sebastian rolls his eyes as he leans forward in his seat. They debate the merits of American football and soccer—he taunts them with the very wrong name. Lucien points out American football uses hands with an occasional little kick, so which has the wrong name. Malcolm and I chime in as they parry.

It's good to relax with those closest to me. The familiar

companionship combined with the best Scotch and cigars makes it an enjoyable evening.

"Now, that fucker…"

Malcolm gestures to the entrance, and we swivel in our seats.

Fucker is right. It's Mattei with a curvy blonde woman on his arm. He saunters in with his head held high, a smirk on his face as though the emperor has arrived and his loyal subjects should stand and salute. Mattei exudes cockiness.

He hasn't spotted me, yet.

"What's his story with the Steeles?" Lucien asks, already bristling.

"A dick who thinks he's God's gift to women. The wrong one being Leonie," Sebastian sneers as he flexes his fingers.

Malcolm nods and adds, "Well, he better keep it moving. I'm in no mood for his shit tonight."

"No worries, I'll take care of it. This is the last time he'll waltz into a Jackson establishment," Lucien says as he rises to his six feet, three inches. His emerald green eyes blaze.

His movement catches Mattei's attention. His smirk falters and he stops mid-stride as our eyes lock. His lip curls up in a snarl. The woman turns to him in surprise. Then follows his glare to me.

I stand beside Lucien as Sebastian and Malcolm flank us.

At the sight of a pack of four Alpha males, Mattei reconsiders his actions as his eyes shift from each of us.

I step forward, but Lucien holds my arm. He nods at

two men in dark suits and they approach Mattei. The baffled woman stands closer to him. Fortunately, he doesn't argue when they escort him from the lounge.

Lucien pulls his mobile from his trousers pocket and says, "No need to let him ruin our evening. What's his full name?"

"Giovanni Mattei," I respond through clenched teeth.

Lucien types on the screen. Then glances up at me.

"I just sent a text to my head of security. He'll alert all of our businesses to deny entry to Mattei."

He claps me on the back and sits back in his chair.

"Time for another round, bros!" Joel chuckles as he pours more Scotch into our snifters.

Yeah, I need to wash the sour taste in my mouth from the encounter with Mattei and end the night on a high note with my boys. Then go home to bury myself in my woman until her body can't take another orgasm and her voice is hoarse from screaming my name.

An even more appealing high note.

ROGER

"*I*t's so beautiful! This was a splendid idea, *Mon Amour!*"

Leonie's smile is brighter than the sun reflecting off the turquoise waters of the Mediterranean Sea shimmering behind her.

We're eating lunch at the restaurant on the terrace of the Château Eza. It sits high above the Jardin d'Eze and lower village. This area is my favorite on the French Riviera. Its borders extend from the Med at Èze-sur-Mer to the hilltop medieval Èze-Village. The villages connect at Saint-Laurent-d'Eze.

Leonie and I arrived in Monte Carlo late last night and went straight to her duplex. Even though it's only over the weekend, we packed a full schedule. Today we drove along the coast and up to Èze. We meandered through the streets, stopping in shops and art galleries.

A beautiful bracelet of gold filigree set with precious

stones caught my eye as we passed a window display for antique jewelry. The bold, yet delicate piece in 18-karat yellow gold seemed made for Leonie. I smile as the sun sparks off of the stones when she claps her hands in glee. I need not see her eyes past the giant glamour girl sunglasses she wears to know the gold flecks in the amber orbs shine.

"Come, I want to take a photo with the water behind us," she says as she beckons a server to the table.

"*Oui, madame?*" The besotted server asks as he bows to Leonie.

"*Veuillez avoir la gentillesse de prendre notre photo, merci!*" She asks him flashing her megastar smile.

"*Absolument! S'il vous pla"t!*" He responds.

I hold back a chuckle as he falls all over himself to take her mobile, so awestruck by her beauty. Leonie rises gracefully from her chair as I help her to her sandaled feet. Even in a tiered eyelet gauzy mini dress, no makeup, and her hair piled atop her head, Leonie is breathtaking. The white fabric and freshly painted white nails make her caramel skin glow. I pull her into my arms and kiss her passionately.

Once I let her loose, her tinkling laughter carries through the air. Other patrons clap at my exuberant display of love. Sappy, I'll claim it just as I claim my woman. Mine!

As we turn to pose for the shot, the server smiles and counts to three. He takes two pictures, then shows them to us for approval. Perfection... Nothing can make *The Lion* look bad.

"Merci, merci beaucoup!" Leonie tells him as she hugs him.

He bows again and leaves us. Backing away to get one last glimpse at her. Then he turns and rushes to the other servers who slap him on the back. He peeks over his shoulder and blushes when Leonie waves and blows him a kiss. The others clap and whoop.

"More admirers for you, Bonbon," I tease.

"Peut-être," she starts as she cups my face. "But you are the only one who matters, *Mon Amour.*"

Leonie brushes her lips across mine. A zing tingles from my mouth to my heart down my spine to erupt out the tip of my dick. It weeps at her loving touch. Her soft purr vibrates through me. I close my eyes as I shudder with need.

"Only you, Roger."

"I love you, baby," I murmur, my gaze landing on her gorgeous face.

She smiles and nods, "I know."

We order green salads to start and fresh fish in a crust of peppers and herbs with steamed coconut and Iberian chorizo as our main dish. It's hearty enough after our long walk up the hillside. But won't weigh us down for the return trek. We sip frothy snifters filled with *Rosé à la Piscine.*

"So delicious and refreshing!" Leonie exclaims as she licks a drop of the cocktail from the corner of her mouth.

A low growl rumbles in my chest. I want to bite it.

"Mon loup must be hungry, *non?"* She giggles.

Before I can answer, the server places our salads in front of us.

"Bon appétit!" He says with gusto.

"*Merci!*" We respond in unison.

More than the food, I enjoy the contented sounds Leonie makes as she relishes her meal. A woman with a healthy appetite is a turn on. Unenthusiastically picking at a plate of lettuce leaves and lemon juice equates to vanilla sex. What a snoozefest.

"What's the plan for the rest of the day?" Leonie asks as she sips her *Piscine*.

I think a moment as I check my platinum Rolex Day-Date watch. We have a few hours before the sunsets. Plenty of time for a pleasant drive along the coast, especially in my gunmetal gray convertible Aston Martin Vanquish.

"Let's drive west along the coast to Cannes. We can stop at Villefranche-sur-Mer, Beaulieu-sur-Mer, Vieux Nice, and Antibes," I suggest.

"Fantastique!" Leonie claps as she bounces in her chair. "The day is perfect for it! Plus, I feel like Halle Berry as Jinx in *Die Another Day* in your Aston Martin!"

I throw my head back and laugh out loud. I always feel the same way whenever I drive one of them. As a collector of vintage Aston Martin vehicles for the last ten years, I've amassed quite the collection. This one is my favorite. Halle is absolutely stunning, but she doesn't compare to my Leonie. But then no one compares to her.

"We must find you an orange bikini," I wink at her.

"*Oui!*" She purrs.

"Pardon, monsieur, would you care for dessert?" The server appears at the table.

I look to Leonie and she declines. So I ask for the check. We head down through the streets back to my James Bond ride. I open the door for Leonie and she slips in and ties a colorful silk Hermès scarf around her head. She smiles at me as I hop into the driver's seat and rev the engine.

The ride is thrilling with the hairpin turns and narrow lanes. A bus looms in front of us and Leonie squeaks. Then she grabs my arm and buries her face in my shoulder. I kiss the top of her head without taking my eyes off the road. Laughing as I switch gears and the engine roars in response. Passengers on the bus wave as we slip past them. The exhilaration is addictive.

We hop out at Villefranche-sur-Mer. Leonie wobbles on her feet like a newly born cub. I wrap my arm around her slim waist and hoist her to my side. With a tinkling laugh, she drapes her arms around my neck and kisses me silly.

"My super agent! You saved us!" She gushes.

"Always, baby," I croon in her ear.

The village is quaint as we stroll through the streets. We detour to *Église Saint-Michel*. The baroque Italian-style church intrigues our love of architecture and design. We marvel at paintings and sculptures in the cool quiet interior. Hushed we stand and admire its beauty in awe.

After a while, we hit the road for more thrills. We stop in Beaulieu-sur-Mer to visit Villa Kerylos. Again attracted by the architecture, we gaze upon its Ancient Greek style set on the edge of the coast like the kingfisher it's named for. Leonie tells me her ancestors were founders of the village as we make our way back to the car.

A little boy and girl—apparently brother and sister—run up to us with a bouquet of flowers. Leonie lowers herself to their eye level and takes their proffered gift.

"*Pour vous jolie dame!*" They exclaim.

"*Oh, chéris merci beaucoup!*" She responds as she hugs them tight to her chest.

I grab my mobile from the pocket of my shorts and snap a quick photo. Leonie is a natural with the children as she converses with them in French. She stands when their mother hurries over and smiles at her. She explains they're helping her in their flower shop and rushed out to give Leonie the bouquet they just put together.

I hand them some euros. But the mother stops me as the children shake their heads vehemently, insisting the bouquet is a gift. We thank them and get in the car with a wave.

As we drive, I think about children with Leonie. I can't wait. My only worry is for her wellbeing given her mother's experiences. As though sensing the unease rising in me, Leonie puts her arm around my shoulder and strokes the back of my head. The comforting move dispels the negative thoughts.

The beauty of Vieux Nice comes into view. Set on the Mediterranean below the primary area of Nice, the vibrant old town looks like a postcard. Its narrow cobblestone streets and pastel-hued buildings line the coast. We stop in shops to buy Niçoise soaps and Provençal textiles. As we head back to the car, we pick up *socca* crepes from the daily market on Cours Saleya.

We take our time walking to the car as we share the crepes. Leonie licks a few crumbs from the corner of my mouth. I turn my head quickly and nip her lips into my mouth. She moans and melts against me. Our tongues tangle as our kiss deepens.

"*Chéri*," she sighs softly. "You taste delicious... Mmm mmm mmm."

When we come up for air, I kiss the tip of her nose and toss the crepes' wrapper in the trash. Leonie's eyes track my moves like a huntress. When I return to her, I slip my arm around her waist to walk us to the car.

"Next stop... Antibes. All aboard!"

She giggles at my antics as she tightens the knot on her scarf. As we pull away from Vieux Nice, she throws her arms in the air and whoops. I join her, tossing my head back for my own shout of joy. People turn and wave at us. Her excitement is contagious.

When we arrive, we take in the Roman-era architecture and marvels. From the aqueducts and their ingenious arches, to the luxury found in the excavated villas. The history and lore surrounding the area pulls us back in time. After a stroll through the magnificent gardens at Villa Eilenroc. The scent of olives, lavender, and eucalyptus mingles in the air around us as we walk hand in hand along the paths. We capture the moment with more photos.

The ride to Cannes is just as majestic along the coast.

The busy city filled with tourists, celebrities, and the wealthy bustles with a vibrancy unlike any other. We park at the STEELE Cannes and walk along the Promenade de la Croisette. The piers and beaches dotted with colorful umbrellas and chaises encourage sun lovers to stretch out.

As we stand gazing across the sand to the glittering waters of the Med, I glance down at Leonie. She stifles a yawn with the back of her hand. Yeah, it's been a long day. She senses my intense stare and glances up with a bright smile.

"Pardon me!" She laughs. "I'm still wide awake and ready for some more action! Where to next, *Mon Cœur?*"

I pull her into my arms, and she snuggles against my chest. As I brush my lips across the top of her head, an idea comes to me. I tip her face up to mine.

"How about we go find you that orange bikini, grab two chaises, and drink some more *Rosé à la Piscines?* Then change for dinner and stay the night at the hotel?"

Leonie dances and shimmies her hips as she claps her hands—her and Lola's signature merry dance.

"That's a wonderful idea! I wholeheartedly agree!"

I pull out my mobile and dial the general manager. I ask her to book the Joséphine Baker Suite and request the concierge to locate an orange bikini, some evening wear options for dinner, and make a reservation. She assures me they will take care of everything before we return. I thank her and end the call.

"One more photo! I want lots of memories!" Leonie says.

We pose with the sparking water behind us for another great shot. The walk back is at a slower pace since we know the rest of the afternoon and evening we will spend in the city. Just as we step onto the STEELE Cannes' property, my mobile vibrates with a call. Pulling it from my pocket, I note it's my mother. I answer right away.

"Hi, Mom. What's going on? Everything okay?"

In the background I hear a boat's horn sound as though leaving port. The last I checked, they were touring the Malbec vineyards of Mendoza with Lucie and Connor Jackson. No water for big boats in that area of the world.

"Oh, honey! Everything is fine! Don't worry," She starts. "Your father and I just boarded *Serendipity*. After being at such high altitudes for the past two weeks, we needed the warm weather of the Mediterranean."

I breathe a sigh of relief. Then nod at Leonie to show all is well. The worried expression drops from her face as she asks me to tell them hi for her.

"Oh, good. I hope you had a good time. Leonie says hi," I respond.

There's silence on the other end.

I pull the mobile from my ear to check the call didn't disconnect. It is. Why would my mother get quiet when she finds out Leonie is with me? As I form the words to ask my mother, her voice carries through the line.

"—told me you were in Monte Carlo. So I told your father we should meet up. Spend some time on the yacht tomorrow. Have brunch, sunbathe, catch up on what's happening in your life. Dress up and go to the casino later."

The call must have faded out. But I have to be certain she understands Leonie and I are together. No way will I abandon her.

"Mom, did you hear me when I said Leonie says hi?"

"Of course! And I said that's perfect. Didn't you hear me?" She says.

Thank fuck! I'd hate for them to not get along. Although they seemed fine at Sebastian and Lola's wedding. Especially with the future I have planned for Leonie and me.

"No, Mom. Your mobile cut out," I respond with a sigh of relief.

She tsks, "Your brainiac brother persuaded me to 'upgrade to the best model on the planet.' So now it blanks out... High tech my butt!"

We laugh at her spot-on impersonation of Harris. Not only a gadget geek, he's a coder. We tease him and Haley for being nerds, but they're wizzes at what they do. I can't wait to get him for giving Mom a whacked-out mobile.

"Let me speak to Leonie," she adds.

I pass my mobile to Leonie. A wide smile blooms on her face as she listens to my mother speak. I can't hear what she's saying. But judging by Leonie's expression and giggles, it's all good.

"*Oui, oui,*" she says. "I'd love to! Okay, see you tomorrow. Bonne nuit!"

She hands the mobile back to me after she disconnects the call.

"Eleven tomorrow morning we're to meet the tender at

the marina in Monte Carlo," Leonie tells me. "I can't wait to see Shelley again. She's so good to Lola. I told her she's lucky to have such a cool mother-in-law."

At the end, her voice takes on a wistful note.

I slip my arm around her shoulders and pull her to me. I bury my nose in her fragrant hair, inhaling deep of the sultry florals with amber and musk.

Leonie slides her palm along my chest. The tip of her fingernail brushes the skin of my nipple. Then tweaks the tip when she feels a shudder run through me. Her hand continues on its path to cradle the back of my head. She tangles her fingers in my hair and pulls my mouth down to hers. The warm air that escapes her lips as she moans softly against mine makes my dick jump. Her kiss is full of fiery passion that zings through every cell in my body.

"If we don't stop, we'll never get to the beach," I growl as my teeth nip her plump bottom lip.

Leonie purrs seductively, "Who says we need the beach? We can make our own waves, *Amoureux*."

My dick agrees as pre-cum splashes from the tip.

LEONIE

"*Mmmmm… Mmm mmm… Aaahhh!*"

My eyes roll. My head flies back on my neck. My legs snap together against the sides of Roger's head. I jackknife off the bed. It's the third orgasm he's pulled from me since I awoke to his tongue laving my pussy. I'm incoherent at this point. My swollen pussy lips and engorged clit can't take any more of his licks, nips, and probes.

"Ooohh, Rogeerrr!" I wail as my body continues to convulse.

He growls his disapproval and nips my inner thigh. Then he adds two of his thick fingers to the mix. The strumming of my G-spot causes another orgasm to rise from the base of my spine.

I cry out from the unexpected sharp pain and toss my head side to side. My bound wrists struggle against the silk belts attached to the ornate wooden headboard. Not only is

Roger *The Responsible*, he's resourceful. He made good use of the sumptuous robes in the suite by repurposing the belts as restraints. I can only move my lower body fully and tug my arms fruitlessly.

"Bad, Kitty," he admonishes as he parts my lower lips to spank my sensitive clit.

The moist sounds of flesh meeting flesh are a trigger for my body to respond with another mind-blowing climax. I mewl as it ignites my body in pure ecstasy.

"Be still or I'll make you cum five more times," Roger threatens.

Ordinarily that may sound like a phenomenal idea. But not after multiple rounds last night and this morning. I hate to admit it, but my body needs a break.

"Rogeerr… Please!" I beg.

Relief floods my system when he crawls up my body, leaving a trail of open mouth kisses on my heated skin. His gray eyes now coal black with lust never leave mine. Hypnotized, I watch his approach. Only when I catch sight of his massive cock in my periphery do my eyes veer from his.

Roger's dick is a sculpturesque piece of art. Hard as steel, covered in velvety soft skin. Veins and ridges stand in relief. The bulbous head reddened with need glistens with a drop of pre-cum on its slit. Its ten-inch length and girth too wide for my fingers to meet. His heavy balls swing at the base like a pendulum. The tantalizing sight makes my mouth water. I lick my lips. He chuckles.

"Hungry for what you see, Pretty Kitty?" He asks as his voice thrums in my ear.

I nod and whimper my response.

He grips the base of his big dick and feeds the tip an inch inside of me.

I groan.

"Open up for me, Kitten. I need to feel your tight pussy wrapped around me, milking my cock," he says in a voice rough with desire.

Conditioned to respond to her mate, my body drains of the tension to allow him unrestrained entry. We groan together as he breaches my passage. Once fully seated, Roger stills. Entranced by the sensation of my pussy clenching around his pulsating cock, we don't utter a sound. Only the rapid beat of our hearts fills the air.

Not until my hips rise of their own accord demanding movement, does Roger pull out to his tip then piston back inside of me. He wanted to give me the time I needed for my mind to catch up with my body in its appetite for more.

"Oh, baby... You feel so fucking good... So hot and wet..." Roger grunts as his passion builds.

I writhe beneath him. My wrists pull against my restraints, aching to wrap my arms around his neck or grip his biceps for stability. Instead, all I can do is open and close my fists on air. He feels so good. So very good. But I need more.

Roger takes one hand from my hip and places his thumb in my slack mouth. Without hesitation, I suckle it with fervor, pretending it's his dick. Once it's sopping wet, he pops it from my mouth and lifts me up onto his thighs as he sits back on his haunches.

Upright, he has more access to my body. His lips trail down the column of my neck to wrap around my fully aroused nipple. At the same time, he pulls my ass cheek to the side and presses the pad of his wet thumb against my puckered hole. My muscles in my pussy and ass tighten. He grunts from the strength of them on his dick.

"Aaahhh!" I scream as he plunders my bottom hole with his thumb and uses his muscular thighs to pump his cock up into my pussy.

My back arches and I keen with each bottoming out thrust. I seem as though I'll break in two from Roger's power. An orgasm comes upon me with the speed of a freight train going downhill with no breaks. A bolt of lightning strikes me. Blinded with my body on fire, I ride Roger like my life depends upon it.

"Fuuuck… Leoonnieee!" He roars as my climax triggers his release.

Inside of me, his dick swells impossibly larger bumping into my cervix before hot ropes of his seed bathe my womb. Another wave crests over us as we continue to pound fiery flesh against fiery flesh in our frenzy to sate our carnal needs. When the last drop of Roger's essence flows from his body to mine, we collapse breathless on the bed in a state of sheer euphoria.

He brushes his lips against my temple as he murmurs in a voice thick with emotion, "I love you, Leonie Beaulieu."

I find the energy to lift my head from his solid chest where his heart beats in sync with mine to gaze into his eyes. I stroke his cheek and rub my thumb across his full lip.

"I love you, Roger Steele."

He kisses my fingertip and cradles my head back to his chest. We fall into a peaceful slumber.

"I LOVE YOUR BIKINI! You look great in it. It reminds me of Halle Berry's in that Bond film."

Since Roger and I had more important matters to attend to, I didn't get a chance to wear my new Jinx bikini in Cannes. Lounging on the fourth deck of *Serendipity,* I make good use of it. Lola told me about the boat and how big and beautiful it is, but I never imagined it was this magnificent. And I've been on some of the best in the world.

Morgan gifted it to Shelley for their thirtieth wedding anniversary a few years ago. They keep *Serendipity* in Posi tano, where their Villa Sogno is located during the season. Then transport her to the Caribbean for the fall and winter months.

Roger told me it's the largest megayacht in the world with a length of six-hundred feet, nine inches. That extra nine just to nudge past the next yacht down. At least for now, *Serendipity* holds the record since everyone competes for the prize of the biggest on the water. There are already rumors that a Russian oligarch contracted a prominent builder specifically to outsize *Serendipity*.

It's definitely a beauty to behold. The all-white, sleek design boasts seven decks. The top for the bridge; the sixth for four palatial suites where his parents, Malcolm, Haley, and Sebastian and Lola stay; the fifth deck for four suites where Roger and Harris and up to four close friends stay, plus our private library, office, family and dining rooms with galley; the remaining decks accommodate twenty-four guests in staterooms, quarters for eighty-eight crew, helicopter pad, submarine and water vehicles and toys garage, swimming pool, spa, gym, barbershop and salon, disco, living and dining areas, and an entertainment deck with a bowling alley, cinema, pool room, cards room, and game room. The open-air decks hold chaises, beds, tables, televisions, and dining spots. *Serendipity* is a floating haven for rest, relaxation, and partying.

I turn on my chaise to smile at Shelley and pat my belly. We just ate the most scrumptious meal and I sip on my favorite aperitif, Lillet.

"Thank you. Even though my belly protrudes over the bottom!" I laugh.

Shelley joins in. But shakes her head.

"Your belly is nonexistent! Flat as a board," she says as she claps her hands together in emphasis.

Roger glances over at us from the sound. I blow him a kiss and he pretends to catch it. Shelley laughs at our hijinks.

"I'm happy that you and Roger are back together. I

worried about you two," she says as she peers at me from over the top of her Ray-Ban aviators.

She's a striking woman in her mid-fifties with shoulder-length, wavy black hair and expressive brown eyes. I smile at the Steele Matriarch who I can tell is the boss of the family. As her feisty New Yorker personality affirms.

"My son is set in his ways. But loves fiercely," she says as her gaze drifts to Roger who sits next to Morgan at the table. "He's always been the child who wanted order and for everyone to get along."

She turns back to me with the same intense stare as Roger's—the only difference in their eye color.

"And he loves you. It would please me to no end to see the two of you together for good. He needs a strong and independent woman like you who challenges him out of his comfort zone. Is that possible, Leonie?"

I'm speechless by Shelley's words. I turn to look at Roger. Can I make that commitment to Shelley? To Roger? To us? We're in a good place now and have been for four months. I just worry that he'll nitpick on me again.

I take a deep cleansing breath and return my gaze to Shelley who sits patiently waiting for my response. One last glance at Roger and he faces me with a smile. I'm a goner.

"Yes, it is possible, Shelley," I respond.

"Wonderful! Salute!" She toasts as she clinks her glass of rosé with my Lillet.

. . .

THE CARESS OF THE RED, open-back, silk-charmeuse gown makes my skin tingle as the material languidly drapes over my frame, ending in a dramatic mermaid train. The five-inch heels of my matching strappy sandals click on the marble floor. The matching diamond suite of a necklace, bracelets, earrings, and hair brooch sparkle.

The extraordinary gift Roger gave to me took my breath away. I told him no; it was too much. But his intense eyes blazed with indignation. He took the jewelry case from my hands as I stood gaping at the enormous diamonds and put the pieces on me.

"You cannot tell me to not give you a gift, Leonie," he growled.

When he finished adjusting each piece to his satisfaction, he turned me to the full-length mirror. Then put his arms around my waist as he stood behind me.

My gaze went from the diamonds to his eyes, glittering fiercely at me in our reflection.

"*Merci, Mon Cœur,*" I whispered as I touched my palm to his cheek.

He nuzzled into my hand. Then turned to kiss my palm. His hands slipped around to press against my lower belly, possessively locking my ass to his groin.

"You are mine, Leonie. If I want to shower you with presents every day, I will. Do you understand?" He asked gruffly.

"*Oui, Mon Cœur,*" I replied as I turned to face him and kiss his lips just as possessive as he held me a moment before. "And you are mine."

Now the James Bond vibe continues from the Aston Martin to the megayacht to an evening at the French Roulette table in the Casino de Monte-Carlo. Morgan, Shelley, Roger and I stride through the casino's lobby. Once again, I think as though I belong in one of the films: sexy boyfriend looking debonair in a custom Tom Ford tuxedo; being led by the general manager to a room reserved for the most high-profile patrons; to die for diamonds. *Incroyable.*

A squeeze to my hand draws me back from my musings. I peer up at Roger, who's smiling down at me.

"You are the most gorgeous woman in the world, Kitten," he murmurs.

I've been in the most fantastic clothes, primped to perfection, and spoiled immensely. Traveled the globe. Hobnobbed with the most wealthy, intelligent, and successful people on the planet. But nothing compares to the pleasure I get when I hear Roger's words.

The saying about being on cloud nine does not even come close. I am beyond the clouds in the stratosphere with my love for this man. I'm sure we'll get into it now and then about his control-freak ways and my sometimes less than focused ways. But in the end, it's more than worth it to me, to us.

As I squeeze his hand in return, I grace Roger with my most dazzling, megawatt smile that shines brighter than the jewelry he gave to me.

"*Merci, Chéri.*"

The general manager opens the doors to a large room

even more elegant than the rest of the casino. Opulent crystal chandeliers hang from the ceiling, adorned with hand-carved woodwork. The walls continue the ornate splendor with even more extensive moldings and reliefs. Plush wool and silk carpet cover the floors, cushioning our steps as we enter the palatial interior.

Men and women similarly dressed as us for a glamorous evening gather around the gaming tables. We follow the general manager to a center table. Three croupiers and a table manager who plays the role of Master of Ceremonies surround the beautifully crafted table. It's as much a work of art as a gaming table with its fine craftsmanship and quality materials.

We join two couples who sit opposite the four chairs reserved for our party. One couple smiles while the other nods in greeting. The table manager turns from his conversation with one croupier and sees us. He grins and steps down from his high chair.

"*Signore* Steele, it is a pleasure to have you join us this evening! I pray all is well with you!" He says as he shakes Roger's hand enthusiastically.

Roger grins and responds, "Good to see you, Signore Moretti. All is well, thank you. And your family?"

"*Bene Bene, grazie!*" He responds, then glances at the rest of us. "Ah, your family, *s*?"

Roger smiles and holds his hand out to his parents and introduces them to him. They exchange pleasantries. Then Roger lifts our clasped hands.

"And this is Leonie Beaulieu, my girlfriend," he says

with a smile.

Signore Moretti beams as he takes my other hand and kisses it.

"Such a pleasure to meet you, *signorina*," he starts, then turns to Roger. "You are a lucky man, *Signore* Steele!"

He bows, then gestures for us to take our seats at the table. The other couples who now recognize the name Steele are more welcoming. The men engage Roger and Morgan on business while the women compliment Shelley and me on our gowns.

I laugh to myself at their obsequious behavior. Shelley taps my leg under the table and I know she agrees with me. Such is the life when married to or dating some of the wealthiest men on the planet.

The game begins. The unrivaled accuracy and high-octane thrill of French Roulette captivates us. It's a theatrical performance of sound and movement. As the three croupiers call out enthusiastically, other patrons flock to our table. The onlookers hang on the croupiers' every word.

Roger and Morgan play like professionals while Shelley and I choose numbers at random. When we arrived at the casino, they gave Shelley and me trays of chips worth hundreds of thousands of euros. Again, I attempted to refuse. But Roger pinned me with his no-nonsense stare, and I gave in. Shelley tittered next to me and whispered to just let it go. I did, and now I play with the chips and have a blast.

After an hour passes, I discreetly tell Roger I'm going to

the ladies' lounge. Shelley asks where I'm going, and she accompanies me. We excuse ourselves from the table.

Two men ask if they may have our seats. I look to Roger and he asks if I'd like to continue to play. I decline for now. Shelley also opts out. So he allows the men to take our seats.

I kiss Roger's cheek and whisper good luck. His smile melts my heart.

"This is a wonderful night," I remark as we stroll through the doors opened for us by two attendants.

Shelley loops her arm through mine and nods, "Yes, I'm so glad that Morgan and I came. It's given me time to spend with you since we were so busy with Lola and Sebastian's wedding preparation."

She squeezes my arm, and I smile at her.

We walk on in silence. When we reach the ladies' lounge, we part. Once we're back in the anteroom, we continue our conversation as we apply fresh lipstick and fluff our hair.

"I know you are an independent woman and are not interested in my son for his wealth, Leonie," Shelley says as she watches my reflection in the mirror. "Roger knows that as well. When he gifts you with something, you do not have to feel as though you cannot accept it."

She pauses and eyes my jewelry, then continues.

"He's like his father and now Sebastian. They are generous men who willing to give to those they love. And Roger loves you."

Shelley stops to allow me to absorb her words before

she goes on.

"I was like you and Lola. Self-sufficient successful," she stops to laugh. "Well, I was a shopgirl and Lola owns shops and you rule the modeling world. But I was making it on my own. So I understand. I too had to get used to Morgan giving me gifts, fancy and simple alike."

She takes my arm and loops hers through it to lead us out the door.

"And now I just go with it. It's their way to express their love and care for you... for us. They don't do it for just anyone. Roger has never done it before. Okay?"

I take a second to reconcile her words. She's right.

"*Oui*, Shelley," I resound as I squeeze her hand in mine.

Her eyes sparkle as she smiles up at me.

When we arrive back at the table, Roger and Morgan stand to offer us their seats. But we decline and stand behind them, preferring to watch. It's even better when not playing since I can see more of what's going on beyond the wheel spinning.

The night goes on with round after round. Roger and Morgan win and lose some. But in the end, we have an incredible time.

Later, after we make love and cuddle in bed in my duplex, I think back on Shelley's words of advice. They remind me of similar ones Lola shared with me about the many gifts Sebastian has bestowed upon her. She too has accepted the situation for what it is—they give to us because they love us.

That's all the explanation I need.

LEONIE

"*O*h, this is just what I needed... Sun, sand, cocktails, and my girls."

Lola says as she sighs and leans back against the chaise lounge. She sips her Tipo Tinto R&R rum and raspberry with a sigh. Her mouth stained red from the iconic Mozambican specialty drink.

Starr, Blair, Haley, Billie, and I laugh at her drama.

"Hold on! You just returned from your two-month long honeymoon full of sun, sand, cocktails, and a sexy as hell husband," I start. "How could you need more two months later?"

Lola swats the pillow away that I tossed at her and sits up.

"Right!" Chorus Blair and Billie.

Starr shakes her head. Her curly, dark brown hair sways along her back as her dimples deepen with her smile.

"Lola, you crack me up! Even I, a staunch believer in self-care, can't imagine why you need a break this soon!"

She throws her pillow and dings Lola on the stomach. She laughs and hugs the pillow to her chest.

"I agree! Give us a break already, Lola!" Haley adds as she rolls her sharp gray eyes behind her glasses.

"Well, so that you know, I've been extremely busy catching up on work I missed while on my honeymoon with my sexy as fuck husband. Now, I need you, Ms. Knight, to work your magic to clear my head and relax me. And boy do you have your work cut out for you, again!"

Lola throws the pillow back and Starr catches it.

"Fine. Challenge accepted, Mrs. Steele!" She replies.

Lola swoons clutching her ginormous engagement ring to her bosom. She's right, it's definitely like her idol Elizabeth Taylor's ice skating rink ring. The nearly 30 carats glimmer in the torchlight.

The ring is a Steele family heirloom Shelley most recently wore. Being Sebastian is the eldest son, he inherited it and will pass it to his eldest son in time.

Lucky girl!

My thoughts turn to Roger. We've been back together for five months, and it's fantastic. Every day proves it was right for us to take a second chance at our relationship. Now, I wonder if we will go further like Lola and Sebastian.

"Leonie… Hello there… Leonie?"

"Girl! Snap out of it!"

"Oh, don't tease her…"

"See, I knew it! He's blown her mind and her back—"

"Okay, okay! I hear you already!" I cut into their chatter with a laugh.

All eyes are on me, varying from expressions of concern to smirks. When Starr called to invite us to her second international fitness retreat, we agreed to make it a Girls' Getaway, too. Time for us to reconnect with our minds, bodies, and friends. Over the seven days, we plan to do just that.

The retreat is at a luxury beachfront resort on Buenguerra Island off the coast of Mozambique in the channel between the country and the Indian Ocean. The island is a haven known for its pristine, white-sand beaches, peaceful vibe, and five-star resorts.

The property we're staying at is the most exclusive with only three cabanas, ten casinhas, and one large villa scattered across eleven acres of beachfront and lush tropical vegetation. Starr's retreat participants and her staff along with us secured the entire resort. It's our private oasis.

Lola, Billie, Haley, Blair, and I claimed the villa since it features five large bedrooms with sitting areas, living room, dining room, and kitchenette. The outdoor areas include a pool, deck area with thatched-roof cabana and chaises, plus chaises down by the ocean. It's stunning and tranquil.

Starr chose a casinhas since she's working more so than relaxing. She needs more space for her staff to meet and for her one-on-one sessions with guests. It's just through the palm trees on one of the sandy paths that crisscross the property.

"Spill. You've been mighty quiet about Roger and you..." Billie says as her green eyes flash.

"Right! I know I've been away and busy. But even so," Lola starts. "You can always call me. I am your BFF!"

"Oh, don't pressure her!" Blair says concerned.

"No pressure, but... Do tell!" Starr laughs.

I smile at my closest friends. Then take a sip of my Tipo Tinto R&R. When I set it down on the side table, they stare at me expectantly.

"I'm in love with the man of my dreams!" I throw my head back and roar. "He's mine, all mine! And I'm all his!"

They holler and stomp their feet.

"Another brother taken so he can get off my back about my love life! Thank you, Leonie! Hooray!" Shouts Haley pumping her fists into the air as she falls back onto her chaise lounge.

Lola jumps up and grabs my hands to pull me to stand. We do our happy shimmy dance around the chaises.

"Yeah, Girl! Strut your stuff!" Starr calls out as she fans herself.

Billie jumps up and joins our parade. Soon we form a conga line and weave in and out of the furniture. Then we head out to the beach, where we form a circle under the brilliant moonlight and star-filled sky. My girls and I continue to dance around as our laughter carries out over the silent, inky black water.

* * *

"LET us end our practice with three oms together. Inhale through your nose gently, hold it for a heartbeat. Then slowly release your breath back through your nose. Let us begin."

Starr's entrancing voice guides us through the last part of our yoga session. We started with breathwork for five minutes to prep us for a vigorous, forty-five-minute flow sequence. My muscles craved the fast-paced tempo. It allowed my body to focus on the asanas and not wander. The ten-minute meditation grounded me.

"Namaste. The light in me honors the light in you," Starr intones.

We bow to each other with palms pressed together at our heart centers. We remind ourselves of the good energy and intention we set forth in our practice. As we sit up and open our eyes, Starr's heart-shaped face beams at us. Her love of helping others reach their best mental and physical potential shines from her sorrel brown eyes.

"That was transcendental," Lola breaths out in awe as she sits cross-legged on her mat beside me staring at Starr.

"She's amazing," I whisper in the ensuing silence, just as awestruck.

"I agree," Blair leans over to whisper.

"This is the best I've felt in a while," Haley says softly as she stretches her arms overhead.

"Yes, she's still the best yoga teacher I've ever had a session with," Billie adds as she wipes down her mat.

We follow suit and clean ours, then hang them on the wooden racks inside the beachside, open-air pavilion. Other students gather around Starr to glean more of her sage advice. Two of her assistants offer adjustments for those who want more instruction.

Starr glances up and waves at us. We wave back before we walk down the steps to the sandy shore. Two other assistants offer us frothy shot glasses filled with refreshing juice made from local fruits. The delicious concoctions cool us down and fill us with energy.

"It has ashwagandha in it. An Ayurvedic herb that many studies show increases energy and reduces stress and anxiety," the assistant with a curly afro tells us.

"This is tasty," Blair says.

We nod and thank them for the elixirs as we place the empty glasses on the table. Our next session for Pilates isn't for another two hours. So we stroll along the beach to our villa. The sun glistens on the water between the island and the Mozambique coast. The waves splashing on the sand call to us.

"Hey, I'm going to change into my bikini and go for a swim!" Lola declares.

We agree it's a good idea and a great way to wash away the sweat from our yoga class. The flecks of gold in Billie's moss green eyes glint as she peeks over her shoulder at us. Then she skips ahead.

"Last one in is a rotten egg!" She shouts.

My long legs easily overtake the munchkins Lola and Billie. However, Haley and Blair who are only two and three inches shorter than me at five feet, eight inches and five feet seven inches tall are close on my heels. Their taunts of being number one urge me to increase my speed.

With a triumphant whoop, I yank my sports bra over my head as I race into my room. I ditch the skimpy yoga shorts and rush to the wardrobe. Snatching the first bathing suit I can reach, I step into the bottoms as I head to the door. Then slide them up over my hips. I don't worry about a top since we're on the secluded side of the island—no paparazzi to snap unwanted photos for Roger to go berserk about. I zip out the door, down to the beach, and dive into the first wave.

"Damn supermodel! You're used to quick changes!" Blair says as she splashes me when I come up from the surf.

"*Absolument! Ma chérie!*" I giggle as I sweep my arm through the water to douse her.

Haley who just ran in, tucks to avoid the spatter.

Lola's laughter as she beats Billie into the water by a hair's length, draws our attention to the shore.

"Ha, ha! You lose, Billie!" She shouts. "*Piu*, you stink like a rotten egg!"

Billie laughs and ducks under the water. When she comes back up, her medium blonde balayage hair cascades down her back in waves. Her pecan-colored skin already browning from the sun glistens.

"Tell her not to worry about it. Patrick thinks you smell divine!" Blair laughs.

The Southern belle from Savannah, Georgia captured the heart of Patrick Rockett, her new Scottish billionaire beau. Sebastian nearly had a fit when he found out Billie was dating the CEO of STEELE International's biggest competitor, Rockett Construction. Lola had to calm him down when she reminded him Billie signed an ironclad nondisclosure agreement and she swore her allegiance to Lola.

"You got that right, honey!" Billie's cheeky reply. "And my brawny babe cannot get enough!"

We crack up as her Southern drawl switches to a Scottish accent flawlessly.

"Your turn, Blair! Leonie and I were on the hot seat last night. Billie fessed up. Do share..." Lola says, splashing Blair.

She splutters as she her face reddens. Her cerulean blue eyes dart everywhere but at us.

"Yes, Ms. Secretive!" I tease. "How are things with *Le Renard Argenté?*"

Blair floats onto her back and closes her eyes before she responds.

"I don't kiss and tell—"

The three of us cover her in a deluge of seawater as we shout at her for being so prim and proper. She flips over and dives under the water, resurfacing a few feet away. She flips her chestnut brown hair over her shoulders, then stands akimbo.

"I won't let you bully me into saying a word!" She declares, but can't hold in her laughter.

After a moment, she wipes her eyes and saunters back over to us.

"You know cheese, wine, leather... They all age well... But not as well as my Silver Fox Luc Montaigne!"

She ends her pronouncement with a two-armed sweep of water aimed at us. We retaliate, and it becomes an all-out, every woman for herself water war. We laugh hysterically while trying not to drown as we jump around splashing in the warm tropical Indian Ocean.

* * *

"How did you like the retreat?" Starr asks as we sit at the outdoor dining table surrounded by fragrant torches.

The other participants left yesterday morning. We stayed two extra days to spend some quality time with Starr off of the mats. Yesterday we went for a long hike through the verdant patchwork of forests on the island. Then had a rejuvenating swim in one of the crystal-clear freshwater lakes.

Now, we're eating a delectable dinner of flavorful local favorites prepared by a chef on the outdoor grill and cooktop. The aroma is mouthwatering. I sip my Tipo Tinto R&R and nibble on a flaky chamussa. The appetizer is just enough to keep us sated until he presents the main dishes.

"You did such a superb job, Starr! I can't wait for the next one," Billie answers as she clinks glasses with our hostess.

"Indeed! I thought nothing could top your first one on Fijian Laucala Island last year. That private paradise is surreal," Lola chimes in.

"It was the best I've ever been on! Fantastic!" Haley says as she rises to give Starr a standing ovation.

"Sign me up for all of them! I feel incredible, thank you very much!" I exclaim.

"Me, too!" Blair says as she raises her glass. "A toast… Here's to good friends, good loves, and good times!"

Everyone cheers and clinks glasses. Lola pauses and peers at Starr.

"What's the latest on your conversations with Malcolm?"

No one else notices the tone in Lola's voice but me. I've known her the longest and can understand what she thinks or feels easily. Right now, she's prying because she knows something Starr doesn't or at least Starr hasn't admitted to us yet. As if on cue, Starr avoids Lola's probing gaze. Starr shifts in her chair and pretends to straighten the napkin on her lap.

Lola is relentless.

"Well?" She demands.

Starr clears her throat and returns Lola's gaze. Defiantly Starr lifts her chin as she responds.

"Malcolm Steele is an arrogant, self-focused cretin!"

Blair, Billie, and I gape at Starr's heated reaction. Haley covers her ears not wanting to hear such things about her older brother.

Our normally quiet calm, namaste, om, center your mind friend now flustered completely. Our gazes dart between her and Lola in shock. What the hell did Malcolm do to Starr?

Lola bursts out laughing. Her last sip of Tipo Tinto comes out on a snort. She pulls back from the table, doubling over in glee. The sight is too comical. We can't help but join in—even Starr.

Once Lola gathers herself, wiping tears from the corners of her eyes, she straightens. She lifts her left hand and waggles her fingers. The ice skating rink on full blast.

"That's the same thing I said about his doppelgänger brother, Captain Caveman... Now look at me, my friend!"

Starr looks just as stunned as the rest of us. But Lola just keeps giggling. She definitely knows something Starr is clueless about. When we question her, Lola shakes her head and sips her drink, laughing to herself.

ROGER

"*H*ey man! Where the hell are you today? You're definitely not here in this ring. Get it together real quick, Steele!"

Norman Green, my boxing coach and personal trainer, yells at me when I practically walked right into his sledgehammer left hook. I've never been more thankful for protective headgear and a mouth guard. The former world heavyweight champion nine years straight—eight by knockout—scowls at me as he flexes the muscles in his massive arms.

"Are you ready for this session, Steele? You've been goofy the last few days, man," Norman continues as he eyes me up and down.

He's six feet, five inches, solid two hundred-fifty pounds of muscle who moves with the grace of a gazelle and the speed of a cheetah. Norman has been my trainer for the last four years. I met him in Las Vegas at a party at

STEELE LV after his final KO match. He told me he promised his girlfriend, now wife, Anita he would stop with this fight. He was at the top of his game with no more to prove. Norman said it's better to leave on high than get carted away low.

I offered him the opportunity to open his chains of branded gyms through STEELE's Entertainment Properties Division. One for underprivileged youth and another as exclusive elite training facilities for the über-wealthy and star athletes.

Born and raised in Harlem to upper middle-class parents, Norman understands the importance of giving back to the community. A mentor taught him boxing after school and his career took off. Being a celebrity athlete, he understands the need for specialized training and the demands on the body. He didn't hesitate and agreed to the deal. A perk for me is I became his first client.

When I moved to Paris, he and Anita came with me and opened locations in the city, London, and Madrid. The States has several besides the New York City flagship including Las Vegas, Los Angeles, Austin, Chicago, and Miami.

My father, Sebastian, and Malcolm are pleased with the profitable revenue stream. Especially since the membership and assorted fees of the elite facilities pay for the community ones. Norman can continue in the sports world and add even more to his multimillions. It's a win-win business partnership for all.

Anita who is a yoga instructor with a flourishing practice just finished culinary school at Le Cordon Bleu and started a meal plan delivery service. Norman added her customized plans to the paid offerings of the elite facilities and complimentary healthy snacks to the youth. She also took over the food services in both chains. They're a dynamic couple who raise the bar in the fitness industry.

"Well... Shall we proceed or do you prefer to go sit in the sauna, Steele?" Norman taunts me as he bounces on the balls of his feet and punches his fist together.

I shake the kinks out of my neck and pound my fists. Then do some jumping high knees to get the blood pumping in my legs.

"Nah, Green. I'm ready for you. Let's go. Ding ding!" I respond and hold my gloved fists out to him.

"Now that's more like it, Steele! Ding ding!" He says as he hits his fists on top and below mine. "Let's go, man!"

We spend the next two hours in the ring, and on the mat sparring and doing drills. We end with a bout on the rower to flush out the lactic acid built up in my muscles. Then follow with stretching and foam rolling. The intense workout was just what I needed to get my head on straight.

As we walk to the locker room, Norman gives me the side-eye and cocks his bald head.

"In the end you made up for your subpar start. You're usually more focused than that, Steele. What gives?" He asks.

I run my towel over my head and face to collect some sweat. Then I turn to him.

"My woman's been out of town for over a week on a

Girls' Getaway at a fitness retreat on an island off of Mozambique," I start. "It's the longest we've been apart in five months. Leonie in a tiny bikini on a tropical island with a bunch of her stunning friends, including my sister-in-law, has my mind going crazy, man. She's got me all over the place."

Norman nods at my confession as he lets out a wolf whistle, "Leonie *The Lion* Beaulieu… That's one beautiful woman you snagged, Steele—"

I stop cold in my tracks and growl at him, squared up, ready to defend my woman.

Norman also stops and raises his hands. Not in a fighter's stance, but held up in surrender.

"Whoa, man… Anita is my childhood sweetheart. She's the only woman for me, and she's more than I can handle. Not to mention she'd have my balls on a platter if I fucked around with another female. Don't let her little self fool you. She scares the shit out of me when she's pissed. No, sir! I am good! Trust and believe."

I give him the side-eye. But he shakes his head no way and mimics Anita's voice.

"Norman! How dare you!"

We burst out laughing, envisioning her chasing him with a frying pan around their Parisian penthouse. I've seen her when she was less than happy. The petite beauty scares me, too. She's more formidable than her champion husband.

I clap him on the back, and we stride into the locker room.

"You can sit in the sauna now that you redeemed yourself, Steele," he teases. "Oh and don't forget the package of meals Anita made for you. The front desk staff will retrieve it from the refrigerator. The meals include her most recent recipes. She wants your feedback before she rolls them out."

"If they're anything like last week's, they'll be delicious," I respond, patting my stomach.

"Thanks, man. Appreciate it," Norman says as we bump fists.

We part and I take a quick shower to wash the sweat off before I relax in the sauna. Yeah, I definitely deserve it after the grueling workout Norman put me through. I sigh as I lean back and close my eyes. My mind drifts to my "beautiful woman." I did snag a good one, I chuckle to myself. And I can't wait for her to get home...

"THE PROJECTIONS SHOW an increase in the demand for residential property in the epicenter of the—"

The chirp of a text message to my mobile interrupts my director of research and development's presentation. I slide it across the conference room table to pick it up from beside my laptop. Leonie's name appears on the screen.

"Excuse me. I have to take this," I say as I rise from my chair. "Please continue. I'll review the transcript and contact you with feedback."

I grab up my laptop and hustle out the door to my

offices. As I pass by her area, Françoise checks her watch. Then arches her eyebrow questioningly since I left the weekly status meeting an hour early.

"Please hold my calls," I ask her before I shut my door.

Once inside, I lock it and darken the glass walls. Then sit on my sofa. Eager to see the message, I fumble with the passcode. When the Messages app finally pops open, my jaw drops.

Leonie is naked, floating on her back in turquoise water, the sun shining bright above. Her hair floats around her head like a halo, undulating with the waves. Her amber eyes stare boldly into the camera, exuding confidence in her bare form.

The days she's spent in the hot African sun toasted her caramel skin tone. The water glistens across it, making her brown nipples stand erect from her ample breasts. They beg for me to suckle them. Her slim waist highlighted by her hourglass hips that lead to her long, toned legs. Spread wide like a starfish, her arms and legs extend in welcome, reaching out to me from the captivating image. She's a goddess come to Earth to seduce us mere mortals with her gloriousness.

I study every angle. Zoom in and out to see all the minute detail of a woman whose body has become my playground. Not an inch of her am I unfamiliar with. This photo of Leonie in the bright sun laid bare on the ocean waves surpasses Botticelli's *The Birth of Venus*.

Finally dragging my eyes from the image, I read her text message.

Wish you were here, Amoureux. xoxo Your Kitten

Fuck... me...

The only reason I didn't race to my private jet to find out in person who the hell took the picture is the position of Leonie's right arm. It shows she's holding a selfie stick to get the shot. If not... all hell would have broken loose.

My cock, on the other hand, didn't give a damn. It hardened immediately at the perfect vision of its mate. My tongue wishes it were lapping at her pussy like the seawater between her thighs. I flex my fingers, wanting to grip her hips as I shove my hard dick between her wet folds to stake my claim repeatedly.

I growl and unzip my trousers. Relief runs through me when I release my weeping cock from the confines of my black silk boxer briefs. I stroke it from the root to the tip as I open my laptop to AirDrop Leonie's masterpiece to it.

The larger image allows me to appreciate truly the bounty splayed before me. Leonie's lush body beckons me. My hand pumps my dick with fervor as my passion builds. I grunt as I grip it harder to squeeze the shaft, pretending my tight fist is her pussy clamping on me.

As my arousal peaks, I fight to hold it back a little longer, to milk every pleasure out of the sensation. I widen my feet on the rug and scoot down on the cushion. The base of my spine tingles as my balls fill with my seed.

I close my eyes momentarily to force back the impending orgasm. A peek at the laptop screen has my hips thrusting up as my head falls back against the sofa. I close my eyes again, the image of Leonie seared on the backs of my eyelids. I no longer need the photo, I've committed it to memory.

My strokes lose the rhythm as my body prepares for a toe-curling climax. I grip my dick tighter as I use my thumb to smear more of the pre-cum around the tip. One last glimpse at Leonie, and I pinch the bulbous head.

My eyes roll into the back of my head. As I anchor my feet into the floor for leverage, my hips jump up from the leather seat. The pistoning of my hips matches the pumping of my clenched fist. Bright white lights spark behind my closed eyelids. My hearing dulls. A deep passionate roar rips from my mouth as my climax hits me like a careening truck. My jizz shots up like a. geyser, then spills over my hand.

I collapse back onto the sofa, sated and spent. I only want to curl into a fetal position and drift off to sleep. A slumber filled with dreams of my goddess Leonie floating towards me on a wave risen from the depths of the ocean. A spectacular gift only for me.

LEONIE

"*L*eonie, babe. It's time to get up. You have to get to the site on time. Leonie…"

I roll over onto my back toward Roger's voice and peel my eyes open. Instantly, I squeeze them shut with a hiss.

Merde!

The glaring sun streaming through the uncovered floor-to-ceiling windows in Roger's penthouse primary bedroom blinds me. Stars flash behind my heavy eyelids. Why the hell did he open the damn blackout curtains so early? I mutter to myself as I flip over to curl into a ball. With a groan, I pull the covers over my head. Burrowed in the bedding, I try to ignore the persistent buzzing of his nagging voice.

"Listen, Leonie, you have to get up, baby," he drones on. "You slept through your alarm. It's already nine fifteen."

He pulls the comforter and sheets off of my naked body, exposing me to the glare of the light and the cool air.

"Seriously, the team is meeting at the property at ten o'clock—"

I snap my eyes open to, amber eyes shooting darts. I growl at Roger as he looms over me and snatch the bedding from his hand.

He's so shocked by my reaction, it falls with ease from his hand. He scowls at me and shakes his head.

"What the hell, Leonie?" He asks.

I mutter curses as I slip back into my cocoon.

"Enough, Leonie. Don't be irresponsible. This meeting is important, and I don't have time to treat you like a little girl who doesn't want to go to school," Roger says as he pulls all the bedding off from the foot.

The sheets slide from me, and I shoot up to a seated position. We lock eyes as we glare at one another. I break first.

"How do you speak to me that way, Roger! I'm not a child! I'm a grown ass woman!"

He snorts and folds his arms over his chest, feet wide apart ready for a fight. He looks me up and down with a smirk.

"Really? Well, you could have fooled me!" Roger snarls. "You're the one who's lounging in bed past your alarm. I try to wake you and you snap my fucking head off!"

I throw two pillows at him. He ducks his head from one and swats the other away. His pale gray eyes darken to slate as he glares at me.

"Oh, so that's how 'a grown ass woman' behaves?" He shouts. "I don't think so, Leonie!"

"Fuck you, Roger!" Stop always trying to boss me around! You... You control freak!" I scream.

I jump from the bed and storm into the bathroom, slamming the door behind me.

Roger bursts in. I glare at him over my shoulder. Rage contorts his face. His chest heaves as he breathes hard.

"I do not know what the fuck is wrong with you this morning, Leonie. But you are pushing it!" He growls.

He uses his much larger body to crowd me against my vanity. I turn around to face him. Then he cages me in, bending his knees to bring us on eye level.

"I am not a control freak. I came to you to wake you up. Why are you flipping the script?" He demands.

I push ineffectively at his firm chest. He's already fully dressed and his cologne fills my nostrils. It's too much.

"Bouge toi! Laisse-moi tranquille, Roger!" I scream, unable to translate my thoughts.

My head is pounding as my heat races. I need air, and I need Roger to give me space. I beat against his chest and shake my head vigorously. Then lower it in defeat. The strength drains from my fatigued body.

"Très bien, Leonie ... Je vais vous laisser tranquille." He whispers, then leaves the bathroom without another word.

The raw pain of hurt in his voice slices into me. But I remain steadfast. I wait until I hear the door click shut before I raise my head. A sigh slips from between my lips. I wrap my arms around my torso and shiver from the cold. Or could it be from the loss of Roger's warmth?

Fuck it…

I shake my head and clap my palms against my arms to boost the circulation. A glance at the clock above the door —leave it to Roger *The Responsible* to have a clock in the bathroom—shows I have half an hour to make it to the meeting on time.

Merde!

Quickly, I walk into the shower and turn on the water. The blast chills, then warms me. Wasting no time, I cleanse myself and don a fluffy cotton towel to dry me. Simple and classic, I think as I choose a crisp white shirt, black pencil skirt, black pumps for my wardrobe.

Selection made, I pin my hair into a bun. Jewelry kept minimal with single pearl earrings and a three-strand necklace. Then I swap the robe for a flesh-tone lace Lola's Coterie bra and panties set. Fully dressed, I grab my pumps and mobile. I run down the stairs only stopping to pick up my handbag and attaché still backed from yesterday.

When I open the front door, I find Eric standing by the elevator. I skid to a halt.

"Bonjour, Mademoiselle Beaulieu," he nods. "Monsieur Steele asked me to drive you to your meeting."

Eric takes my attaché from my hand and rings for the elevator, and it opens immediately.

I'm gobsmacked by what he just told me. Despite our nasty argument, Roger still thought to have his driver take me to the site visit. He must have figured I would have a hell of a time getting a hired car or cab at such brief notice during this time of morning. Mr. Responsible... My face heats in shame as I mutely nod and slip my shoes on.

Like a chastened child, I meekly follow Eric into the elevator. The ride is quiet as we study the floor display. Even though I'm pissed by his comments, I make a note to call Roger when I get a chance.

The doors open to the level of the underground garage reserved for the Steele family's vehicles. Roger has four including a Black Badge Rolls-Royce Cullinan, the most gorgeous SUV ever crafted, and the powerful and sexy Aston Martin DB7 Vantage. Several other cars of all colors, brands, and models line up along the wall. Four motorcycles cluster in another area.

We make our way to Roger's Rolls-Royce Corniche, already positioned to face the exit. No time to waste. Every detail well thought out. Eric opens the back door for me. I slip onto the buttery soft leather. He places my attaché on the floor by my feet. As he shuts the door, I thank him.

A faint hint of Roger's cologne lingers in the air. It wraps me in a comfortable, familiar embrace. I lean back against the seat and let it cradle my head. My eyes close as I take a deep inhale the combination of the leather scent and Roger mingle pleasantly.

"We'll take the fastest route and arrive at the property in ten minutes, mademoiselle," Eric states once he settles in the driver's seat. "Would you prefer the partition up or down? I can also diffuse some lavender or lemon in the air to relax you before your meeting."

I sit up and open my eyes to meet his gaze in the rearview mirror.

"Perfect. Please put it up and lavender would be lovely, *merci*," I respond with a smile.

Eric nods and the partition rises soundlessly. As the soft scent of lavender wafts through the air, the vehicle's filtration system removes the last vestiges of Roger's cologne.

I rest again as the dull ache in my head increases. Thankfully, the tinted windows lessen the sunlight filtering through the windows, the quiet interior, and the soft seat recreate the cocoon of the bed. I drift off to a dreamless catnap.

"Mademoiselle Beaulieu? Mademoiselle? We're here."

A gentle tap on my shoulder rouses me as the sound of Eric's voice reaches my ears. Momentarily disoriented, I glance around confused. When my eyes land on his face, he smiles encouragingly.

"We're here, Mademoiselle Beaulieu."

He steps back and offers his hand to me. I take it gratefully as I slip my Birkin on the bend of my elbow and pick up my attaché.

"*Merci beaucoup*, Eric," I reply. "What time is it?"

He glances at his watch, a sleek Cartier Tank in gold with a black alligator-skin band.

"It's just 9:59, mademoiselle. But don't worry. At Monsieur Steele's request, I sent a text message to the assistant to inform her you're here."

Again, my face flushes. Then I remember I didn't send the text message to Roger. *Merde…*

"You're the best, Eric. Enjoy your day," I tell him as I hurry to the front door of the majestic apartment building.

"Oh no, mademoiselle, I will wait for you—"

"*Merci*, but that's all right. I can get a ride with a colleague," I interject thinking there's no need for him to wait for so long.

"My apologies, Mademoiselle Beaulieu," he shakes his head. "Monsieur Steele asked me to drive you around today. I'll send a text message to you, and you can reply when you're ready."

I nod and thank him, again. On the way up into the lobby, I deftly apply lipstick and mascara. Blair would tease me about my modeling quick-change skills, I laugh to myself. Once inside, I spot the Design Team. They wave me over and I join them.

"I apologize for my tardiness—"

"No worries, Leonie, you're right on time," Clinton the design director on the project tells me with a kind smile.

"Ah, *oui*. But to be early is to be on time; to be on time is to be late; to be late is unthinkable," I respond with a grin.

They laugh, and Clinton says he'll add that nugget to his list of adages. I notice Delia just stares at me, her expression unreadable. Unfortunately, Clinton chose her to join this project. So I've seen more of her than before. I smile, not wanting her to sense my disdain. Roger may be an ass, but he's my ass. And I don't share.

"On that note, let's review some specifications for this renovation," Clinton says, looking at each of us.

This is one of my favorite buildings in Paris. Near to my duplex and Lola's penthouse in the *seizième*, I pass it frequently. This arrondissement is renowned for the ornate nineteenth-century buildings, wide avenues, prestigious schools, museums, and spacious parks. French high society has flocked here for their places of residence for years. The *seizième* is comparable to the luxurious Kensington and Chelsea neighborhoods in London. French popular culture has coined the phrase *le 16e* as association with great wealth.

I share some of my insight with the team. They're impressed with my knowledge of the history and culture. Others contribute their thoughts so we have a lively discussion.

"Excellent observations. Now we'll go to some common areas, sample flats, and the courtyard," Clinton starts. "Be sure to note the original details, fixtures, and elements that we can preserve or recreate. STEELE wants to keep the property as true to the original as possible. As you know that's their trademark with historical buildings."

We pull out our tablets and prepare to make sketches and notes. Then Clinton tells us to partner up for the walk-through. When we return to the office, we'll meet in the conference room and discuss our findings and initial recommendations.

Brandon Eliot, an architect I've had lunch with a few times strides over to me. He's a handsome man in his early forties. I smile at him as he gets closer. His arctic blue eyes brighten.

"You intrigued me with your knowledge of the building. I have some ideas that you could help me flesh out. Would you like to do the walk-through together?" He asks as he runs his fingers through his wavy, sandy blond hair.

"That would be great, Brandon," I respond returning his smile.

We head off to examine the inner courtyard to get a feel for the exterior and what elements we may incorporate in the interior areas.

"I've always loved the style of the nineteenth century," Brandon says as he covers his eyes with his hand to gaze up at the facade. "The detail is incredible."

"Yes, *La Belle Époque* is my favorite…"

Brandon and I chat amiably as we go from one section of the property to the next. We're so absorbed in our conversation and tasks, the two hours pass by quickly. We rejoin the group in the main salon of the ground floor.

Delia peers at us, shifting her gaze between Brandon and me. I look at her pointedly, daring her to insinuate something happened between us. She must sense that I'm not in any mood for her shit today. So instead of making a snide comment, she turns away.

"We'll meet in the conference room in thirty minutes that should be enough time for everyone to return to the office," Clinton says.

"Also, we're ordering lunch in, so please send you order

by text message to my mobile," the assistant tells us. "I sent the menu to you already."

My stomach rumbles at the mention of food. I didn't have time to eat breakfast or grab one of Anita's protein bars. I pull out my mobile to scan the menu and to send Eric a text to let him know I'm ready.

"Would you like to share a cab back?" Brandon asks.

I forgot about him beside me, so focused on getting something to eat. I glance over at him and shake my head.

"I have a ride. Would you like a lift?" I ask.

Brandon nods and smiles as he responds, "That would be great, thanks."

We leave the building. Eric is right where I left him. I wave and he opens the back door.

"Eric, Brandon Eliot is a colleague who'll ride back to the office with me," I tell him as I slide onto the seat.

Eric nods, and Brandon thanks him as he joins me.

"Nice car. A design marvel of its own," Brandon says, admiring the handmade luxury vehicle.

I feel awkward telling him it's Roger's car when he's the president, so I just smile.

Now that I'm still, I realize I haven't heard from Roger. I unlock my mobile to double-check for a message or missed call. Nothing. He's probably still angry I behaved "like a little girl." I get irritated with him all over again.

"—compile our notes and come up with some ideas. Your extensive travel really is an asset."

I glance at Brandon and tuck my mobile back into my handbag. Focus, Leonie! Remember… prove Roger wrong!

"That sounds good, Brandon. Let's compare what we jotted down before we get to the office," I answer as I remove my tablet from my attaché.

"Excellent," Brandon says opening his crossbody bag to retrieve his device.

We spend the next fifteen minutes on an outline. When we arrive, Brandon doesn't wait for Eric to open the door. Instead, he hops out and offers his hand to me.

"*Merci*," I smile, then turn to Eric, "Thank you so much! Enjoy your day, Eric."

"Of course, Mademoiselle. Have a good day," he responds, then gets back into the driver's seat without a word to or glance at Brandon.

We stroll inside the building. The lobby is bustling with activity. So we hurry to the elevator bank for the STEELE floors. Other companies have their offices in The Tower. Just as we arrive at the elevators for the top floors, one opens and we duck inside. Brandon tells a joke about move slow, you blow, and I laugh heartily.

Other members of the team enter the conference room shortly after us. Clinton stands at the head of the table with the whiteboard behind him. He lists headers for tasks with slots for names to handle the duties. When the last person settles at the table, the assistant shuts the door and Clinton clears his throat.

"Now, we'll get to business of expectations, budget, organizing activities, and creating the project schedule. As you know management set occupancy for six months from today…"

We dive right in. A slideshow presentation takes us through the history of the building from construction to remodeling. We review the schematics and other construction details. Then get into the parameters for the job.

It's thrilling.

The assistant steps out and returns with our lunch orders. The delivery person helps her to set up the credenza where we'll pick up our food. My nose doesn't appreciate the varied smells as they blend in the air. I take a sip of water and try to concentrate on the discussion.

"Everything is ready," she tells us.

While several colleagues head to the credenza, I hang back. The smell is overpowering. When Brandon sits down with his egg salad sandwich, saliva fills my mouth. In a panic, I jump up from the table as I cover my mouth. I rush out of the room to the hallway that leads to the ladies' room.

"Leonie! Hey, are you all right?"

I can't risk answering Brandon for fear I'll retch all over the place. Instead, I increase my pace. He catches up to me just as I stumble from a wave of dizziness.

"Hold on, I'll help—"

"Leonie!"

A powerful arm grips my waist and hauls me against a hard body. The sudden movement proves too much for my resistance. With a surprising burst of energy, I push away from him and rush into the bathroom.

I barely make it to the first stall. My entire body shudders as spasms rock me. I feel hot and cold. On a moan, I heave into the toilet bowl. My empty stomach emits nothing but the water I drank. I moan pitifully.

"Baby, it'll be okay. Just breath, baby."

Finally, my mind registers it wasn't Brandon who held me. It was Roger. How did he know, I wonder? I don't have time to ask since another wave hits me. It's too much. I sob.

"Françoise! Call the medic to the ladies' room on the twentieth floor!"

I try to wave my hand to stop Roger from calling for the doctor. But I feel too weak. I wonder if I caught a bug in Mozambique.

At last, my body stills. I sit back on my heels and wipe my mouth with toilet tissue. How embarrassing, I think and groan.

"Can you stand?" Roger asks softly, stroking my hair.

I nod, and he lifts me up. He leads me to the sinks. He fills a disposable cup with cool water, then hands it to me.

Shakily, I put it to my lips and rinse my mouth out. Roger's gray eyes search my face intently. I blush from the scrutiny, knowing I must look a fright. I duck my head and bend to rinse my face off. The water cools my heated skin.

Roger rubs my back in circles, easing the tension in my body. I glance at him in the mirror. He looks worried and starts to speak, but the door opens.

"Monsieur Steele, what's happening?"

The doctor hastens to my side when he sees my reflection in the mirror.

"Mademoiselle, tell me what happened," he says.

"I'm fine. I just... I haven't eaten yet. That's all," I

respond, straightening my clothes and brushing my hand over my hair.

"Leonie…" Roger starts.

I glare at him. But before I can speak, the doctor cuts in.

"Monsieur Steele, please be so kind as to wait for us outside"—he raises his hand to stop Roger's response—"She is a patient and I must respect her privacy."

Roger looks flabbergasted. But the doctor holds firm and shakes his head. Then points to the door. Roger looks to me. But I offer no consolation. He leaves without a word.

"Now, tell me what happened," the doctor says.

I tell him about not eating and the smells upsetting me. He takes an assessment of my vitals, including blood pressure and temperature. I mention my thoughts of a bug, and he nods.

Finding nothing untoward, he tells me to go home, have a light meal, and rest. Should my symptoms worsen, I'm to go to hospital for a full checkup. I thank him and we leave the bathroom.

Roger, Brandon, and Clinton stand just outside the door. They turn in unison when they hear it open. I offer a wan smile. Roger curses and strides over to me.

"I'm taking you to the hospital," he declares. "You don't look good."

I roll my eyes and sigh, "Gee thanks. Just what every woman likes to hear…"

The doctor coughs to cover his chuckle. Then responds, "Monsieur Steele, Mademoiselle Beaulieu should be fine with a light meal and some rest at home. I told her to go to hospital if her symptoms worsen."

Turning to me, he pats my arm and wishes me good health. I thank him again and he leaves with Françoise, who also wishes me a speedy recovery.

"Yes, Leonie, you should go home. Don't concern yourself with the project right now," Clinton says, concerned.

"I'll keep you up-to-date. Don't worry," Brandon adds with a smile.

Roger gives him the once over. But doesn't respond. Down, caveman…

"Leonie, are you all right?"

We turn towards the voice. Delia stands there with an expression of concern on her face.

I don't buy it.

"*Oui, merci*," I respond.

Roger puts his hand on my lower back and guides me past them. He nods at Clinton, who inclines his head slightly.

When we're out of their line of sight, Roger pulls me close and kisses my temple, brushing his nose against my hair. He takes a deep inhale and sighs.

"You scared the shit out of me when I saw you run past the conference room I was in for a meeting. Françoise took your things upstairs. Let's go home, Kitten."

As soon as we arrive in his bedroom, Roger leads me to the bathroom where he carefully strips me and wraps me in my robe.

"Are you okay to freshen up while I fix you something?"

he asks, touching his fingertips to my cheek in a caress. "I'll bring a tray for you to eat in bed, okay?"

I close my eyes as I nuzzle against his hand and nod.

Roger sighs and kisses my lips before he backs out. His stormy gaze never leaves mine until he turns to walk out of the door with a nod.

When he returns, I'm snuggled under the covers wearing one of his t-shirts. He sets the tray on the bench at the foot.

"Do you want to eat a little something or at least drink a bit of ginger tea to settle your stomach?" He asks.

"*Oui, merci,*" I respond as I sit up.

Roger fluffs the pillows behind me. Then places the tray over my legs. He waits for me to take a sip of the tea before he sits facing me.

"I'm sorry, Leo—"

"Forgive me, Roger—"

We speak at the same time. I giggle, and he chuckles when we talk over ourselves again.

"You first," he says.

I take another few sips of tea; the ginger eases my nausea. The scent of Roger's cologne and the softness of his worn cotton t-shirt comfort me.

"Forgive me, *Mon Cœur*. I was a brat, and you didn't deserve it. I love you," I say, overcome with emotion.

"Baby!" Roger exclaims as a tear rolls down my cheek.

He moves the tray to the bench and sits next to me as he pulls me onto his lap.

I snuggle against him, inhaling deeply.

"I love you too, Leonie. So much. I don't want to control you," he says, then adds. "Well… Aside from in bed."

My shoulders shake as my tears turn into snorts of laughter. Only Roger, the love of my life and sometime control freak.

ROGER

The nightmare from two weeks ago of Leonie sick is a distant memory as I sit on the sofa in my penthouse's primary bedroom watching her rush around. It's the morning of her graduation ceremony. In fact, it's an hour and fifteen minutes before the commencement starts. And as always, Leonie is late getting ready.

I learned my lesson the morning she took ill. Instead of reminding her over and over, I told her when I came in ten minutes ago we need to leave in twenty minutes. Well...

"Roger! Where's my makeup case?!" She storms in from the bathroom wearing a Lola's Coterie sheer silk, flesh-toned bra and thong set.

Fuck...

My dick comes to life at the sight of her. My eyes wander languorously from her toenails painted white to her shapely, long legs over her belly to the swell of her hips. I tilt my head as I stare at her chest.

Is it my imagination or do her breasts damn near spill from the bra cups? The nipples more prominent? Her tits appear more lush than before, or is it the push-up bra, I muse as I lick my lips.

"Ow, fuck!" I exclaim as I rub the side of my head.

"Stop ogling me! I asked you a question, Roger!" She bellows as she prepares to launch another missile at my head.

I peer around me and spot her hairbrush on the floor by my feet. I didn't even see it coming. She has spot-on aim. Damn.

"Was that really necessary, Leonie?" I ask petulantly.

Her eyes widen. Then narrow to shoot amber flames in my direction. If I could combust, I would from the heat of her glare.

She flings her arms up in disgust. Then goes on a tirade, screeching French obscenities as she stomps off to the bathroom.

My dick jumps at the sight of her round ass jiggling with each one of her steps. I glance at my watch, debating whether we have time to temper her poor attitude with a quick fuck or not. Not, I realize when I note we now have less than an hour and fifteen minutes to the start of the ceremony. I rise from the sofa and sigh.

"Leonie, I don't care if you get pissed. But I will not let you be late to your graduation, babe," I tell her as I stand in the doorway to the dressing room.

She stormed in here after a fruitless search in the bathroom didn't reveal her missing makeup case. She's now dressed in a strapless white jumpsuit and skin-tone strappy sandals. Her hair cascades down her back in silky waves. It's gotten longer these past six months as it now reaches her waist.

I want to grip it in my fist and fuck her really hard. Use it as leverage to bend her body to my will. I run my hand over my burgeoning bulge that aches to drive deep inside of my Kitty's tight, wet heat.

She spies my action and growls at me. Even lifting the corner of her lip to flash her incisor.

Damn if it doesn't turn me on more. But I can't help a chuckle. My *Lion* is fierce today. And I have just the thing to tame her. I slip my hand in my trousers pocket and run my thumb over the velvet box.

"Besides, you're glowing, Kitten. You don't need any makeup. Let's go," I add a with a touch of command.

Leonie glances up and gives me the once over. Then nods to herself as though she's decided to not argue with me.

"Fine, let's go," she says as she sweeps past me like a queen.

I shake my head and chuckle some more.

"I heard that!" She snarls.

I duck as I come out of the bathroom, not wanting another ding to my head. Fortunately, Leonie stalks out of the bedroom door with her cap and gown in her hand.

I notice her mobile still plugged into the charger sitting on the nightstand by her side of our bed. I shake my head as I snag it. Then follow her out of the door.

"Congratulations, Mademoiselle Beaulieu!" Eric exclaims as Leonie and I step off of the elevator to the Steele family private garage. "I wish you much success!"

Leonie no longer a temperamental lioness beams at Eric.

"Merci beaucoup, Eric! How kind of you!" She says as she gives him a big hug.

He inclines his head as he reddens from her attention. He can't meet my eyes knowing how possessive I am of Leonie. But I know he's happily married with two sons. If he were not...

Leonie slips inside of my Black Badge Rolls-Royce Cullinan as Eric holds the back door open. I help her inside. Then walk around to the other door. We're picking up her parents on the way to the school. So we need the additional third row.

For now, I sit beside Leonie. She smiles at me and takes my hand.

"Thank you too, *Mon Cœur*," she says. "I didn't mean to bite your head off."

I lean in to whisper in her ear, "Later, you'll have my other head down your throat. So don't fret."

She snorts and slaps me on the chest.

"You Steele men are cretins without a doubt!"

Not sure what she means—but not caring either—I bring her hand to my lips and kiss her palm. Then slide them to her inner wrist where I kiss it softly.

She whimpers and strokes my face with her fingertips.

"I love you, Roger, so much," she whispers. "You've

supported me and believed in me. Even when I argued with you. The completion of my degree would have been a lot harder and taken more time without you. You pushed me and made me realize I could do better if I just focused more. *Merci, Mon Cœur.*"

Fuck… I have to look away as my eyes fill with tears. Damn, this woman gets to me. I close my eyes and lean back against the headrest.

Leonie gives me a moment to collect myself. She just strokes my face gently.

I inhale deeply and turn to face her. I cup her face in my hands and slant my mouth over hers. She opens up to me. My tongue slides into her mouth to draw hers to mine. She moans as the passion of our kiss increases. Sparks zip from our dancing tongues to my heart.

So caught up in our love, we don't notice the SUV stopped until Eric's door opens and closes. He hops out to get the door for Josy and Guy, who stand in front of their mansion.

I pull back and kiss the tip of Leonie's nose. Then move to the rear bench. Leonie's mother will sit in the bucket seat I vacated. Her father will sit in the passenger seat up front with Eric.

"*Mon Trésor!*" Her father bellows as he gets in the SUV. "We are so proud of you, Leonie!"

"*Oui, Ma Chérie! Félicitation pour ton passage!*" Josy says, hugging Leonie when she settles in her seat.

Leonie tears up, and I pass my handkerchief to her. She smiles gratefully and dabs her eyes.

Quietly she responds, *"Merci, Maman et Papa."*

"Bonjour, Roger!" Josy says with a bright smile so like her daughter's as she shifts in her seat to face me. "Thank you for picking us up."

"Bonjour, Josy. No worries," I respond. "Leonie would have it no other way."

"Yes thank you, Roger. Good to see you," Guy adds, glancing over his shoulder at me.

I nod and answer, "You're welcome and good to see you too, Guy."

The rest of the ride Leonie shares stories about some of her memorable times at the Paris American Academy. She's so happy, we listen attentively.

We pull up to the drop off area with ten minutes to spare. Leonie hops out and blows kisses to us as she follows the other graduates to their section of the auditorium. I watch her rush off, slipping her gown on and straightening her cap on her head. Once she's through their entry, I turn to her parents.

Josy smiles at me warmly. Then loops her arm through mine and Guy's. We make our way through the crowd to the section Leonie reserved for her family. Already seated in two rows are my parents, Sebastian, Lola, Malcolm, Harris, Haley, Luc, Blair, Billie, Patrick, Starr, Lucien, Joel, and Hettie. They wave us over, and we sit just as the faculty walk onto the stage.

The New York City crew and Starr, Billie, and Patrick flew in last night on Sebastian's and Patrick's private jets. My parents are staying in their penthouse at The STEELE

Tower Paris. Sebastian and Lola claimed dibs on the one below theirs. While the others, except for the Paris locals, stay at STEELE Place Vendôme where we'll have dinner after the graduation finishes.

I scan the crowd of students for Leonie. With everyone in caps, it's impossible to find her. So I settle back in my seat and listen to the presentations. I feel a poke on my arm from behind.

Lola grins at me like the Cheshire Cat. I glance to her left to Sebastian who's purposefully ignoring my stare as he studies the graduation program. My gaze moves back to Lola and I smile at her. But shake my head and turn around to focus on the stage when she starts to speak.

She huffs and mutters how I'm no fun.

I hold back a chuckle. No need to encourage her. Besides, I don't want to miss a thing.

My mother who sits beside me leans in to whisper to me.

"When are you going to introduce us to Leonie's parents?" She asks, then sits back and arches her eyebrow at me.

Duh! In my haste, I forgot to make any introductions. I mouth an apology to her and turn to Josy and Guy.

"Please forgive me. I was so busy focused on the ceremony I forgot to introduce you to my family and friends," I whisper.

Josy pats my arm and Guy nods.

As quietly as possible, I share everyone's names and relationships to me. Josy is especially happy to meet

Shelley and vice versa. Guy and Morgan appear equally pleased. Good.

Everyone else makes Josy and Guy welcome. Now that I've made everyone acquainted, we continue to listen to the ceremony.

A little over an hour in, the president steps to the podium to announce the student speakers. He explains how the faculty selects one based on their academic grade point average and the other selected by the graduates.

"For the first time in the history of Paris American Academy, the student with the highest grade point average and the student voted upon by their peers is the same individual."

He pauses as a hush falls over the crowd. He glances out at the students, then continues.

"Please join me in congratulating this year's valedictorian... Mademoiselle... Leonie Beaulieu!"

The crowd erupts in applause. The students jump to their feet and clap for Leonie.

Everyone around me goes wild with whistles, hoots, and clapping. I'm so stunned I don't move until my mother grabs my arm to force me to my feet.

My mind reels when I see my woman sashay across the stage. She owns this platform just as she does the fashion catwalks all over the world. Leonie waves and the cheers increase in volume. Once she reaches the president, she hugs him and he proudly holds her hand up in the air in victory.

Flashes from mobiles and cameras capture the moment.

Leonie shines like a megastar. I'm so proud of her achievements. Career switch to study in a different field. Balancing modeling while completing studies for her bachelor's degree. Mentor to young girls and teens. The addition of her part-time junior designer position to the mix. With all of her hard work, she deserves her honors.

I join with whoops and clap louder than anyone else. That's my woman!

Leonie stands before the podium and motions for silence. The auditorium quiets. She glances around those seated until she finds us in the crowd. We wave and blow kisses. She bows her head, overwhelmed.

Then she straightens her spine and recites her speech from memory. Just as she shared stories with us in the Cullinan, she shares some now. Her words of farewell to her classmates and faculty inspire all. Her speech enraptures everyone in the audience.

At the end, she thanks her parents, Luc, and Lola. All four are in tears when she finishes her praise for them. Leonie focuses her gaze on me and my heart skips a beat. Our eyes lock.

"Also, I thank the love of my life. His support and belief in me was unceasing. Even when faced with my fierce lioness."

The audience laughs, and Leonie smiles as she continues.

"Without him, my completion of my degree would have been a lot harder and taken more time. He pushed me and made me realize I could do better if I just focused more. You are so dear to me, Roger. *Merci, Mon Cœur. Merci pour toujours.*"

I rise from my seat and in a clear voice heard throughout the auditorium I respond, *"Je t'aimerai pour toujours,* Leonie Beaulieu."

She holds her fist to her heart, brings it to her lips, and kisses it. Then releases it towards me. I catch her love and kiss with my fist and bring it to my lips and to my heart. She bows to the audience and strides off of the stage.

Exhilarated, I take my seat. Her father shakes my hand and her mother kisses my cheeks. Lola hugs my neck while my mother kisses my cheek. My father also shakes my hand, and Luc claps me on the back. Everyone is excited about Leonie's pronouncement.

We settle down and listen to the students' names as they're called to receive their degrees. Once again, the crowd cheers loudly for Leonie. Our section is the most rambunctious. She waves again, bursting with joy.

As soon as the president calls an end to the ceremony, we make a beeline for the reception area. When we arrive, Leonie is waiting for us by the door. I hurry over and sweep her off her feet. She holds my face between her hands and kisses me silly.

We only come up for air when we hear the wolf whistles. Leonie throws her head back and laughs. The sound makes my heart swell with satisfaction.

Lola tugs on my arm to let Leonie down. Reluctantly, I

set her on her feet. She's surrounded by our families and friends offering their congratulations and well wishes. I stand aside and bask in her glow. Her eyes meet mine and she winks at me. I chuckle as I return one to her.

After a while, we leave the reception and go to the restaurant at STEELE Place Vendôme. It's one in Lucien's stable, so he prepared all of Leonie's favorite dishes and desserts. As we enjoy after-dinner drinks in the private room, Leonie calls for everyone's attention. We turn expectantly towards her as she stands before us.

"Thank you, everyone for celebrating my big day with me. It marks a new page in my life. So, I want you to be the first to know my plans."

She pauses and smiles around the table before she continues.

"As of now, I plan to work full-time at STEELE Paris as a newly promoted project designer. I will model only for Lola's Coterie and for the global cosmetics company."

We offer more congratulations as we toast her, and Leonie beams.

I notice her expression pinches for a moment. But she seems to shake it off. I gulp down the rest of my Jackson Special Blend Scotch and set the snifter on the table. Then stand and take Leonie by the hand.

She follows me to the center of the room.

I bring her hand to my lips and kiss it. Then drop to one knee as I pull the little navy blue velvet box out of my trousers pocket. I take a deep breath and open my mouth.

"Leonie!"

Lola's scream makes me falter. I swing my head around to look at Lola. She's ashen with wide eyes and pointing at Leonie. I turn back around and stop breathing.

There's a red stain blooming on the white of Leonie's jumpsuit. Her eyes follow my stare. Then widen when she notices the blood.

What the fuck?!

I must have spoken out loud because Leonie drags her frightened eyes to mine. She whispers my name as she touches her stomach and reaches for me. Then she faints in my arms.

All hell breaks loose as screams resound around the room, chairs crash to the stone floor, and Guy shouts. Above it all, I hear a high-pitched wailing.

It's not until my father and Sebastian try to lift Leonie from my arms do I realize the sound is coming from me. The wail turns into a growl as I cradle Leonie with one arm and use the other to push them away from my mate.

She moans from the jostling, and I freeze.

Josy kneels before me and gently takes her treasure from my arms. She rocks Leonie's limp body against her bosom for what seems like an eternity. But in reality is only ten minutes, as long as it takes for the ambulance to arrive.

The medics bustle in and within moments have Leonie strapped to the gurney, wheeling her out of the room. I rush behind them, focused on her pale face. Every so often she winces in pain and moans.

Before they let me into the ambulance, they ask if I'm her husband. I tell them her fiancé. One tells me family only and I almost punch him in the throat. Guy steps up and demands my entry or he'll sue them for endangering his daughter's life with their delay over semantics.

I nod gratefully to Guy and hop on board. I sit in a corner while the medic sees to Leonie. I answer his questions to the best of my ability. I send a prayer for her well-being as my eyes never leave her face.

She moans what sounds like my name and I call out to her, I'm here. I yell for them to go faster. But the medic ignores me as he calls in to the hospital, issuing details in code I don't understand. He's also speaking in French, and my mind is far beyond the capability to translate right now.

Only moments later we stop, and the doors open. I jump out of the way as nurses and doctors take over. I rush after them as they wheel Leonie inside the hospital's emergency room. I hear my name called. But I don't stop. I have to stay with her.

At the end of the corridor, we arrive at swinging double doors. A nurse steps in front of me and puts her hands up to stop me from going any further. I glare at her and try to get past. I won't hit a woman. But I will move her aside.

"Monsieur, you cannot come into the OR! Please come with me," she insists.

I glance behind her, debating my chances of getting around her smaller frame when a hand on my shoulder holds me in place. I whirl around with my fists at the ready to strike.

It's Sebastian, with Malcolm and Harris beside him. They shake their heads and I snarl at them.

"I need to know what the fuck is going on!" I shout, spinning around to the operating room.

"Stop it right now, Roger! You're not helping the situation. Leonie needs their full attention and not you going crazy."

At the mention of my love's name, my knees buckle and I collapse to the ground. On my hands and knees, I punch the ground. But Malcolm pulls my arm back before my fist can connect and I break my hand on the hard, unforgiving tile.

I drop my head and sob.

My brothers lift me up like a rag doll and half carry, half walk me to the waiting room. I drop into a chair and lower my head into my hands. I can't think of or see anything but the bright red bloodstain on Leonie's white clothes.

What the fuck happened? Was it the food? Did she cut herself somehow?

I shake my head, unable to wrap my brain around what's going on. This is a nightmare I cannot wake up from.

"Roger, honey?"

I can't look up at my mother or I'll break down. I shake my head and cover my face, my cheeks aflame.

Understanding I cannot speak at the moment, my mother sits beside me and rubs my back soothingly. Haley sits on my other side and strokes my hair.

After a while, the room comes into focus slowly. Softs cries from Josy and Lola filter through first as Blair tries to console them. Followed by the murmurings of my father, brothers, and Lucien. Guy's footsteps as he paces back and forth in the middle of the room. Luc on the phone speaking in French urgently.

Billie, Patrick, and Starr enter the room with trays of coffee and tea. Joel and Hettie help to pass them out. When Hettie offers a coffee to me, I shake my head. My mother and Haley also decline.

How the hell did we get to this? One minute Leonie's sharing her future plans, and I'm about to ask her to share her future with me. The next minute, we're sitting in the waiting room of a hospital with Leonie in an operating room.

What the absolute fuck is happening?!

Abruptly, I stand. I can't sit around and not have any answers. She's been in there for an over an hour! Somebody is going to tell me something right now.

"Roger!" My mother cries as I storm to the door.

Suddenly the door opens.

A doctor in surgical scrubs walks into the waiting room and removes his cap. His expressionless eyes scan the area, observing one anxious face after the other.

He takes a deep breath and says, "Monsieur et Madame Beaulieu…"

* * *

Roger & Leonie's Story Continues: *Stoke My Desires*

Turn the page for the Steele Family, Author's Note, and Previews of *Stoke My Desires* **and of The STEELE Series Book 1** *Fulfill My Desires Sebastian & Lola Part I*

THE STEELE FAMILY

STEELE INTERNATIONAL, INC

Multigenerational, multibillion-dollar business luxury real estate development and management corporation

Headquarters & Family's Primary Residences:

The STEELE Tower, New York City

A modern, gray-tinted glass fifty-seven story mixed-use skyscraper on southwest corner of Fifty-Seventh Street and Fifth Avenue within Billionaires' Row

Global Offices:

- The United States of America (New York City, New Jersey, Chicago, California, Miami, Las Vegas)
- The Caribbean (St. Maarten, St. Barth's, St. Lucia)
- The French & Italian Rivieras (Nice, Cannes, Positano, Capri)
- Monaco (Monte Carlo)
- The United Arab Emirates (Abu Dhabi, Dubai)

STEELE FOUNDATION: A STRONG AND SUPPORTIVE HOUSE

Builds and manages attractive, affordable housing for urban, lower-income families

Available for download at **bit.ly/STEELEFamily**

Author's Note

Thank you for reading Part I of Roger and Leonie's sexy, sizzling romance! I hope that you enjoyed the start of their passionate love affair. If so, I'd love to hear your thoughts, please share a review at **bit.ly/CLBooksSI3Review** and tell your friends.

Click below for what's up next for this darling duo:

Stoke My Desires Roger & Leonie Part II

Also, did you catch on to the dynamism of Sebastian and Lola? Well, you'll have your answers!
Visit books2read.com/u/3RLy0D

Fulfill My Desires Sebastian & Lola Part I Preview

At **CharmaineLouise.com** take the *Four types of lovers. Which are you?* **Quiz** to match your Sexy Fantasy: sub, Voyeur, Dominatrix, or Dominatrix sub Switch.

Follow me on social media including my CLBooks Coterie Fan Club below or on your favorite channels below and subscribe to my newsletter at **bit.ly/CLBooksNewsletter** for a **Free Book**.

Fulfill Your Desires.

xoxo

Charmaine Louise

BB bookbub.com/authors/charmaine-louise-shelton

f facebook.com/CharmaineLouiseBooks

instagram.com/charmainelouisebooks

tiktok.com/@charmainelouisebooks?

g goodreads.com/charmainelouisebooks

STEELE International, Inc.
A Billionaires Romance Series Book 4

Stoke My Desires Roger & Leonie Part II

Click on the link below or visit books2read.com/u/3n51dx
to get your copy.

Stoke My Desires Roger & Leonie Part II

Books in the Series:

Discover My Desires Sebastian & Lola Prequel
(Available Exclusively to Subscribers)

"*I* am so very proud of you, Leonie. You've accomplished your dream, babe. You did it and everyone will celebrate with you tomorrow. I love you so much."

"*Merci, Mon Cœur, je t'aime aussi.*"

Roger's words from earlier this evening linger in my mind as I lie here wrapped in his powerful arms. The heat of his body still consumes me after we made soul-stirring love for hours. I bask in the glow of our lovemaking and in his praise. Both mean the world to me.

I snuggle deeper into his embrace and smile to myself as even in his sleep Roger tightens his grip to hold me possessively, never wanting to let me go. He murmurs my name and rubs his cheek against my hair with a sigh of contentment.

My mind turns back to how far we have come from almost two years ago.

. . .

THE MEETING my best friend Lola Lewis had to expand her lingerie company Lola's Coterie with STEELE International, Inc. set off a chain reaction for her and for me. She met the love of her life, Sebastian Steele. I met his younger brother, Roger.

I giggle to myself as I think back to his initial reaction when he walked into the wrong conference room and came upon my half-naked voluptuous body. To prepare for the fashion show portion of Lola's presentation, the models, glam squad, and I were using the room. Roger caught more than an eyeful as I stood before him in a thin, silky thong that covered my bare mons and nothing else.

His mouth gaped and his gray eyes popped out of his head comically. An impressive bulge grew to punch against the zipper of his bespoke trousers.

"They're only breasts, *chéri!*" I teased him as I cupped them in my hands for emphasis. "No need to look so stunned!"

Transfixed in a daze, he licked his lips. Then beat a hasty retreat when someone cleared their throat.

During the fashion show, Roger sat in the correct conference room with an unblinking intense stare. His expression never changed as scantily clad models strutted past him—me, *The Lion* included. His gorgeous eyes tracked our moves. But he didn't show interest or displeasure. He was a hard read.

Boy, was I wrong...

Who knew my being the spokesmodel and sashaying my way through the fashion show would result in an unexpected two-month-long relationship?

Our insta-attraction sparked further when Roger blocked other suitors from me at LEVELS New York. Lola surprised me with her purchase of seven-day All Access membership passes for us to experience the flagship of the three luxury BDSM and dance club—Paris and London have locations, too. Global and Local All Access Membership or Dine & Dance Membership options for the über-wealthy and high-profile people who prefer discretion.

On a night I ventured alone, Roger absconded me. We moved from the Peepshow banquette to one of the private suites. Our tryst turned into an evening of sharing our lives and goals. A release of our souls to the other. I'd never felt so connected to a man as I did with Roger.

We ended my week in New York City bound for Paris on his Gulfstream 650 and bound at the hip.

While in the city—where funnily enough we're both based—our relationship continued to flourish. Roger guest lectured one of my classes at Paris American Academy. It was a natural fit as he's the President of STEELE's Residential Properties Division, and I was completing my interior design bachelor's degree. Of course Dalia Shaw, another student, flirted shamelessly with Roger. Later that night, he and I role-played naughty schoolgirl punished by her professor at LEVELS Paris.

Despite the good times, Roger's control-freak ways drove a wedge between us as he constantly nitpicked my coursework ethic as too lax. When he publicly harangued me, then had a fight with my seat mate Antonio Vasquez at our end-of-the-semester reception, marked the beginning of the end.

Roger apologized to me. He paid for Antonio's medical costs and gave him a sum of money in recompense. In addition, Roger had STEELE Paris' Human Resources team set up an annual paid internship program for two students awarded in perpetuity.

Happy to move on, our relationship progressed until we had the horrible blowup. The last argument that led to the end of our short-lived relationship. Sadly, the immediate electricity of what I thought was our *coup de foudre* fizzled.

A shudder runs through me as I recall how the numbness of despair hooked its tentacles into my heart. Then ripped it out when Roger so callously told me he wanted "a serious-minded partner and not a wayward woman who cannot stay focused for over five minutes."

As I made my way from the pleasure we had just shared in the surf at Palmilla Beach to the luxury villa beside STEELE Cabo San Lucas, I could barely keep the tears from falling. It made my pain even worse when Roger refused to relent as he pinned me with his stoic stare. That damnable intense expression he gets when he's being pigheaded. So, I left.

Three weeks later, my tender heart cut anew when at the Grand Prix after party in Monte Carlo I saw Roger cozy up with Verónica Casal. The Spanish supermodel had her claws in him, and he didn't appear to mind at all.

Despite me being with Giovanni Mattei, the anguish was genuine. After the Cabo fiasco, I couldn't help but return to the arms of my on-again-off-again paramour. I needed some way to soothe the pain in my heart.

Gio and I fell back into our agreed upon relationship: to the public we were the hot, passionate couple; in private, our amorous encounters never reached intimate penetration. So once again, I put up with his seeking full release with others as long as I was not a witness to his rendezvous.

Yet, it was not enough.

Eight months later, Roger insisted upon speaking to me. Until then, I ignored his phone calls and text messages. Finally he reached me while I was visiting Lola at Sebastian's penthouse duplex in The STEELE Tower. The clan occupies the top floors of the mixed-used property where their company's headquarters are on Fifty-seventh Street and Fifth Avenue—Billionaires' Row. I was in New York to help Lola with her wedding plans.

Roger was adamant to make amends.

"Please Leonie. For the sake of Lola and Sebastian, let's set our situation aside. Put their minds at ease about how we'll behave at their wedding. I promise I will not bother you. Okay?"

I agreed. The mind-blowing kiss he gave me to seal our agreement reignited my desire for my love.

Ever the fighter—Roger trains as a boxer—he and Gio

came to blows at Lola's Coterie Dubai's opening night party just two months later. And a week before the wedding...

After which, Roger left a heart-wrenching voicemail asking me to forgive him and to tell him what to do to make things right with us. I couldn't resist him.

I can never resist him.

FORTUNATELY, that was then, and this is now.

Roger and I realize we need each other and respect each of our ways: Roger exacting and me more carefree. We truly are *un coup de foudre*—a second chance version. So we've learned to adapt to one another. But also to take on some of the other's qualities. Roger loosened up and doesn't have to stick to a regimented way. I focus more on the tasks at hand and not flit around. We make our relationship work.

And it does.

Over the last six months we've been back together, Roger and I have grown and our relationship has matured. We get it and each other. At last.

"ROGER! WHERE'S MY MAKEUP CASE?!"

I yell as I storm in from the bathroom wearing a Lola's Coterie sheer silk, flesh-toned bra and thong set.

It's hours later and I'm trying to get dressed for my

graduation ceremony. Nothing is going right so far: I forgot to set the alarm; my toe decided to jam itself against the cabinet when I kicked it closed; cramps battling my insides. Now my makeup is missing...

Merde!

Roger of course is all cool and collected, fully dressed as he sits on the sofa in his primary bedroom. Meanwhile, I'm running around like a madwoman.

He has the absolute audacity to eye me from my toes up my legs over my belly to my hips. Then he tilts his head as he stares at my breasts, transfixed again. This fool is eye fucking me!

I let him have it.

"Ow, fuck!"

He exclaims as he rubs the side of his head.

"Stop ogling me! I asked you a question, Roger!" I bellow as I raise my comb to take aim at his stupid head since my hairbrush wasn't enough to knock some sense into him.

Can't he see how stressed I am??

I nearly blow a gasket when he asks if it was necessary to ding him upside the head. I refuse to answer. Instead, I pivot on my heels and storm into the bathroom as I mutter obscenities in French

No sign of my makeup case, I head to the dressing room. At least my strapless white jumpsuit and skin-tone strappy sandals go on without a hitch. I let my mahogany hair loose from the topknot to cascade down my back in silky waves to my ass.

D'accord!

"Leonie, I don't care if you get pissed. But I will not let you be late to your graduation, babe," Roger says.

I turn around to find him standing in the doorway to the dressing room. Damn is he sexy... all six feet, three inches of him.

Roger Steele could be a male supermodel. His sultry gray eyes and ebony hair slightly long, cut to skim his ears and neck along with the angular cheekbones and cleft chin of his clean-shaven face. The olive skin tone doesn't completely hide the shadow of hair beneath the surface.

But at this moment, he makes the mistake of running his hand over his burgeoning bulge. Does he think of anything besides sex?!

I growl at him as I lift the corner of my lip to flash my incisor. *The Lion* is not pleased with her mate.

He chuckles, not at all bothered by my histrionics.

"Besides, you're glowing, Kitten. You don't need any makeup. Let's go," he commands.

I glance up and study him. I decide he's not fucking with me. So I nod and not argue with him. My golden caramel-colored skin is flawless thanks to genetics, clean eating, and regular exercise. My mother is Tunisian and my father Parisian. They taught me at an early age to treat my body well.

"Fine, let's go," I respond as I sweep past him.

Roger shakes his head and chuckles some more.

"I heard that!" I snarl as I stalk out of the bedroom door with my cap and gown in my hand.

We take the family's private elevator at The STEELE Tower Paris to the garage. Similar to the New York City Tower, it's mixed-use with commercial and residential space plus the largest mall in Paris. Being in the *quinzième* with spectacular views of the Seine and of the Eiffel Tower adds to its appeal. Location. Location. Location.

Roger's driver Eric Vogler has the Black Badge Rolls-Royce Cullinan ready. We'll pick up my parents Guy and Josy Beaulieu from my family's ancestral home *Le Beaulieu Manoir* in the wealthiest neighborhood of the *seizième*. Eric offers me congratulations and I thank him with a hug.

Once settled in the plushy SUV, I relax. Then smile at Roger and take his hand as he sits beside me.

"Thank you too, *Mon Cœur*," I say. "I didn't mean to bite your head off."

He leans in to whisper in my ear, "Later, you'll have my other head down your throat. So don't fret."

I snort and slap him on the chest, "You Steele men are cretins without a doubt!"

He brings my hand to his lips and kisses my palm. Then slides them to my inner wrist where he kisses it softly.

I whimper and stroke his face with my fingertips.

"I love you, Roger, so much," I whisper. "You've supported me and believed in me. Even when I argued with you. The completion of my degree would have been a lot harder and taken more time without you. You pushed me and made me realize I could do better if I just focused more. *Merci, Mon Cœur*."

Roger takes a moment to collect himself from the

effects of my words. I truly love this man more than he can ever imagine.

He kisses me with such passion that we don't realize we've arrived at my parents' home until they get into the SUV. Now it's my turn to feel overwhelmed as they praise me. I can only whisper my thanks. Roger gives his hand-kerchief to me to dab the tears from my eyes. My heart bursts with joy surrounded by my loved ones.

We arrive at Paris American Academy. I rush to join the other graduates, slipping into my gown and placing my cap on my head. My nerves have my stomach in knots. I feel queasy, but ignore it.

The excitement is palpable as I make my way to the side of the stage. I peek out to spot my crew. I'm so excited everyone came to celebrate with me.

Lola and Sebastian along with Roger's parents Morgan and Shelley, his second oldest brother Malcolm, Harris and Haley fraternal twins and the youngest flew in from New York City. Plus Blair Thomas and Billie Chandler Lola's personal assistants-cum-close friends, Starr Knight who became another close friend after we attended her fitness retreats came on Patrick Rockett's private jet—Billie's Scottish billionaire beau. The Paris locals include Luc Montaigne Lola and my billionaire mentor and Blair's not-admitted *Le Renard Argenté*, Lucien Jackson, Roger's cousin, and Joel Bailey and Hettie Fuchs, Roger's close friends.

Boy, will this surprise them, especially Roger...

"For the first time in the history of Paris American Academy, the student with the highest grade point average and the student voted upon by their peers is the same individual."

The Academy's president pauses as a hush falls over the crowd. He glances out at the students, then continues.

"Please join me in congratulating this year's valedictorian... Mademoiselle... Leonie Beaulieu!"

The crowd erupts in applause.

As I sashay onto the stage, I wave and smile at the audience thrilled they're delighted for me. It took more time than usual since I maintained my modeling career full-time. And I didn't focus as I much as I could have...

The president and I hug, then he raises our hands in victory. Yes, this is a tremendous success for me. I deliver my valedictory of anecdotes and inspiring stories. It's well received. I end in thanks to my parents, Lola and Luc, and Roger.

"Also, I thank the love of my life. His support and belief in me was unceasing. Even when faced with my fierce lioness."

The audience laughs, and I smile as I continue.

"Without him, my completion of my degree would have been a lot harder and taken more time. He pushed me and made me realize I could do better if I just focused more. You are so dear to me, Roger. *Merci, Mon Cœur. Merci pour toujours.*"

I'm ecstatic when Roger rises and responds, "*Je t'aimerai pour toujours,* Leonie Beaulieu."

My happiness reaches its peak as I blow a kiss to him and he catches it.

Once the ceremony ends, the graduates and faculty go to the reception area to await the guests. I take a spot by the door to get an unobstructed view of my family and friends. Roger hurries over and sweeps me off my feet. I cradle his face between her hands and kiss him fervently.

Wolf whistles draw us apart, to which I throw my head back and laugh.

Roger puts me down reluctantly when Lola wants to hug me. It's a glorious moment as everyone shares their congratulations and well wishes.

I glance around for Roger and see him standing to the side, watching me intently. My amber eyes meet his gray orbs, and I wink. He chuckles as he returns one to me.

The reception is lovely. But we're ready to go to the restaurant at STEELE Place Vendôme. Lucien—*The Sexy Chef*—runs the restaurant along with several other businesses that Jackson Corporation partners with STEELE. As a surprise, he prepared all of my favorite dishes and desserts. While we enjoy after-dinner drinks in the private room, I call for everyone's attention. They turn expectantly towards me as I stand at the table.

"Thank you, everyone for celebrating my big day with me. It marks a new page in my life. So, I want you to be the first to know my plans."

I pause and smile at everyone gathered before I continue.

"As of now, I plan to work full time at STEELE Paris as a newly promoted project designer. I will model only for Lola's Coterie and for the global cosmetics company."

They offer more congratulations as they toast me, and I beam.

A sharp pain zings my belly. It's enough to make me cringe. But I ignore it, not wanting to ruin the moment.

Roger distracts me when he stands and takes me by the hand to lead me to the center of the room.

I smile at him as he brings my hand to his lips and kisses it.

My vision blurs just as Roger drops to one knee. The pain is excruciating. Bile rises in my throat as a warm sensation seeps from my core.

"Leonie!" Lola screams.

Roger swings his head towards Lola, who's pointing at me. Then he turns to me.

Confused, I glance down as my eyes follow their stares. A red stain blooms on the white of my jumpsuit. My eyes widen in fright when I notice the blood—the source of the warmth and pain.

"What the fuck?!" Roger yells.

I drag my eyes to his as I touch my belly, stricken with another zing and reach for him, feeling faint.

"Roger—"

My vision goes black as I fall into his arms.

* * *

Click the Link Below for Your Copy

Stoke My Desires Roger & Leonie Part II

PREVIEW SERIES BOOK 1: FULFILL MY DESIRES SEBASTIAN & LOLA PART I

*S*ebastian

"Good evening, Mr. Steele," one of the two stunning greeters purrs as I step into the lobby for LEVELS New York.

This is the flagship location of the global, luxury, members-only BDSM/dance clubs in Manhattan's Meatpacking District. They chose the historic location as a play on the area's name. Put a club where men pack their meat into willing women and willing men allow women to pack them with their toys. The theme for the lobby is minimal and industrial. The fixtures and furniture that appear well worn are high-end, modern replicas used to add authenticity without the grime of old pieces. The two sides have coordinating greeter stations that allow access to the separate Dine & Dance levels and the BDSM levels. The other greeter turns her head in my direction and briefly smiles at me before she returns her attention to a couple entering the BDSM side.

My cousin Lucien Jackson cooked up the idea and roped my younger brother Malcolm into it. Lucien literally cooked it up since he thought of it as he finished his hospitality and culinary training at Le Cordon Bleu in Paris.

Who the hell goes through that prestigious training to come up with a titty bar? Well, five years later his idea proves it's bigger than that and has a high profit margin with more locations in Paris and London. That's all that concerns me: will it add to STEELE International's bottom line? Yes, well, it's a go. No, then no go.

LEVELS is one of many business partnerships that STEELE has with Jackson Corporation. World-renown for their award-winning eateries, choice cigars, and distinguished liquors and wines, their products pair well within STEELE's casinos, hotels, resorts, and residential and retail properties.

On the personal side, my mother is best friends with the Jackson matriarch. They spent most of their adult lives together forming a closer bond than they have with their blood siblings and relatives. Not sharing DNA doesn't keep our families from being a close-knit group.

"Good evening," I respond as I make my way to the D&D elevator.

Once inside, I place my keycard against the panel to select the third floor for the Level 4 Restaurant. I'm a Global All Access member. I can choose from any of the seven levels: 7th Sky Lounge that offers a stunning, 360-

degree view of Manhattan and across the Hudson River to New Jersey's shoreline, a bar, restaurant by day dance club by night, a coverable pool that's open during the warmer months, and a glass-retractable roof; 6th and 5th multilevel dance club with two bars and a lounge for food and drinks; 4th Level 4 Restaurant and bar open for breakfast, lunch, and dinner; 3rd has twelve private suites for members to continue their pleasure apart from the BDSM levels; 2nd Peepshow for BDSM with seating alcoves, primary stage, mini-stages, performance rooms, and a bar that serves non-alcoholic mocktails; below ground the Cellar a BDSM dungeon with mocktails bar. The Dine/Dance members only have access to the party levels—Sky Lounge, Dance Club, and Level 4 Restaurant.

Tonight, I need to eat and fuck hard in that order. I'm bound to find a female at the restaurant or bar who's willing to be my pet for the evening. One night only, maybe two if she's not clingy or a gold digger, but two fucks is my maximum. I'm not looking for a relationship and damn sure not marriage, just enough time to satisfy my Dom needs and my physical release for the moment. A short-term encounter to balance out my business-focused life.

As president of the Retail Properties Division of STEELE, I bust my ass fourteen hours a day to make it super profitable and to prove that I deserve my future role as CEO of the entire luxury real estate development and management company when my father retires next year. It's not just my last name getting me into the head position.

I'm damn capable since I've worked my way up the ranks to learn our multigenerational, multibillion dollar business combined with my Harvard undergrad and MBA degrees.

My father, Morgan, trusts me to carry the legacy into the future and my younger brothers and sister respect me and accept my leadership. Each sibling works at STEELE: Malcolm president of the Entertainment Properties Division; Roger, president of the Residential Properties Division; Harris and Haley, fraternal twins, co-founders of the subsidiary STEELE Technology and Cyber Security. At 35, I take my role as the eldest seriously, so I don't have time for nor care to get involved in a relationship. Thanks to Lucien and Malcolm, LEVELS provides exactly what I need.

As I step off of the elevator, I take in my surroundings. The bar is bustling as usual with the crème de la crème of society. They hobnob with top-shelf drinks. Seating ranges from the leather and black metal stools at the long, reclaimed-wood covered bar to the dozen high-top tables styled to match. The bar along the right wall features a floor-to-ceiling mirrored wall of shelves of only the best spirits and wines—most are from the Jackson labels. The bartenders serve signature cocktails. Tables on the left complete the layout of the open-plan room. A path between the two areas leads to the LEVEL 4 Restaurant's maître d' station. There, the patrons eat delicious meals prepared by chefs trained by Lucien. My destination awaits.

As I stride towards the maître d', my gaze alights on

several recognizable faces enjoying nightcaps at the bar area's high-top tables. Tonight, the U.S. Attorney for the Southern District of New York, the former governor of California, and a high-powered female CFO of a Wall Street investment bank are present. The club caters to the most wealthy and influential in society. They prefer the relative safety that one can expect from the ironclad nondisclosure agreement that LEVELS requires every member and their guests to sign.

I smile and nod in greeting—every Steele is instantly recognizable—but keep it moving as I'm not here tonight for small talk. As I approach the hostess at the dining area's maître d' podium, I also notice several pairs of lust-filled eyes including those of a few men track my movement as I walk past them. Sadly for the men, I'm strictly a female to a male individual. As I approach the station, the maître d' on duty tonight looks up with an alluring smile on her pretty face.

"Good evening, Mr. Steele," says Susan, as her name tag denotes. She angles her chin down to allow her to peek up at me from beneath her long eyelashes without direct eye contact.

"Your usual table, Sir?"

I don't miss her emphasis on Sir as a sub innuendo. Susan is one of many LEVELS employees who want to have my marks on them and my dick in every one of their holes. Disappointingly for the staff though, I don't mix business with pleasure. That can only end in a messy situation and unnecessarily complicate matters—doesn't fit with my trajectory.

"Good evening, Susan. That's good, thank you," I reply.

Susan's full lips curl up into a dazzling smile as she visibly preens. Her reaction as though I petted her head for a job well done after I fucked her throat and she didn't spill a single drop of my copious amount of cum. Susan seductively sways her hips, long legs stressed by stilettos and her form-fitted, black mini dress molded to her curvy body. She leads me to my table in the center of the room with an unobstructed view of the large dining area and of the bar. A spot from which I can easily observe all the patrons to cherry-pick my companion for tonight. However, the sight before me has me second-guessing my no business/pleasure rule. Susan deliberately bends over the table to straighten the napkin, giving me a visual of her cuffed to my pommel horse and a cane in my hand. Damn if my cock didn't just twitch from looking at her plump bottom and grip-worthy hips. Fortunately, I hadn't unbuttoned my suit jacket, or my piqued dick would be on full display.

I give the heads, on my neck and at my groin, firm, shakes to clear the vision. Then, without making eye contact, I thank Susan, take my seat, and pick up the menu discouraging further attention.

With an audible sigh, Susan bids me, "Enjoy your dinner, Mr. Steele," and walks away. Then on second thought she turns and offers, "Should you need anything at all, please let me know."

Keeping my gaze on the menu, I nod, and Susan dejectedly walks away with less sway to her hips, albeit still an eye-catching vision. Sorry, sweetheart.

If I'm not entertaining business associates or attending social gatherings like charity functions, I frequently dine at Level 4. I prefer that then eating takeout at home or hiring a personal chef to cook for only one person. Both are extravagances that I can afford, but why waste resources with my mutable schedule that changes as often as I change boxers.

Dinner out at whatever time is convenient in a city with thousands of excellent restaurants suits my lifestyle. Level 4 is one of them with a menu that offers the expected fare typical of Continental cuisine of pastas, meat, and steaks with favorable sauces. Lucien complements the usual dishes with appealing specials that change daily to keep the choices fresh and habitual guests like me from getting bored.

The client care is impeccable. So, I don't flinch when the server quietly appears at my side and places a napkin-covered basket with an assortment of warm, fresh-baked breads on the table. I glance up to see a youthful man who is model-perfect and well-groomed with a clean-shaven jaw, slicked-back ebony hair, and intelligent brown eyes. His all-black uniform of a long-sleeved shirt, pants, butcher apron, and shiny Oxford shoes is spotless—the de rigueur fashion for LEVELS employees.

"Welcome to Level 4, sir. My name is Andrew and I'll be your server this evening. May I take your drink order?"

"Thank you, Andrew. I'll have a bottle of Pellegrino," I respond with a pleasant smile.

"Very good, sir. We have some lovely specials tonight. May I share them with you?"

Since I plan to play tonight, I select a light meal comprising the tossed salad to start and the grilled langoustines with white wine sauce entrée. A clear head is best for my evening plan of play.

As Andrew heads to the kitchen to submit my order, my gaze wanders around the room admiring the décor. Just as with the lobby and the bar, Lucien and Malcolm stayed true to the original use of the warehouse. Clean lines and antique pieces for the decor: floor-to-ceiling mullion windows allow natural light to filter through to the room during the day, now dimly lit for dinner; light fixtures hang from the ceiling where the dark metal duct work and copper pipes are visible; exposed brick walls; the floor poured concrete; the well-heeled patrons sit on antique leather chairs at wooden tables. The guys really did a hell of a job with their enterprise. Few can pull off and maintain a high-end, respectable establishment, especially one that's a combo BDSM/dance club with a restaurant.

Perfectly situated for visibility by those at the bar and within the dining room, sit two lovely beauties laughing and tossing their long, glossy hair over their shoulders. Their eyes roam the vicinity hoping to connect with potential partners. The duo is more focused on attracting company for the evening, then on eating the salads that they absentmindedly move around on their plates.

The blonde spots me watching them, and a grin appears on her face lighting up her baby blues. As she nods her head to show her friend she's spotted a potential hookup, her little pink tongue pokes out to dampen her glossy, lush lips.

I wonder if her pussy is as shiny and wet as that mouth.

Her friend shifts slightly in her seat to adjust her position casually. As she runs her red-manicured hand through her sable-colored, shoulder-length hair, she spies me. The green darkens with lust when I wink at her. With a smirk, I turn my attention to Andrew as he places my salad in front of me. Now that I have the attention of both women, I nod and eat. I know they're interested, so no need to rush my meal. They'll be a double order of tonight's dessert special.

I spend the next thirty-five minutes purposely ignoring them. I only allow my gaze to shift occasionally in their direction, never direct eye contact. That dominant behavior—and who I am—will keep them intrigued. As they cross and uncross their legs, the movement affords me a better view higher up their toned thighs. Green Eyes has on a clingy, silk wrap dress that showcases her ample cleavage, the red color complementing her bronze skin. The blue of Luscious' eyes, enhanced by the cobalt color of her strapless, stretch-jersey dress, make them as prominent as her pebbled nipples. Delightful.

First item on tonight's agenda is complete—dinner eaten, now it's time to fuck.

They automatically place the bill on my membership account, so no need to waste time signing the check. I stand and take my time to button my suit jacket, drawing the attention of my pets. Once our eyes lock, I walk past their table to head to one of the high-tops at the bar.

Susan gives me a wistful stare and bids me, "Good night, Mr. Steele. We look forward to seeing you again soon."

"It was a pleasure as always, Susan. Good night," I offer her in consolation.

Moments after I settle at the closest available table, I feel one hand caress my back and another hand lands on my forearm.

I glance to my left and am greeted with a sultry, "Hello." Green eyes glitter in the candlelight like vivid emeralds.

A squeeze to my forearm draws my attention to my right to see freshly glossed lips beaming, "Hello. There aren't any other tables available, would you mind it if my friend and I share with you?"

"Would your friend and you mind sharing me for a fuck?"

Without missing a beat, Green Eyes responds breathlessly, "Absolutely."

***

Click the Link Below or Visit books2read.com/u/ 3RLy0DFor Your Copy

Fulfill My Desires Sebastian & Lola Part I

I dedicate this novel to never giving up on coupe de foudre and second chances.

Fulfill Your Desires.

xoxo
Charmaine Louise

WELCOME TO
CHARMAINELOUISE — THE
SENSUAL LIFESTYLE

GLITZY. GLAMOROUS. STEAMY.

CharmaineLouise New York, Inc. invites you to indulge in *The Sensual Lifestyle* through **CharmaineLouise Books** and **CharmaineLouise Intimates**. CLBrands immerse you in *Sexy Fantasies* with CLBooks contemporary romance novels and give you *Sexy Under Things & Loungewear* with CLIntimates.

Charmaine Louise Shelton the Founder, CEO & Author of CLNY loves all things classic, elegant, feminine, and of course with an erotic edge! Favorite outfit of choice is a cashmere cardigan, leather pencil skirt, and seamed silk stockings with stiletto heels. Sexy Fantasy Type: sub with a dash of Voyeur. When not writing and designing, Charmaine Louise travels and spends time with her Maltese buddies, ZIGGY and Jynger.

CharmaineLouise — *The Sensual Lifestyle*

~ Visit online at **CharmaineLouise.com**

~ Subscribe to **CharmaineLouise Newsletter**

~ Find us on Facebook **@CharmaineLouiseNewYork**

~ Instagram **@CharLouNY**

CharmaineLouise Books *Sexy Fantasies* launched summer 2020. Sizzling, contemporary romance with your soon-to-be favorite Alpha Doms, Powerful Billionaires, and the women they lust after and love for second chances, insta-love, enemies-to-lovers, and more.

Want to chat it up and share your thoughts with other CLBooks Lovers? Read our blog, join our Charmaine-Louise Books Coterie Fan Club and follow us on my author pages and social media to be in the know about the book release dates, exclusive content, giveaways, contests, and more!

~ **Purchase your eBook and paperback novels from my Author Page by clicking here!**

~ Read and subscribe to our blog *The World of Sex*

~ Connect on **Amazon Author Page**

~ Goodreads Author Profile

~ <u>BookBub Author Profile</u>

CharmaineLouise Intimates *Sexy Under Things &* *Loungewear* debuted in 2003. Inspired by the sensuous sirens and sylph swans of the past and present, the hand crochet cashmere and silk collections are for the sexy: hence, the line names Ginger — Bombshell; Diana — Showstopper; Jackie — Timeless; Lena — Classic. Also known as The Movie-Star from Gilligan's Island; Ms. Ross The Boss; Mrs. Kennedy Onassis; Ms. Horne.

Do you thrive on seduction and being sexy lounging at home? Read our blog and follow us on social media to receive the tips, the latest additions to the collections, private sales, and more!

~ Read and subscribe to our blog *The Art of Seduction*

~ Find us on Facebook **@CharmaineLousieIntimates**

~ Instagram **@CharmaineLouiseIntimates**

Fulfill Your Desires.

www.ingramcontent.com/pod-product-compliance
Lightning Source LLC
Chambersburg PA
CBHW071755110726
47908CB00006B/1807